BLOOD CURSE

BLOOD LEGACY SERIES PREQUEL

ELISE HENNESSY

Flutterbye Trail Press
797 Sam Bass Road #2541
Round Rock, TX 78681

First edition

Editing by Red Loop Editing
Cover Design by FrostAlexis Arts
Published by Flutterbye Trail Press

ISBN: 978-1-7345137-0-7 (E-book)
ISBN: 978-1-7345137-2-1 (Print)
LCCN: 2020903576

Feedback: Encounter a problem with this book? Let us know at
elisehennessyauthor@gmail.com

BOOKS BY ELISE HENNESSY

Blood Legacy Series

Dream Walker
The Winter Key
Queen's Return
Court of Illusions
Shadow Dance
Rule the Night
Blood Curse

BLOOD CURSE

BLOOD LEGACY SERIES PREQUEL

ELISE HENNESSY

1

GWENDOLYN

---

*The Fell invaded our world through portals, showing no mercy.
They had magic. No, they were magic. Either we fought them, or
we died, and there simply was no in-between.*

-From Lucia's Journal

G wendolyn Firetree walked the palace gardens in search of
any flaw that could disrupt her daughter's wedding.
Hundreds of lanterns hung from the trees, creating pinpoints of
light within their dark home.

No sun ever rose over Nyixa, so named after her daughter,
Nyah. The island was shaded in an impenetrable cloud of darkness, blocking out the heavens. There was no sense of time past
the bell towers calling the hour. Counting the distant tolls coming
from the palace, she acknowledged her work needed finishing
soon. Fatigue dragged at her frame from another sleepless night.

On the heels of her exhaustion came a wave of hunger,
gnashing her belly in a spike of pain that couldn't be ignored.
She gritted her teeth, and covered her middle as she nodded to
dismiss her assistant for the evening, hoping he wouldn't notice

her moment of weakness. That assistant was at her side for her most unreasonable moments. Nyah's wedding had to be perfect, and Gwendolyn used her newly acquired muscle as royal advisor to make it so.

She walked to the altar, which was set up in a pavilion the island's former residents had made. That was where she found her future son-in-law slouching over the bottom steps. "What are you doing? You're going to wrinkle your suit," she said, bustling over to him on a second-wind of adrenaline.

Adrius, king of vampires, stood immediately like a chastised child. His appearance was that of a younger man, immortalized in his prime. Though she'd known him for over a decade, the only thing that'd changed about him was the fading of sun-tanned skin and the darkening of his eyes to pitch-black. He was built like a solid oak, broad with muscle and towering over her. Holding still for her inspection, he allowed her to adjust his fine suit.

At least he'd followed her directions and sat for someone else to groom his cap of dark curls and braid his beard. "I apologize. It seems I'll never be ready for this." He gestured to their surroundings with a sigh, sounding more like an uncertain youth than the military leader and king of a budding nation. He was, she realized, frightened.

A chuckle left her lips. Adrius was a hero and an incomparable warrior. Mere months ago, he'd led the charge to take Nyixa from its first inhabitants, the Fell, and had slain the Fell Emperor. While the island was a functioning, ideal city for the vampires, it was made to meet the needs of a different, otherworldly race.

Despite fervently studying what they could of the Fell, much was unknown of the creatures and where they came from. It was Gwendolyn's theory that they'd come from a wasteland of their own creation since that was what they left in their wake. Fell were emaciated, ravenous creatures that fed on humans, ripping throats and drinking blood with overlarge mouths lined with shark-like lines of teeth. Entire civilizations were wiped out or threatened by these creatures. A lone Fell could take down four armored men, shearing breastplates with claws like long knives.

Survivors often had a parting gift, as the Fell's corrosive black blood burned its way into any open wound. Adrius was one of the first afflicted in such a way, transforming from a common mercenary into a vampire. Once it was known that humans could take in the blood of their enemies and gain a fraction of their strength and a facsimile of their magic, his condition spread. The more blood they took in, the stronger and more unstable their powers were.

Gwendolyn had found him as he searched for similarly afflicted individuals to form an army. It was Adrius who led the mad hunt for more. He became leader of the Fell hunters, a title given only to the first vampires who hunted Fell like animals.

She'd traveled with the Fell hunters in a different capacity, watching bloodlust nip at the heels of each and every vampire. They'd traded humanity for the ability to fight monsters, accepting power that shook hands with unnatural hunger and madness. The moment they drank a drop too much of Fell blood, she was there to stop them from turning into what they hunted.

Gwendolyn used to be a rare force of great faith, a half-angel filled with heaven's light. She represented heaven's wrath, wielding light magic that was devastating against photosensitive Fell and errant Fell hunter alike. She'd left ashes in her wake. The budding Fell hunter army had bowed to her, a woman, and even Adrius had feared and listened to her every word.

Together, they'd destroyed countless Fell. She'd lost her husband Gabriel, a valiant warrior himself, a year ago in one of the final skirmishes that led them to Nyixa's shores and accepted that fighting to take the island would reunite them.

She'd helped lead a full army of trained Fell hunters to Nyixa. There, they'd faced an endless tide of death, but they'd triumphed. Only eight of the original Fell hunters had survived with them, the rest were respectfully buried on the far side of the island.

Her light had left her the moment she'd seen death's shadow, but accepting Adrius's blood allowed her to continue fighting. A vampire's unnatural hunger now coiled at the base of her stomach, demanding blood with needle pains as she had her moment of mirth at Adrius's fear.

He'd faced off and defeated the worst creatures that'd tried to despoil their lands and successfully staved off the ravenous hunger of a hunter who'd drunk too much Fell blood. But assemble the couple hundred vampires that were part of their rebuilding society and the foreign human dignitaries whose governments weren't scared to acknowledge them, and Adrius was nervous.

Still, his big, calloused hands engulfed her own to stop her from picking at every tiny imperfection still marring his suit. "It'll be all right. No one's going to notice a couple of wrinkles. You know why?" He dropped his voice to a gentle tenor. It was how many presumed to speak to her now, seeing her as broken without her husband and magic. Not wanting to be snippy with him right before the wedding, she fought back her initial reaction of raised hackles.

She wet her lips, already anticipating what he was about to say. "Why?"

"Because they're all going to be looking at Nyah. The palace tailors are making her a dress of legends, right?" She'd teased him for weeks about his bride's dress being labored over by a team of masters. Its mention tugged a smile back on her face. "But how can Nyah enjoy her big day when you're so obviously worn out? When was the last time you fed?"

She bit her lip, realizing her mistake as the action exposed an unsheathed fang. "You know I don't like indulging in such behaviors," she hedged. She didn't like how good it tasted to have another's life force on her tongue. It was anathema to her nephilim nature when she had sworn to do no harm to innocents.

"Let's find you a host," he said, giving her hands a squeeze before parting from her.

He headed out of the garden with her talking to his back. "Adrius, no. I'm not hungry," she lied. Only the spur of starving desperation would push her to take blood.

Ignoring her, he found a young man trimming back last-minute growths along the walkway. Her protests trailed off to an unhappy sigh as Adrius bartered with him, passing him a couple of coins that had the servant's eyes widening.

Nyixa was a mix of cultures with currencies that spanned the known world. They'd moved to a new standard upon taking control of the island, swapping out various coins and bills for discs hewn from the otherworldly white stone that made up the island's foundation and every structure. Gwendolyn was dubious of stone currency at first, but like all things Fell, it wasn't as it appeared. Nothing could break it. They could only be formed by a special potion brewed in the alchemy lab, so the coins could hardly be counterfeit—but that meant that they were still rare compared to their demand. Most of Nyixa's subjects bartered their goods and services instead of paying with coin.

The servant bared his neck for her without hesitation, and she did her best to block out her senses, telling herself she didn't enjoy the warm taste of his youth. When she was done, he went back to his business, whistling happily with the coins clacking in his pocket. Vampires didn't need more than a few sips daily to sustain themselves but only if they kept up with the hunger.

Adrius had to pick out a strong, young man she could take more from. The liquid meal settled over her needling stomach, finally soothing that near-constant ache. "Not so bad, right?" Adrius asked, offering his arm to escort her properly.

"I do feel better," she said, slipping her arm in his.

"Good. I'm glad." He flashed her a warm smile, walking her away from the gardens. It was a relief to leave them behind, knowing they were prepared for the ceremony that day. They headed toward a structure gleaming with distant torchlight.

On a joyous day, neither of them should visit it, as it stood as a reminder that their occupation of Nyixa wasn't completely secure. But even their brightest moments needed tempering by vigilance.

2

ADRIUS

They called their magical foci a word that translates poorly to our language: occultarus. These orbs hang suspended within a sundial-looking holder inscribed with the thirteen symbols of Fell magic. Accomplished, silver-blooded Fell played this object like a lute, raining destruction in their wake.

-From Lucia's Journal

Adrius's feet led him to his greatest preoccupation besides the upcoming ceremony. He stopped before the dormant Grand Occultarus, a massive orb that towered over him and Gwendolyn. Their reflections wavered in its surface, though the grim thing played tricks on his eyes. Shadows seemed to surround them, silent mouths open in mocking laughter.

He hated this thing and wished it was something they could destroy. Its metal was as indestructible as Nyixa's stone foundation; he'd found that out the hard way. Their greatest minds sought to harness its power and control it rather than figure out how to disable it. The hair on the back of his neck rose at the thought of anyone being able to wield it in full.

The Grand Occultarus had a base of bronze metal upon which were inscribed five unknown symbols. Lucia was still researching their meaning, poring over untranslated texts to find anything that looked like them. From the base rose an elegant stem like the neck of a wineglass which shaded to silver as it slashed out in a crescent moon curve. Thirteen more marks were carved into that curve, but at least those were discovered and understood as the different symbols for Fell magic. Suspended within the crescent moon was a gigantic orb of magic with a glass-like surface, dormant as of yet. When it spun, it became a portal, and Fell poured through like a river of death.

The whole structure was three stories high, large enough to hide someone standing on the other side. "Lucia?" he said, spotting the telltale silver of her favored robe. The woman lifted herself off of the ground and dusted off her knees. Lucia, their resident Sorceress, scowled as if they'd both interrupted her.

Lucia had undergone a dramatic transformation mere months ago, and still the sight of her made him do a double take. She'd bargained with the Fell Emperor, receiving and drinking a more concentrated form of his blood. It'd turned back time for her, erasing fifty years of life in mere moments. In the prime of her life once more, she favored hip-hugging robes in shades that complimented her otherworldly silver eyes. He was too used to the bent-over crone who'd had little patience for him, so deep was she in studying the Fell corpses and artifacts left behind from his army. Now, she simply stared when he had her attention. Those eyes pierced him to his soul.

He rubbed his arm self-consciously, feeling more like the boy he'd been when they first met rather than the king of a budding land. "What are you doing here?"

"Studying. Important work." Her brow lifted, and her gaze flitted to Gwendolyn briefly. "It's such slow going with our last specimen deceased. If only I could get my hands on one more, there's so much I would ask him…"

"The portal is supposed to be closed. Do not wish danger upon us," Gwendolyn said. Shadows seemed to dance in her eyes, dulling them further. Adrius was used to seeing the bright yellow-orange of nephilim magic in her eyes and the gold of her skin and hair, but she was wan compared to her old self.

In their battle for the island, Gwendolyn had laid down her life and magic to close the permanent portal created from the Grand Occultarus, cutting off the flow of monsters. If it weren't for her, they all would've died and the Fell Emperor would still be receiving human sacrifices for his daily feast.

Adrius had been present for her miracle and watched the life start to fade from her eyes as the portal collapsed from her sacrifice. After closing the eyes of so many fallen brothers and sisters in arms, he couldn't bear to do the same for her. He'd stripped off his gauntlet and cut his palm with a fang, offering her the bleeding wound.

On death's door, she'd chosen to return as a vampire. But things were different. Her otherworldly assurance was gone, replaced by a haunted expression as she gazed up at the Grand Occultarus. "Have you figured out why it's still making portals?" she asked Lucia.

Adrius understood the defeat in her voice all too well, feeling the same pressure on his shoulders. Despite her sacrifice, it wasn't enough to silence the giant orb completely. It would still activate on occasion, allowing the Fell to send small groups through to weaken what remained of the vampire forces.

"I'm still working on that," Lucia said. She seemed tired as well, and her journal was open to her incomprehensible scrawl of notes scribbled atop more notes.

"I was just activating a sigil for the wedding. Look." Lucia pointed upward where a triangle glowed a faint silver halfway up the dial. It was the sigil of tongues, representing magic that helped everyone who lived on Nyixa understand each other and speak the same language.

Even newcomers to the island would understand each other once Lucia cast her spell over them. Adrius clapped a hand over her shoulder. "Thank you for your dedication. I don't know what we'd do without you," he said. Lucia dropped her gaze to her hands with a coy smile. "Shall we leave you to your work?"

"If you would. I still need to freshen up for your wedding,

and I dare not be late for the event of the century." Now she winked Gwendolyn's way before turning back to the alien structure.

Adrius turned away with a shrug, heading back to the palace. If there was light in this place, the palace would cast a giant shadow over the island. It rose to the heavens on spiked peaks, its white stone façade glowing in the gloom. They were still finding nooks and hidden corridors within. It had more than enough room to keep their entire island's population living there.

He was king of that palace now, and he saw distant figures descending from the front steps and heading down into the garden. He would need to entertain these guests, be their king while he waited for the reveal of his bride and the fine gown Gwendolyn spoke of.

Nyah could marry him in a potato sack, and he wouldn't care. He wanted the woman, not the extravagance, but he could hardly say that and disappoint his future mother-in-law. So, he simply smiled and nodded, ready to give a show worthy of his station as a new king. He wore his finery, and Nyah would wear hers. As he parted ways with Gwendolyn for her to take care of other last-minute details, he found himself circulating amongst the crowd, entertaining as best as he could while missing his fiancée dreadfully.

In truth, they didn't need a wedding. They had been drawn to each other from the start and were already attached in a way that was unique to vampires. When they were near each other, they could sense the other's feelings and the tone of their thoughts, in tune on a level they'd never experience with another person.

Lucia had investigated this pull between them. While subjected to her tender mercies, a Fell had explained the phenomena in detail. Fell did not mate for life unless they found their "soul match," which was exceedingly rare for them. It was a shock for him to learn that Fell were capable of love, but the explanation translated well to human expectations and was one nice thing left within their poisoned blood. It seemed that, like Fell, they could find their perfect matches.

Nyah called him her lifemate, and the word stuck. Other

vampires now sought their lifemates, wanting to know what it was like to meet and love their perfect match. He encouraged it. If they had to live forever, no vampire should go lonely for eternity.

3

LUCIA

They say breaking a Fell's pact will result in a fate worse than death. Fell seal deals with magic, carefully crafting their words so they'll never be caught in a lie. I wish I'd done the same.
  -From Lucia's Journal

Lucia was finishing her spell as Gwendolyn returned alone. "Nice day for a wedding," Lucia said, lifting a miniature version of the Grand Occultarus to use as her focus. It was the Fell Emperor's before it became hers. While she could perform magic on her own, with the help of a focus, she could cast spells at double their effectiveness and even command the Grand Occultarus itself to respond to her whims.

She channeled her power through it, sending a pulse of magic out of the massive magical tool, and set off the sigil she'd activated. The magic would settle over the whole island, imbuing new visitors with the ability to understand each other no matter the language. It was her favorite spell, removing the inconvenience of living with a group of vampires and mortals who didn't all share a common language.

Mortals poured into their island, fueled by rumors of the honorable vampire race. They came curious of impossibly strong people and immortality. Some wanted to fight, but most sought protection and to rise over their impoverished status in a new land. Lucia could respect that, coming from a destitute village herself.

"Did you take your medicine?" Gwendolyn's voice cut into her thoughts.

"What medicine?" Lucia's voice was saccharine.

"I left a vial right next to your journal."

"Oh, yes, that."

Lucia waited, a smile teasing at the corner of her lips as the other woman's stare burned. It was a relief to see a measure of fire in her friend, even from simple teasing. "I took it," she said, earning a sigh of relief. "You think I'm going to ruin Nyah's big day?"

Nyah was as beloved to Lucia as a niece, but that didn't make her a good ruler. *Lucia* should be queen, a fact that burned in the back of her throat even on the eve of the wedding and coronation. She was the most powerful vampire on the island, the only one who could wield the Fell's alien magic. Their small council of advisors and Blood Princes had voted Adrius in as their leader though, agreeing with his plan for vampire kind's future over Lucia's. He'd taken up his crown mere months ago.

Adrius was a naïve fool when it came to the nature of their people. He wanted to fade into the shadows and become a protector of mortal kind, holding them all to the high ideals of knighthood that he'd learned from Gwendolyn and her late husband, the indomitable Gabriel Legion, so named for the amount of Fell he'd killed in his time as a Fell hunter.

But realistically, the vampires were a race of humans both blessed and cursed by Fell blood. They were immortal, beautiful, and vain but kept those traits by feeding off of human vitality. They weren't protectors. Before she'd become a Sorceress, Lucia had long observed their true nature as a mortal outsider.

Once she had a taste of power, she knew. They were conquerors, destined to rule the world as a superior race with the strength and immortality stolen from Fell blood. The council had not agreed.

"What is it like? Does the Emperor's voice whisper to you from the grave?" Gwendolyn asked.

"Don't say such things. He's dead." Lucia dropped her voice. "There is no curse." And if she kept talking so freely about whispers, insanity claims would follow Lucia like the blowing breeze. Especially if Gwendolyn murmured in the ears of the right people.

Gwendolyn's brow rose, but she sighed, adjusting her skirts. "You need to freshen up for the event, yes? Why don't we have a chat on the way back to the palace?"

"Yes, why don't we?" Lucia muttered, letting go of her small occultarus. It started to orbit her slowly, moving with her as she walked. It was attuned to her, answering her every whim and desire for her spell crafting needs.

"You and I have clearly documented Fell talking about a broken pact," Gwendolyn began after they cleared the earshot of the guards.

"It's the worst thing that can happen to a Fell, yes. But I'm not a Fell. I'm hardly a vampire. I don't need to drink blood even. There's no grounds to say that I'm cursed because I broke a pact with the Fell Emperor."

Gwendolyn regarded her with quiet disappointment as if speaking to a lying child. "How do you explain the darkness we've cleansed from your eyes?" They'd only seen veins like it in the eyes of the Fell, which were black in iris and sclera alike, pools of darkness in their inhuman faces. Lucia had come to her friend for help when her eyes began turning the same way, and one of Nyah's potions had safely cleaned the darkness from her.

Those black veins hadn't returned, and Lucia resented them being brought up again. "They were a complication fixed with medication." She shrugged. "Please, we know eyes are the windows to all manners of magic. Yours glowed with a nephilim's light, and now that the power is gone, so is the glow." Gwendolyn winced, her gaze falling to her hands which had once burned the unholy with blasts of heavenly fire. "Nyah's are gold, yet she drank the same blood as I, and mine are silver. Is it because of her heritage?"

"She drank a more processed version of the Emperor's

blood," she said. "Perhaps that is why she's an Alchemyst and you're a Sorceress." Lucia had been reluctant to share the Emperor's blood, as scarce as it was. She'd wanted to remain the only Sorceress. After all, Lucia was the only one of them clever enough to make a pact with him and receive an influx of Fell magic rather than the bloodlust that hampered the Fell hunters.

Once the impurities were burned from it, the blood was also given to Nyah, as the future queen deserved magic according to the council. To Lucia's relief, she manifested a completely different skill set, her golden blood capable of brewing the strongest of potions.

"My point is we don't *know* anything for sure. We know almost nothing about the Fell. They've left us their secrets as puzzles in their old texts and experiments." Lucia sighed, running a hand through her hair as she pushed it back from her face. "Maybe their silver-blooded Sorcerers developed black veins as well. Perhaps they start out young and silver and degrade to black-blooded as they age."

Gwendolyn sucked on the inside of her cheek, regarding her with dubious disbelief. "We've seen enough Fell to know that's not true."

"Be that as it may, I'm *fine*, Gwendolyn. Really. Whatever it was is gone, and I'm not going crazy," she said firmly.

It wasn't what the other woman wanted to hear, but it was truly all Lucia planned to disclose. She didn't need her to know that she was already frantically reading Fell tomes at night, searching for the cure to whatever dark thing ran alongside her silver blood.

She had a different reason to believe there was some foul magic afoot within her, but she wouldn't sign off on her own execution by admitting to it, especially to someone already suspecting something was off about her.

"I haven't bothered Adrius or Nyah about the black veins. Not with their wedding so close," Gwendolyn said, leaning in as her voice dropped. "But if you give me any more reason to suspect something's wrong, I will." A chill settled over Lucia as she imagined how quickly Adrius would use this to remove Lucia from her position as advisor. It would be a step back from her goal—the moonstone crown of vampire queen gracing her brow.

"Very well. You shall not suspect a thing," she said. She seethed inside as she shut herself in her rooms to freshen up. She stood before her full-length dressing mirror, inspecting herself for any flaws as she passed her occultarus from hand to hand.

No dark veins. She was perfect. Young, without a sign of wrinkles nor a wisp of gray in her dark hair. Powerful, so powerful, with the occultarus under her command. A few whispered words to it and she could send the island into a spiral of chaos from her command over light and dark, the elements, or—

"No. I can't," she whispered, shaking her head. But Nyah was about to receive her crown. She had to do *something* before it was too late.

Lucia should be queen. It was written in her blood as the strongest, most capable vampire. No one else could command Nyixa to move as she could. Oh yes, the island moved, but only on commands issued from the Grand Occultarus.

She smiled in the mirror and watched it grow to the too-wide grin of a Fell's. For a moment, she imagined sharp teeth lining her mouth like the bite of a piranha and recoiled, screwing her eyes shut as she looked away.

Gwendolyn could never know the truth. There were no whispers, not with the curse she suspected was taking root in her. The thoughts were all her own, spoken in her own mental voice. She turned back to the mirror, seeing her own terror as she hyperventilated before the glass. "Gwendolyn is my friend," she said slowly, clutching the front of her gown.

Gwendolyn was...her enemy. She was pathetic, weak, and ready to stab Lucia in the back at a moment's notice.

"What?" she whispered, shaking her head. That's not what she thought. She *liked* Gwendolyn, one of the only people who had always treated her kindly.

"I want Adrius to be a good king to our people."

I would be a better, stronger queen. He was a fool that'd nearly gotten himself killed countless times.

"Nyah is like a daughter to me."

She took a deep, shuddering breath, waiting for the

conflicting thoughts to press in. When nothing came, she started over. Gwendolyn was her friend. She wanted Adrius to be a good king. She wanted sweet Nyah to enjoy her wedding.

A black speck bloomed in the corner of her eye like a burst blood vessel. She chanted on without noticing it, wanting to believe her own words.

4

ADRIUS

Today's specimen confirmed our worst fears. There will be no stopping the invasion unless we do it by force. Nothing remains but a smoldering ruin where the Fell hail from. They've destroyed their land, and now they've come to destroy ours.

-From Lucia's Journal

When the music started playing and Adrius at last beheld Nyah, it felt like his throat was in a vice. She was gorgeous, floating in on her mother's arm. Even through the wedding veil, he knew her eyes glimmered with awe from the display of lamps as she passed through a split tide of vampires and servants. Everyone they could invite was there, both from the island and those who could travel to it on short notice. Hundreds of eyes admired the future queen of Nyixa, but she only had eyes for Adrius as she ascended the stairs and placed her palm in his.

Her blonde hair was woven into a graceful bun, individual strands framing a glimmering moonstone circlet. The prized dress Gwendolyn had crowed about had a corset that fit tight to her chest with moonstones and pearls sewn into the material all the way down to her hips, where the skirts flared into a starburst of white fabric trailing into gold, giving her a train like the tail of a shooting star.

He lifted her veil and cupped her delicate cheek, which was painted a rosebud pink. Everyone would admire his beloved tonight, he thought, ready to kiss her right out of turn.

"Mother says you've been waiting out here for hours." Her voice was high and sweet like music.

"For you. And every moment was worth it," he said, searching her face for any sign of regret and finding only her devotion glowing back at him. It was the same thing he felt from their mating bond, delving deeper than the physical ceremony they were about to perform. Their love for one another twined together as their friend Jaromir recited the vows in lieu of a priest.

Jaromir was one of the eight Fell hunters that'd survived their siege of Nyixa. The other seven bore silent witness in the front row. Gwendolyn waited with the ring box to Jaromir's right, and Lucia stood in the other place of honor to his left, her hands clasped tightly before her as she beheld Nyah's splendor with gleaming silver eyes.

When it came time for the rings, Nyah reached in first, placing the ring he'd meant for her onto his finger. They'd chosen to give each other symbolic rings of the Fell Keys they had in their possession. There were thirteen in total, though the Fell hunters had only eleven, the other two lost.

Each Key had its own story, wielded by a Fell Sorcerer for maximum destructive effectiveness. The Keys were a set of rings, each with a stone from the Fell Lands, capable of granting the wearer magical abilities. They'd been entrusted to Lucia as the only vampire Sorceress, unable to reach their maximum potential when wielded by anyone else.

Nyah slipped the Shield Key on his finger, and it magically grew thicker and heavier to compliment his masculine hand. "Are you sure?" he murmured, touching the tiger's eye stone at its center. He'd meant it to be symbolic of his protection, and to have her change plans at the last moment threw him.

"You're the one always charging into danger. I want you to be protected," she said. It was the earnestness of her voice that had him nodding and slipping the next ring onto her finger.

"Then I'll give you good luck and new life," he said. The Autumn Key represented harvests and fertility and was meant to symbolize the richness of his new reign. But he had to admit the ruby ring suited her and her temperament quite well.

They turned to Lucia for her to bind the rings to them. She'd stated the magic was in one of her books where she could "attune" the Key to answer only to them. As she reached out to take his hand, a gentle rumble shook the earth. Onlookers murmured amongst themselves.

Adrius went on high alert, though he didn't dare jerk away from the spell Lucia wove over his hand until it was finished. It felt like the ring tightened on his finger as he turned, his preternatural senses focused beyond the chattering of the crowd. He could faintly pick up a *swish swish* sound on the breeze.

"Do you hear that?" he whispered to the only one close by who would know what it meant, Jaromir, who looked pale in his fine suit.

"Yes," Jaromir said. "It's a portal. They're attacking *now*."

The other Fell hunters pushed into motion, rushing toward the Grand Occultarus before anyone could panic as the hum and swish of an activating portal grew in intensity.

Adrius turned back to his bride, watching the emotions flit across her face. Though torn, she met his eye and nodded. "Finish the ceremony so you can go. Lucia can bind my ring later," she said.

Jaromir announced before the crowd, "I now pronounce you man and wife. You may now kiss the bride!"

Now everyone knew something was wrong. Someone screamed, and panic seemed to descend at the same time Adrius pulled his new wife to him. They shared a quick mash of lips, nothing like the romantic kiss he'd imagined hundreds of times over.

"Do what you have to do." Nyah's quick fingers undid the buttons of his fine jacket, pushing it from his shoulders. He was still about to ruin the finest thing he ever wore with Fell blood, but there was no time for regrets.

He broke the peace tie on his sword and took one last glance at her before turning to Lucia. "Let's go." Only she could close the portal.

She inclined her head with a sigh, but he swore she was smiling as he turned away and shouted a path through a gaggle of panicking socialites. Most startled out of the way when they saw him coming though. Despite the finery, he was still over six feet of solid muscle and fury. His fangs lengthened as he anticipated the fight to come.

After drinking the Fell Emperor's blood, he knew he was at capacity for the amount of otherworldly power he could hold. He'd taken in so much he'd had to share with the other remaining Fell hunters. Otherwise, it would've killed him. He still craved the taste and power. Maybe he'd have just a little more from these invaders...

By the time he reached the portal, there was already a pile of bodies, mostly Fell. The majority hadn't made it ten paces from the portal before encountering arrows and steel from the elite force of Fell hunters and their available trainees. They'd been lucky, with most of the island inhabitants at the wedding.

Sirius, his brother, slashed forward with his blade, taking out a Fell about to spring at him. Its head, stuck in a wide rictus grin displaying two rows of fangs like a bear trap, rolled to Adrius's feet. "Protect the Sorceress!" he called, heading into the fray.

The Grand Occultarus's massive orb spun faster than the eye could place, its surface black and rippling like liquid as more and more Fell piled through. He remembered them rushing through like fish in a river, but this was a tepid stream, as if they weren't prepared to siege.

He knew it wouldn't last, so he lifted his sword and joined the fight, placing himself between them and Lucia as he carved a path toward the portal. He hadn't missed the foul, sulfurous smell of their homeland so thick his eyes watered. They noticed him flinching and pressed their advantage, coiling back on legs long and jointed like a frog's. A dozen sprang at him and Lucia at once.

An arrow whipped by, impaling two through their heads. Chandra, a veteran Fell hunter, stood atop one of the nearby buildings, loosing and reloading rapidly. Adrius stood his ground; the creatures would sail into Lucia if he ducked. He killed several, dropping their bodies before they could bite or claw him. But three found their mark, sinking those bear trap maws into his flesh.

He grunted as his blood flowed freely. Each Fell feasted from him in great, sloppy swallows, stealing his strength. He crushed their necks with his bare hands, the world spinning as he tossed the last body away. More Fell turned to him, hissing as the smell of fresh blood hit their slit-like nostrils.

Most of them were emaciated without recognition, mere husks of bone and muscle. The situation in the Fell Lands must be dire. He seized the next one that leapt at him and bit into its neck, its blood flowing like liquid electricity down his dry throat. His injuries were severe, so he justified the taste before hefting his sword once more and slashing his way toward the portal.

It closed when he was within three strides of it. A great shriek came over the remaining Fell, all of them turning back toward the Grand Occultarus, surprise in their flat, black eyes. Adrius helped make quick work of the stragglers, but he was just as shocked.

Lucia hadn't touched the portal, so she didn't cause its closing. And the Fell wouldn't be stupid enough to close it when they had the advantage in numbers, especially while desperate and starving.

Only one answer came to mind as he helped finish off the stragglers. Gwendolyn had given every ounce of her magic, and nearly her life, to close the portal between Nyixa and the Fell Lands. Perhaps it would never open fully again. Her sacrifice was not in vain, not to the extent she beat herself up about it. He assumed she'd damaged the orb enough for it to close on its own.

He turned a bloody smile toward his friends. They, too, were injured but grinning, victorious and flush with power once more.

Lucia glanced around and huffed. "Don't you brutes know I need live test subjects?"

5

NEALA

Neala sat within the palace laboratory a few days after the wedding, watching Nyah work as she finished mixing a potion with a couple drops of her golden blood. Magical light suffused the brownish liquid. "It's not the prettiest, but it should chase away your symptoms," she said, passing it to the woman who sat next to Neala. Prince Chandra, the Dreamer, had dark bruises under her eyes from her dreams turning to nightmares.

Neala was also a veteran Fell hunter, one of the few who's survived the siege of Nyixa. She'd taken the title Prince Wraith, rolling her eyes every time she was referred to that way. Being a Blood Prince was a formal title and thus gender-neutral despite its masculine slant.

Things were quiet on Nyixa with the wedding party dispersing back to their homelands. Unfortunately, the mortals who'd dared take a chance to visit would be going back with tales of Fell and an active Grand Occultarus. Neala left the political concerns to the royal family and their advisors, instead seizing the opportunity to take some time with her two friends since Nyah was already back to work.

"Thank you," Chandra said, pinching her nose as she swallowed the thick liquid. She'd come to Nyah seeking help with her magic, having a unique problem.

The nine Fell hunters who'd succeeded in capturing the Fell Emperor had all shared a portion of his blood magic. Adrius was the only one to sip from the Fell's veins directly, and the attempt to hold all that power nearly killed him. The Blood Princes took what they could from Adrius, saving him from a grim fate in what was otherwise their finest hour.

Being the last to drink, Chandra had received the dregs, sharing snippets of abilities that filled her body with half-formed power. Her most notable skill was a talent to enter and manipulate someone else's dreams. With that as her only claim to a bloodline, she'd been titled Prince Dreamer.

She often complained of nightmares though, and the ability to cause those was something Elandros, otherwise known as Prince Legion, was perfecting. Neala hoped that this would be the end to that particular piece of magic within her.

Chandra was the only Blood Prince who'd survived their war without taking up a sword, meaning she and Neala hadn't had much time to get to know each other until recently. She was an archer with an uncanny knack for lucky shots. It kept her alive even though she was a newer recruit and was a relative unknown compared to the other surviving Fell hunters.

She was lithe and athletic underneath her bright teal sari, a wide smile showing pearly teeth and fangs as the potion soothed her lingering pain. Neala appreciated her presence, as it uplifted the laboratory which was close to a dungeon with its low walls and questionable smells. "I think it's working," Chandra said. "You need me to stay?"

"Unfortunately, you should suffer my company for another hour so we can check for side effects." As Nyah spoke, Chandra made a face of playful horror.

"Such a hardship. I don't know how I'll take it. Do you?" She turned to Neala, who smiled silently as she watched them banter.

They were expecting a reply, so she swallowed and cleared her throat, speaking with effort. "We'll be bored for certain." Her voice was nothing more than a quiet rasp. Nyah turned back to her station, mixing up a new potion.

When she set the finished vial before Neala, she earned a raised brow. Coating her voice in scorn, she picked it up and rolled around the thin liquid, watching the air bubbles bob from side to side. "Another one?"

Nyah was as dear as a sister to her. Gwendolyn had raised them together with Neala as her ward. Hope glimmered in the other woman's golden eyes as she drank the potion without any other hint of complaint.

Though Nyah didn't know why Neala's voice was stricken from her throat at an early age, she'd done everything in her power to give it back. Nothing worked, not even the preternatural healing bestowed on a vampire from drinking pure Fell blood.

It didn't help that Neala refused to reopen the book about her past, before Gwendolyn had found her begging and covered in dirt by the side of an old trail. Back then, at the height of her nephilim power, Gwendolyn had seen something in Neala—some potential—which spurred her to take in a mute child. She would say it was fate, some part of her sensing what Neala was to become.

The lack of voice didn't hinder Neala's success. She'd followed in Gabriel Legion's footsteps and became a Fell hunter, emulating him in sword work and Gwendolyn in her nephilim ideals. As a Fell hunter who'd traveled with Adrius since the beginning of the vampire race, she was comparable in height and musculature to a man. The Fell blood had changed her over time, replacing delicate femininity with physical prowess and an ease with her vampire abilities.

Strength was something Neala embraced when her voice would hinder. She could not rely on a woman's silver tongue nor an inheritance from the parents she didn't acknowledge. So instead, she was one of the men. She wore no glamor, the power to influence how a vampire was perceived, even though Neala was perfectly capable of influencing minds to see her as a great beauty.

Day after day, she wore her true face. Thin-lipped, with squinty eyes and an overlarge nose gracing her face, which was made less flattering with how she constantly scowled. Her hair was raggedly cut by the edge of a blade, a lazy afterthought for her thick, red mane.

Like Chandra, she had eyes as red as blood. Drinking Fell blood directly influenced them. Red for Blood Princes, silver for Lucia.

Black for Adrius, who drank in all the power of the Fell Emperor and lived with help from the Blood Princes sharing the burden with him.

And for Nyah...Neala wasn't exactly sure why hers were golden when she was also turned by the Fell Emperor's blood after his death and Lucia's pact with him. Nyah had cleaned and purified it, reducing quarts down to a few vials that were safe to consume. Without the impurities, perhaps she was the result, as Lucia's sorcery resulted from a drink of raw blood.

They may never know for sure, as the remaining vials were considered too precious to give to a mortal. Even a drop could magnify a vampire's power and blood-based abilities, which was a siren's call not even Blood Princes could resist.

Having golden blood blessed Nyah as an Alchemyst, able to mix potions that could alter and bless other vampires. She'd helped purify the most maddening part of being a vampire, the endless thirst for the vitality of others. Neala was able to feed off of mortals without hurting them, which was a blessing when compared to the Fell, who were never satiated.

As Nyah's most recent potion worked its way through Neala's body, she coughed, feeling it all the way in her lungs.

"Well? Did it work?" Chandra asked, patting her on the back.

"I don't know. Is this better?" Neala croaked. "I can't tell if it hurts to talk because of the potion or if it's just me." Though most potions did the same thing to her, showing a glimpse of potential and healing before leaving her voice as broken as before.

"Why don't we wait a day and test it?" Nyah suggested. "Maybe get some fresh air."

Neala bobbed her head in agreement, standing to her full, intimidating height. "Would you like to come, too?" she offered to the last person in the room. Lucia was in the back, stooped over a portion of a Fell's corpse. Her gaze rose, face blank from deep thought.

"I'm all right. I'll have a new pile of reagents for you when you return," she said, her gaze unblinking as she spoke mostly to Nyah. Neala shifted uncomfortably for a moment.

"Suit yourself," she murmured, leaving the room with her friends in tow. Servants bowed as the three of them passed through the main corridors of the palace on the long trip down into the city and the gardens Nyah loved so much.

"It's not going to work, is it?" Neala asked as the breeze hit them, tinged with the brine of the sea. Her lungs prickled with pain as they descended the near-endless stairs toward the palace gardens. For all of its splendor, getting to and from the city left even Neala winded.

Chandra nudged her, smiling. "Let's enjoy the flowers and butterflies. Nyah's made a bunch of them, don't you know?"

A blush rose to their queen's cheeks. "I don't want *everyone* to know I've been breeding butterflies!"

"How?" Neala glanced between them, confused.

Glancing around as they ventured off the path and into the greenery of her garden, Nyah lifted her sleeve to show a second Fell Key next to the Autumn Key bound permanently to her finger. The Spring Key—granting the ability to shape shift. "Put two of these together and you can make life," she whispered. "It's a secret, okay? No one needs to know that two of these things together are that strong."

Neala blinked, her brows rising high. "As you wish. You're making butterflies with that though? Of all things?"

A cluster of the little, colorful creatures fluttered by, luminescent in the dark of Nyixa. She imagined their glow was made special. "Why not?" Nyah smiled. "I am a queen, after all. I require butterflies."

6

LUCIA

I began to notice a change in myself. I could see events unfolding in the future when I closed my eyes. Some were daydreams, far away madness, but others were happening just moments from where I existed. I was privy to conversations, the invisible fly on the wall. More power for me to wield when I am queen.

-From Lucia's Journal

Lucia scoffed as she returned to her work. "She is queen, after all. She requires butterflies," she said in a mocking undertone. In the blink of an eye, she'd seen how the afternoon would play out for Nyah and her two friends as a vision of the future. When she first realized what her strange daydreams were, she was excited for the opportunity to use her future sight to plan and manipulate.

However, most of the time, it delivered her snippets no more useful than background noise. She did not need to be present to know the three women were out having a pity party for Prince Wraith. Lucia knew the truth. There would be no returning voice, not if Fell blood had not already healed it.

Nyah was wasting her time, naïve child that she was. She could be exploring the depths of her gift, brewing potions or discovering new ones. But no, she had to have her butterflies. Using Lucia's priceless artifacts, no less.

Lucia finished her last incision, studying the laid-out chest cavity of a deceased Fell. There were harvestable parts here for certain invocations and elixirs, but that's not what she cared about. Fell had different organs than humans, and it frustrated her that she had not yet had a live subject to vivisect and see how those organs worked in harmony together. She'd seen them many times before in their inert form, shriveled or pierced from cause of death. The bodies were usually chopped to bits by Fell hunters who only wanted the creatures dead, not to understand them.

How was she to understand their magic in full if she didn't understand how their bodies had adapted to wield it?

She turned away with a scoff, intending to finish this work later. First, she would need to move the box where she stored the rest of the Fell Keys. If Nyah had found and taken one of them, then it required a new home. Lucia was forced to surrender two Keys to the royalty and one to Gwendolyn, but the rest, she coveted like the precious gems they were.

Turning to one of the cabinets full of empty materials, she started setting aside beakers and vials, reaching into a hidden compartment in the very back. She tweezed her tongue between her teeth as she felt for a tiny latch. "Lady Lucia?"

The sudden voice startled her. Glass shattered as she turned sharply toward the speaker. "Elandros. What do you want?" She hardly hid her sigh, knowing exactly what he would ask.

The man was nothing if not persistent. Her fingers drifted away from the latch, glad he hadn't snuck in as she'd taken a peek at her little treasures. "I was wondering if you had a task for me to repay my debts," he said. Tall and handsome as any Blood Prince now—*save Prince Wraith,* she thought with a snicker—the way he bit his lip betrayed his anxiety. It was worse every time he came to ask.

She remembered him before he became a Fell hunter, a gawky teenager squiring for Gabriel Legion himself. A little glamor and a few years suited him well even though she saw the unsure boy in him every time they were alone. He'd claimed his Blood Prince name, Legion, was in honor of his old master, but she knew better.

"There's nothing I have that needs your special skills," she said, a touch of saccharine to her tone as she smiled his way.

"I can't wait forever for you to pick a task." His face twisted into a scowl. *That's how he looks on the inside, squinting and ugly,* she thought. That impatience was something she could use, though it often irritated her.

She tisked at him as if he were an errant child. "I kept Gwendolyn from knowing what you did. Fancy an execution block instead?"

For that was where he'd be without her. She would win this silent stalemate every time it came up, much as it frustrated him. It wasn't her fault he'd chosen to assassinate his mentor in a fit of treachery. She didn't know the specifics except that he'd tried to hide the evidence behind her makeshift laboratory in the Fell hunter camp right before a skirmish.

The idiot owed her for helping him frame a Fell for the murder. And now that he was a Blood Prince, seemingly free of faults, Elandros was worth more under her thumb than the religious old man he'd betrayed. He just tended to squirm as he realized how much she owned him.

Elandros turned a shade paler. "I just—"

"I *will* call for you when I need you and not a moment sooner." She turned her back to pick up some of the larger glass shards. The hair lifted on the back of her neck to feel him looming over her, watching with arms crossed.

"As you wish." On those murmured words, he backed away.

"Elandros," she said before he could take more than a few steps. He stopped and glanced her way. "How much Fell blood has Adrius consumed recently?"

As one of the first responders when the portal opened on its whims, he would be one of the most likely to know. "He finds a reason to drink from one every time there's a fight. Why?"

"Mighty unwise for someone who couldn't handle all of the Fell Emperor's power." She made the remark casually, gliding past him to set the shards aside for disposal later in a safer place.

Elandros hesitated. Considering the implications, she hoped. "You do not have the same problem that we do. Fell blood is an addiction. Power is a drug."

"How long before he goes mad with it?" She stepped closer to him, her gaze imploring but, unbeknownst to her, unblinking. Nerves seemed to steal over him. "And who would you stand with if that happened?"

"I would adapt to the situation as it happens," he said, a nervous quaver to his voice.

She nodded approvingly, reaching up to pat his shoulder. "As would I. Now go. I have important work to be doing."

"Yes, Lady Lucia." He hurried from the room as if burned while she smiled to herself. That was one less Blood Prince to worry about when it came time to take her crown. Elandros wouldn't dare to cross her for fear of what she knew of him. She also had the heart of Prince Taryn, the Blade, though he wasn't quite a willing ally at first. She'd stolen a high-powered love potion to make it so, bending his emotions to utter servitude to her.

That left six Blood Princes to stand in her way. Mostly, they were weak sycophants, allowing Nyah her butterflies and Adrius his dreams. Who'd put children in charge? Why, the council of Blood Princes, skipping to Gwendolyn's lead.

She blew out an angry breath as she retrieved her Fell Keys, setting the open, nondescript box next to her current project. Created personally for her, the jewelry display within held thirteen slots for the magical rings they'd reclaimed from certain high-ranking Fell. At one point, each slot was filled, burning with power.

They didn't know how the rings were forged or how they'd come to represent Fell magic. Lucia salivated at the thought of interrogating live Fell now that she knew more about them. She and Gwendolyn had questioned subjects in the past, but back then, Lucia had agreed to their executions afterward, each a mercy killing for sharing a glimmer of understanding in their race. *Foolish*, she thought now.

Since the set was assembled and put in her care, she'd lost two and assumed they were beyond recovery—the Keys of Day and Summer, which allowed the withstanding of two of the Fell's greatest weaknesses, daylight and fire. Two Fell hunters had died wearing them, and their corpses were recovered without them. Some lucky Fell was still on the other side of the portal, bathing in that power.

The Portal Key was in Gwendolyn's trust and most notably used to close the Grand Occultarus the first time. Lucia was suspicious that she'd broken it as part of her *great sacrifice*, pouring all of its power in with the tidal wave of her nephilim light. It was a terrible loss, as their army had once relied on it to traverse the land quickly and intercept Fell before they could overrun villages and townships.

With the Shield and Autumn Keys permanently attuned to Adrius and Nyah until their deaths, Lucia considered the ones she had left. She drank in the feeling emanating from the box and how it weighed far too much for a combination of wood, velvet, and metal.

She wondered if any of them could be paired, as Nyah had paired Autumn and Spring, to create an effect even grander than what they'd originally been created to gift. The Keys representing combat, darkness, weather control, flight, universal language, restoration, and mesmerization lay before her. She figured she could create a great fighter or one gifted to be a living hurricane with the proper combinations, but she would test them all.

She donned her favorite, the Language Key, and admired the triangle-shaped pink sapphire set within it. It looked like a tiny tongue in the right light. As she put it on, it adjusted to her finger, its band hugging her skin as power flowed from it through the rest of her. She laughed with the heady rush, feeling like a goddess, able to strip language from another's head or fill it to bursting with words from countless ones.

Her first experiment became clear as she slipped on the Mind Key, which governed mesmerization and mental communication. Plucking her personal occultarus from its orbit, she put her palm on its orb, giving it a spin while her thumb rested on the symbol for "portal".

Distant screams rose from the city. A too-wide smile split her face as she let her eyes close, lost in countless visions. She was pleased to have some useful ones, seeing the path ahead more clearly now. The Keys hummed on her fingers, transitioning more power through her occultarus. It was the longest and—her future sight showed her—most devastating invasion yet.

Within an hour, a desperate Adrius came to her with a live test subject.

7

GWENDOLYN

The Fell was quite forthcoming, given the right motivation. I learned that Fell magic consists of three domains. Body, mind, and soul. The most advanced form they've created is that of body with their shapeshifting and preternatural strength. Mind, we all can harness in one degree or another with glamors. But soul is something only Nyah and I control. She can alter a vampire's magic, and I can wield Fell magic.

We've started experiments in mental communication. It seems Prince Wraith will have her voice back, after all. I should be happy for her.

-From Lucia's Journal

G wendolyn didn't know of the new test subject for a day until Lucia mentioned it offhandedly as she scribbled in her journal.

"You interrogated a subject without me?" Gwendolyn said in surprise. She'd taken the day off to rest her body.

The silver-eyed woman shrugged, hardly looking up from her

writing. She did that often, fixated on writing every tiny detail as if fearing they would fly from her mind like fledgling birds. "I wanted to use new techniques on it. It's been so long since we had a live one."

Standing, Gwendolyn leaned on a walking stick. Her whole body ached with the motion. Jaromir, their resident doctor, warned that she needed to drink more blood else her body would continue to age and eventually fail. The vampire curse acted like an illness if not properly treated, he'd explained, and blood was the medicine to fix it. Though she had great self-control compared to other vampires, she would eventually be compelled to sate her blood hunger.

She was four days into another fast, finding that her body agreed with Jaromir's diagnosis. Her limbs felt heavy as she limped toward the door, addressing one of the guards on duty. "Send a page to fetch me a plate of meat scraps. I'll be in the dungeon." He saluted in acknowledgement.

Hopefully, she wasn't wasting food on this captive Fell. Nyixa did not have a stable food source yet, so everything was imported from neighboring countries. Adrius ensured that the crown incurred the expense, as they had to feed the population of humans that lived on Nyixa for the vampires to have a food source, too. Humans stayed on the island for the food and honest work, living in harmony with the Fell hunters. They were some of the only mortals that acknowledged vampires as advanced humans rather than monsters one step below Fell. The vampires needed to focus more on diplomacy if they wished for approval beyond Nyixa's boundaries.

Gwendolyn headed toward the back of the laboratory. "Please tell me you don't plan to vivisect our prisoner," she said to Lucia as she eyed a staircase descending into a square of pitch darkness. The Fell creators of the palace had linked a row of cells to the laboratory. She and Lucia had hurriedly cleansed its contents before Nyah could see rotting remnants of some grisly experiments, corpses of Fell and human alike forgotten in this dank pit. It still smelled rank; the enclosed space was impossible to air out completely.

"Of course not. It's much more interesting to me alive. Right now, at least." Lucia came up behind Gwendolyn with a lit torch, following her down into the dungeon. Three sets of cells lined either side of the small space, and a hiss came from one in the back.

Gwendolyn threw her friend a suspicious look as Lucia locked the torch into a sconce at the base of the stairs. Any closer and they risked burning the Fell's paper-thin skin.

"So does this mean you're planning on doing so later?" she asked.

Wetting her lips, Lucia shrugged again. "Probably." She didn't wither under Gwendolyn's judgmental look. "This is science, not religion, nephilim."

An uneasy feeling crept over the back of her neck as Lucia returned her stare, unblinking. Something was truly not right with her, and it was about time she shared her misgivings. Now that the wedding and coronation were finished, the royal couple could give the matter the attention it was due. "Promise me you'll keep the subject alive," Lucia said.

"As long as it is not suffering, I will allow it to live," she hedged. Fell captives lasted hours at most, gnashing their shark teeth over any loose objects as they tried desperately to sate their oppressive hunger.

"Very well. Let us compare our findings when you're finished," Lucia said, leaving her alone as she returned to her notes. It was a gamble, Gwendolyn thought, to leave her alone with their captive and assume that she wouldn't end its suffering. In the past, she did so quickly, taking pity on the creatures that so quickly faded to mindless, starving beasts.

She limped her way to the last cell to her left, where a live Fell crouched in a darkened corner where the torchlight didn't reach. Its pointed teeth gleamed pure white as it panted in panic. The smell of burnt flesh haloed it, courtesy of the golden chains binding its wrists.

Nephilim chains shackled its magic, leaving it hopelessly weak and starving in this cell. They'd sized down with magic to squeeze the Fell's emaciated wrists, glowing subtly to show the outline of a thin, shivering frame. Rags covered its loins but not the exposed ribcage and grayish skin on its chest. It was male then. She eyed the chains on him with a soft sigh. She'd created them, once able to channel heaven's light into any metal and make it sturdy enough to shackle and cripple the wicked.

The dozen or so pairs she'd made would be the only nephilim chains the Fell hunters would ever have, barring the extraordinary circumstance of meeting another nephilim. A pang hit her heart at the reminder, leaving her staring at her feet.

"Please, hunter." The voice came into her mind as she hesitated there, drier than desert sand. She'd only ever spoken to a handful of Fell, but its voice was unmistakable. Cursed with eternal thirst, they all sounded desperate for a drink of water.

"Please what? You came through a portal seeking to claim mortal lives. To *feast* on us." She squared her shoulders, fixing her face into a fierce scowl. How she missed her eyes blazing with holy power, warning the wicked of what kind of judgement they were facing.

It pressed itself further into the wall with a fearful hiss. *"Please, mercy. No torture. I will talk."*

So Lucia's "new techniques" were torture, she thought. While Gwendolyn didn't like it, she had to acknowledge it was a necessity to crack open their enemies and retrieve the information they'd needed. But she'd never left them alive afterward, knowing the combination of pain and hunger was an undue cruelty. Was Lucia's insistence on that very cruelty pragmatism, or something worse?

"Very well. Let us talk." She leaned on her staff, wishing one of them had had the foresight to bring a stool.

The Fell's face was impassive, and they had a staring match as the bells chimed the hour. She knew he would talk the moment she had food to offer. It came slowly, but eventually a page arrived with a plate piled high with a butcher's scraps.

The page fetched her a stool to sit upon, his skin pale as he avoided looking into any of the cells. Gwendolyn gave him a coin for his troubles and sat herself right across from the cell, watching the Fell turn his full attention to the plate in her lap.

She tossed him a scrap, which disappeared whole down his throat.

"What do you wish to know?" he asked. A smile played faintly at her lips. She, too, could use a different interrogation method with this Fell.

His question opened a mountain of possibilities, a dozen questions coming to mind immediately. She knew so little of the Fell. Their captives were never alive and forthcoming long enough to share more than a glimpse of their culture and ways. During the war, she and Lucia had interrogated for information to help their cause, but now that the Fell hunters had won, there were so many additional possibilities.

Lucia would've asked him about magic, the only thing she cared about with her new transformation into a Sorceress, so Gwendolyn didn't waste precious time repeating questions of that nature. "Tell me about you. Who are you?"

"Me?" he echoed in surprise. In the resulting pause, she wondered if there wasn't actually more to him. Maybe he'd been spawned in some dark crack in the Fell Lands, a monster with one, singular purpose. She felt a measure of pity for him, for such a life was hardly one worth the air it breathed.

"My name is Typhos," the Fell said, each word an uncertain croak. Gwendolyn nodded, heartened that he at least had a name. She'd never known a Fell by its name.

"Were you always a Fell?" It was strange to speak casually to one of her longtime enemies, but out came the question that burned brightest at the back of her throat. She tossed him another scrap.

"No, I was born in Faerie. My father was leader of the Jeweler's Guild, and I was apprenticed to him when our kind were cursed." He tilted his head, pitch-black eyes staring, unblinking. It was eerily similar to how Lucia had taken to looking at her, she realized uneasily. *"You do not know the story of our curse, do you?"*

"No. This is also the first time I've heard about faeries," she said. She'd met superstitious folk who'd sworn faeries existed and were responsible for countless misfortunes but hadn't taken one seriously. There was no proof, not like her first-hand witness of wicked demons and selfless angels.

At the same time, she'd always known that Fell were something outside of her black-and-white world of heaven and hell. As awful as they were, they weren't demons. Demon kind made Fell look like kittens by comparison.

"Allow me to inform you then," Typhos said on a weary sigh. *"I used to be an astral fae like many of the original Fell. In your tongue, we are called the Exalted Ones, masters of mind, body, soul, and the four elements. Each of us are blessed with magic. Some have very little, like myself. Others are born with a great amount of magic and become our Sorcerers."*

"Those Sorcerers—they have silver blood?" she interrupted, immediately fascinated. The Fell sounded like he believed every word of his tale, but she would still press for every detail to get a complete picture. If he told the truth, he would be able to enumerate it all.

"Fell Sorcerers do, yes. Astral Sorcerers had silver eyes that glittered like a thousand stars." He sounded wistful, clasping his hands as he spoke.

"What about gold blood? Or eyes?" She leaned forward in her staff, betraying her eagerness as she thought of Nyah and her incredible skill with magical potions.

"You speak of astral Archfae. There is ever only one, an ascended Sorcerer that serves the Faerie King as a political leader." The creature's chest rattled as he took a deep breath. Gwendolyn flinched away from him, though she was fizzing to share this news with Nyah. It was only right that her daughter was the vampire equivalent of an Archfae.

"Our Archfae, Izell, was the strongest of the Arch Council, and her proximity to the Faerie King's side caused...this." He gestured to himself, his too-wide mouth stretched into a grimace. *"I am not privy to the whole story. All I know is that she stole his crown and pried the gems from it. He cursed every astral fae he could find for her crime, for his wrath and cruelty are a thing of legend."*

"That seems quite extreme," she remarked, raising an eyebrow. Judging by the numbers of Fell they'd slain, he'd damned thousands of souls with this curse. What could provoke such a reaction?

"It is the fae way. He punished us all with eternal hunger to be a

constant reminder of Izell's treachery. We were supposed to turn on
Izell and return his gems to him. He promised to lift the curse once he
had all thirteen of them."

"I take it you didn't do that." Else he wouldn't be here, and
the Fell would've never invaded human land.

A dry cough wracked his emaciated body. *"We tried at first.*
Izell was a prisoner to our new leader, the Emperor, but she'd hidden the
gems in the most clever location she could. Here."

Gwendolyn traced an unfinished carving on her walking
stick. Where was *here*? Thirteen gems, all precious enough that a
ruler would destroy an entire population to have them
returned. She wet her lips as she reached into a secret pocket in
the lining of her robe, withdrawing a gold band and shards of a
gemstone.

Just looking at it made her stomach turn and reminded of the
terrible moment she'd given everything to silence the Grand
Occultarus. The Portal Key rested in her palm. What remained of
it, at least. The amethyst that'd graced its band lay in three
jagged pieces. Without its magical glow, it'd dulled to an ashen
gray.

"You're talking about the Fell Keys," she said, certain now.
The woman he spoke of, Izell, had stolen the thirteen Fell Keys
and scattered them through the world for humans and Fell alike
to hunt for. "What could be so important that she would take
away your salvation?"

The Fell stared at the broken Key in her hand, his mouth
hanging open. He didn't respond, instead shuffling forward,
daring to step into the circle of light reaching into his cell. His
knife-like talons smoked upon exposure to firelight. *"Please, let*
me hold it," he begged, swiping ineffectually, unable to bridge the
gap of distance between them. *"What does it matter if I touch it? It*
is broken."

Her eyes narrowed with suspicion. "Back to your corner. I
shall allow you to hold it if it pleases me." Only when he'd
cowered back from her did she speak again, taking in the grisly
sight of smoking wounds over his exposed skin. "Can this be
fixed?"

If she had the Portal Key restored, she could finish the job once and for all. No more Fell to overrun their lands. Her oath to eradicate the Fell threat would be properly finished.

"No, it cannot." The Fell crushed her hope for a breathless moment, as effective as a punch to the sternum. *"However, magic is never lost, hunter. There is hope for my people still. This vessel has broken, but the magic will transfer itself to a new one. How did it break?"*

She regarded him with a twist of her lips, already assuming the vessel the magic now inhabited—the Grand Occultarus itself, still capable of creating portals with the remnants of the Portal Key within it. But she answered anyway. "I sacrificed it to close the permanent portal between your land and mine."

"Then as the one who destroyed it, you now hold its power."

She couldn't help snorting a disbelieving laugh. He sounded serious! If it were so simple, she would surely notice that she was containing power that she shouldn't. But she reached into herself, toward that pit where her holy light used to shine, and came up with an empty feeling. She was no longer a vessel for the power she cared to have.

"What did it represent? Make the symbol with your hands," he insisted.

"It was the Portal Key." She was still chuckling, but it tapered in her discomfort as she shoved the remnants of the ring back into its secret pocket. The Fell made a circle with his index fingers and thumbs, overlapping them to create a perfect circle.

"Imagine a small item and make this symbol. If it teleports to you, you are the new vessel." He leaned forward into the light again, hands clasped in earnest eagerness.

Feeling foolish, she mimicked his earlier gesture. "I'm imagining my quill," she told him, waiting.

A feather fluttered to the ground before her stool. She glanced up, looking for the trick, but there was no errant bird nor anyone else in the dungeon capable of making a quill appear. She picked it up, recognizing the ragged end where it'd broken after rubbing her chin thoughtfully one-too-many times while writing. It was specifically her quill.

Her heart started to race as she turned the simple feather over and over in her fingers. "Impossible," she breathed. It fluttered to the ground as she stood, her whole body protesting the sudden motion.

"Here, a reward." Her voice sounded numb to her ears as she slid the plate of meat into his cell. She needed to find Adrius and Nyah so they could see this for themselves.

8

ADRIUS

I know Gwendolyn will suspect me for our subject's death, but I don't care. Her suspicion is much less damaging to my plans than the information it could've shared.

-From Lucia's Journal

Adrius sat at the head of a conference table as Gwendolyn repeated everything the Fell had told her. He'd called at a council meeting mere hours after she'd burst into the royal chambers, demanding he and Nyah go with her immediately.

The Fell she'd meant for them to listen to was dead, its head buried in the remnants of a pile of meat. "Its stomach must've burst from all that at once," Nyah had suggested, but Gwendolyn's face had drawn into a grim line. She'd shared more with him and his wife than she did in front of the whole council, not telling the group of her newfound ability nor her suspicions of Lucia. It was a prudent move with the other advisor sitting across from Gwendolyn, hands steepled as she considered.

"You think this thing was telling you the truth?" Lucia scoffed immediately. "It thought it was going to be tortured. It lied through its teeth about its magical knowledge when I had a turn with it."

"I believe that in all tales, there are elements of truth. Now we will not know for sure. Will we?" Gwendolyn's question was sharp and aimed right at Lucia.

Lucia shrugged, popping a square of hard cheese into her mouth. She and Nyah still needed mortal food unlike the rest of them, so a light snack of bread and cheeses was set out specifically for them. Adrius itched to try it, but food was on a premium when Nyixa wasn't producing its own. His desire to chew and taste something different than coppery blood would need to wait.

"I do wish you hadn't fed it so much at once. You don't put a starving man before a feast. It's the same concept," Lucia said.

Nyah held up her hand, drawing attention away from the two advisors. "If what it told my mother is true, this changes everything." Adrius felt her blooming compassion over their mating bond, so different from his own reaction.

Gwendolyn's possession of the Portal Key's magic meant they could permanently disable the Grand Occultarus. Adrius's brooding gaze was set on a replica of the city, a diorama they'd found upon taking over the palace. The otherworldly tool in question sat at the very center of the island, glimmering like a cut gem. Around it, the diorama gradually sloped upward from the beach to houses and other structures, to the great palace which took up so much of the island, striking grandly into the sky with its impossibly high towers.

The Grand Occultarus could not be destroyed. It was the pulse of Nyixa, capable of spreading magic over the island or moving it across the sea. Lucia alone could control it, and she'd anchored them like an island-sized ship in a location just off the coast of China. If they could disable the tool, he would be okay with the island staying where it was.

Though he wouldn't admit it out loud, he also wouldn't mind if it sank to the bottom of the ocean instead. With their bridge to human lands gone, the Fell could go terrorize each other for all he cared.

"Apologies, Your Majesty, but I don't agree," said Korin, now known as Prince Bane. The dark-haired man was like a second brother to Adrius. His eyes, like all Blood Princes, were a blood red, though they'd shadowed to maroon, unfocused in the middle distance.

Perhaps he relived memories as Adrius did of the countless battles they'd had and the desolation the monsters left behind when not opposed. Fell were no friends to humanity.

"Really? We have eleven of the Fell Keys." Nyah put her palms down on the table, leaning forward earnestly. "What if we gave them back to the Faerie King?"

A laugh spluttered from Elandros. He swayed in his mirth even under the full attention of the whole council. "Give them back? How are we going to do that?"

Adrius reached under the table and squeezed Nyah's knee as her hands balled into fists. "Be careful how you address your queen," he warned. Without the mocking twist though, he too wondered how they would go about giving the Keys back. They hadn't even known of the Faerie King until this day.

Elandros straightened, schooling his face until his lips stopped twitching. "My apologies, Your Majesty." He'd switched to a courtier's simper in a blink.

"I…" Nyah shot Adrius a desperate look. "I'm not sure *how*. I just think we should."

Sirius spoke what he could not. "Is it wise to empower the man who created the Fell? *If* our captive was telling the truth, which I doubt, the Keys were stolen and sent to us for a reason."

Nyah shook her head hard enough to shake loose a jeweled pin. It was one of the few they could afford to bedeck her in, a shining, frivolous thing she immediately dove to retrieve from the floor. "If we give them back and the Fell give back the two they have, then there will be no more Fell. They won't attack Nyixa anymore. No one else has to die." She fiddled with the silver tines of the ornament, meeting everyone's gaze in turn. Her golden eyes softened as she turned to Adrius last. Through their mating bond, his reluctance and doubts could not hide, but her determination shone back at him.

"Maybe he was telling us a tale," she continued, "but if there is even a small chance that it's true, how can any of us sleep at night knowing a whole group of extraordinary people not unlike ourselves is suffering just so we can wear these." She flipped her hand around, showing the Key she wore as her wedding band.

"This is war," he whispered in a private undertone. "We don't worry over what happens to our enemies."

"We've defeated them," she answered loud enough for the group to hear.

"Can we say that when they still have the ability to come here?" Qin, known as Prince Ascended, was usually quiet in group meetings, but he spoke with a speculative glance between the royal couple. The Chinese man leaned back in his chair, running a white coin between his fingers idly.

Adrius sighed to himself. Qin spoke the same rumblings that circled amongst Nyixa's civilian population. As king, he wanted to say that the war had ended and the Fell hunters had won. But men died every time the portal opened itself out of turn, and fewer mortals were stepping forward to become the next generation of Fell hunters. They needed to do *something* to end this threat for good.

"I'm not saying we throw the Keys at them the next time they come attack us." Nyah sat back as she uttered a sigh of her own. "Some diplomacy is in order. We need a way to confirm the story about them first."

For the moment, the whole council, royalty and advisors alike, was silent. Adrius appreciated the split second to think, though it was Jaromir who spoke first. "I first joined the Fell hunters for their strong principles. We weren't knights, but with Gabriel as one of our leaders, we were held to a high standard of chivalry nonetheless. Is that not a legacy you wish to uphold?" He didn't aim the question toward anyone in particular, but the Blood Princes, former soldiers of Gabriel Legion, sat up straighter at his mere mention.

"Of course," Adrius answered for them all. Every day, he sought to fill two pairs of boots—his own and those belonging to the deceased knight who'd been a beacon of faith in more uncertain times. He wished Gabriel had lived long enough to give his blessing for Adrius to wed Nyah.

"Then we must do the honorable thing," croaked Neala, glancing to Nyah with a nod.

Bolstered, the queen sat straighter. "Diplomacy is the honor we need to follow."

"With all due respect, but how do you intend to go about this?" Lucia asked. "Fell come out of that portal looking for flesh and blood to consume. Do you want to capture another to interrogate or feed the lot of them with the cattle we've had shipped here? They aren't likely to stop eating to listen to you if you go the latter route."

Adrius shook his head, seeing that neither would get the results they were looking for. "I can see how it could work," he said for his wife. "They are more intelligent than we gave them credit for. If we circle the portal with our men and demand their leader, either they comply, or they die. It's worth a try."

There was a general murmur as he asked if there were any other objections. He flashed Nyah a smile as no one spoke up. "Then we are in agreement. Inform our men to stand ready. This meeting is dismissed."

The Blood Princes stood to leave while he, Nyah, and Gwendolyn remained seated. "Lucia, if you would stay behind for a quick chat," Gwendolyn said. The Sorceress raised her brows but sat once more, glancing between them.

Once they were alone, he began the conversation. "Gwendolyn has shared some concerning news with me. Were you cursed?" He opted to be frank, seeing the surprise flit across the silver-eyed woman's face before she schooled it to a calm façade.

"I made an agreement with the Fell Emperor before he died, you recall. His Sorcerer powers for myself in exchange for his life," she said.

"And then I killed him," he said.

"Yes, you did. I did not fulfill my side of the bargain." They all knew this, having been there. He couldn't allow the Emperor to live, and despite her deal with him, they'd already closed the portal back to the Fell Lands. "However, because you were involved, I don't think there's anything to worry about. How could I be expected to get him to safety if he died from someone else chopping his head off?" she reasoned.

He fought off an uneasy feeling as she stared at him. He wasn't so sure she had the right of it, especially after what Gwendolyn had shared. "So why did you start developing black eyes like those of the Fell?"

Lucia opened her mouth to protest. "Don't you dare refute that," Gwendolyn interjected.

"If I knew I was about to go on trial, I wouldn't have stayed here," the Sorceress said indignantly, knocking over her chair in her haste to rise.

"Your actions are very suspicious. Sit, or I'll have the guards drag you to the dungeons," Adrius commanded. He was convinced now that his mother-in-law was onto something when it came to their resident Sorceress.

Lucia gathered up her chair and obeyed, crossing her arms. "We only want what's best for you," Nyah said, the gentle counterpoint to him. "We thought it best to give you a break from your duties for a while. Just so we can observe you and make sure everything's okay."

"A break. You're putting me in prison then?" She scowled. "What do you think is so bad about this so-called curse?"

"If you're cursed to become a Fell, it would explain the black eyes," Adrius said, meeting her glare with one of his own.

She cursed under her breath. "Of course, I'm turning Fell. Maybe you're turning Fell, too, with how much you crave their blood," she hissed, stabbing a finger toward him.

"Enough. Guards!" he called before she could say more that she would regret. Her words dug into his chest like barbs, echoing his own fears back at him. Every time the Fell attacked, he ended up with their blood sliding down his throat.

Two guardsmen came in, going to Lucia as he gestured. "Lock her in her chambers. She isn't to leave."

"Yes, sire." They took her by either shoulder, pushing her from the room as she writhed and struggled.

He sagged in his chair as her protesting voice faded into the hallway. "It was the right thing to do," Nyah said, resting a soft hand over his. "We need her whole and hale."

As he laced his fingers with hers, he hoped she was right.

Gwendolyn understood Lucia's strange actions better than he, and he trusted her implicitly. But he also knew Lucia. She would hold a hearty grudge even if Gwendolyn's accusations were unfounded.

9

GWENDOLYN

To look straight into the Grand Occultarus is to know madness. It is a tool that mocks any who try to harness its power. A firm hand can guide it, but a weak hand will be crushed.
  -From Lucia's Journal

G wendolyn forced herself to feed, relieving her body from its aches and giving herself a second wind. As she made her way to the Grand Occultarus, she kept reliving the moment when Lucia was dragged away by the guards. How she'd glared with a viper's venom at Gwendolyn and the others.

This was not the way Lucia acted before she become a Sorceress. She'd been on the cusp of succumbing to old age, a friendly hedge witch who'd taught Nyah and Gwendolyn alike what she knew of herb lore. The silver blood had changed something in her, and Gwendolyn found new determination in fixing it, be it a curse or a shift in attitude with Lucia's turn of fortune.

But first, she had a more pressing problem. Adrius and Nyah followed as they headed into the city where the Grand Occultarus loomed. Its surface shimmered from constant torchlight in the city square. Several guards watched the structure, hands at the ready on sword pommels or horns to sound the alarm should a portal open. These tense men turned to watch as Gwendolyn stopped at the base of the structure.

"I'm not sure what I'm supposed to do. If I have a Key within me, I can't feel it," she said quietly to Nyah, gesturing to her hand. "You're wearing two Keys. How do you use them?"

"Oh, it's pretty easy. They're eager to do what I want them to. Like they *want* to be used."

"I can't feel mine at all. It just exists," Adrius said, shrugging.

"Here, Mother. Wear this and see if it helps." Nyah pried the Spring Key from her finger, offering it over. It resized itself to fit as she slipped it on, filling her immediately with an awareness of the life around her. Not just the vampires but the rats that scampered between buildings and the butterfly that fluttered by her head, glowing with faint magic of its own. There was far more life on Nyixa than she'd given credit for.

"I can feel this much stronger than whatever is inside of me." She pitched her voice for privacy as she searched within for a sister feeling to the powerful Spring Key. Standing a few yards from the Grand Occultarus, she found it, a drop of power that vibrated on a magical level somewhere within her core. As she focused on it, she realized the tool before her was vibrating to the same frequency.

She stepped forward, trying to place her hand on its bronze base. A force stopped her palm inches from the metal. Tingles and static worked their way down her arm in a numbing wave.

"Mother!" Nyah's cry was distant as if she shouted through water. Gwendolyn's gaze was focused upward as the sphere above her swirled with shadows that pointed and mocked her soundlessly. So fixated on those shadows, she didn't realize the glass was moving. It spun faster and faster.

Her reflection warped where the shadows didn't, smiling at her and holding up the Fell symbol for a portal—index fingers and thumbs curled into a perfect circle. Fire burned to life around the reflection. No, not fire. Wings with feathers so brilliant they blazed.

The next thing she knew, she was lying on her back, stars

gathering behind her tightly shut eyelids. "Are you all right?" Adrius demanded. He loomed over her as she registered the sound of the Grand Occultarus slowing its spinning with a metallic screech.

"Infernal device," Gwendolyn muttered, blinking rapidly to ward off sunspots and tears alike. It had used no words, yet it had effectively popped the scab over her emotions with one simple image. She didn't believe it a thinking, reasoning thing, simply a tool meant to cause as much pain as it could.

She pushed herself to standing, all too aware of the laughing sprites gathering on the Grand Occultarus's surface to watch her. Adrius used his bulk to shield her face from a crowd forming, watching the otherworldly object as its spinning ceased.

"I believe I know how much of the Portal Key is within it," she whispered for Adrius and Nyah alone. "I can no more command it than it can command me."

She shook her head in disbelief to even say it. The captive Fell had suggested she held all of the Key's power, but if that was so, she should've been able to command it without trouble. "Between it and I, we have split the power equally."

Adrius muttered a curse.

"Does that mean you can get the other half back?" Nyah asked, elbowing him in the ribs.

"I will try," Gwendolyn said. The image of her as an angel burned behind her eyelids with every blink. What was it if not the opening salvo from an item intending to keep its power?

She shot a dour look at the Grand Occultarus. It could not be allowed to keep its half of the Portal Key and continue putting her new home at risk. Whatever it took, she would see it go dormant for the last time.

10

LUCIA

Soon, I won't have to hide. All will tremble and throw themselves at my feet. Gwendolyn will be one of the first for locking me away.
   -From Lucia's Journal

L ucia sat in her chambers for days, relying on the distant call of the hour to piece together how long she was into her confinement. Gwendolyn hadn't visited. In fact, no one had, save for Elandros, thinking this was his moment to be free from her at last. She'd sent him away with a baleful look each time.

Rumors had to be circulating over the palace about why Adrius had confined his Sorceress and advisor without having shown so much as a hint of displeasure toward in her public. She didn't devote a moment of her future sight to the possibilities, instead using her magic for other purposes.

She made a circle with her fingers as she lounged in bed, summoning a vial of golden liquid with her Sorceress magic. Without her occultarus, she had to resort to the same simple hand gestures that most Fell used. A guard had locked up Lucia's focus⸱ at Gwendolyn's direction. The other woman probably thought that contained Lucia's ability to cast spells, not realizing that the Sorceress could perform all manner of spells with her hands instead.

She teleported a purification potion made from Nyah's blood, strong enough to silence the bloodlust urges of even their *illustrious* leader. It was a backup stored in the laboratory just in case any of the Blood Princes needed one.

Lucia knew that Adrius still took these regularly. It curbed the bloodlust of one so flush with a Fell's power. Scoffing to herself, she stood and dug into her trunk, pushing aside her dresses and cloaks until she found a weathered pair of boots. Flaring from one boot was a thick pair of horsehide gloves, which she donned before digging inside of the other boot and coming up with a sealed tin of monkshood powder. She popped open the potion and added a generous pinch of poison.

"Soon," she whispered to the vial after she recorked and shook it to dissolve the deadly dose. She hid the vial within a fold of cloth and sat on the trunk as she heard voices outside her door.

One of the Blood Princes opened the door, shooting her a smitten look. Taryn, now known as Prince Blade, was completely loyal to her, though not completely of his will.

Sacrifices had to be made, Lucia thought, rising to her feet as Gwendolyn sailed into the room. "It's about time," Lucia said, forcing her expression into an angry scowl. She couldn't seem too pleased with things—that would make the other woman even more suspicious of her.

"I apologize for keeping you waiting," Gwendolyn said on a sigh, dropping onto Lucia's sofa. Dark rings painted the skin under her eyes. Though she didn't walk with the assistance of a walking stick, she seemed frail enough to need one again. "I thought we could just talk, you and I."

"Whatever about?" Lucia asked. They were a few yards apart, but the channel between them seemed to widen by the moment.

Voices swirled in her head as she eyed Gwendolyn.

She is weak. Kill her and take her power.

Lucia shook her head, her nails digging into her arm to

remain present. "Just like we used to. Would you be opposed to that?" Gwendolyn said.

"You have had me locked in here, without cause, for days, and now you wish to talk like we're still friends?" Lucia raised a brow, unimpressed. Her friend used to cause grown men to cower in her shadow, and this was the best she could do? She'd practically walked into a wolf's den with her neck already bared.

"That is part of what I wanted to discuss. Answer me one thing, Lucia. Why did you kill the Fell captive?"

"I didn't," she lied with a straight face. "Where is your proof for such an outlandish claim?"

"Oh, indeed, proof. There were only two people with access to the captive, and I didn't kill him." Gwendolyn pinched the bridge of her nose.

"And the butcher and the page that brought the Fell's feast. Four people," Lucia said. "You forget that I had much more planned for the captive."

Gwendolyn turned and stared at her, shaking her head. "I wish I could've visited you sooner. We've needed your magical expertise, but…" Trailing off, she drew a battered, leather-bound book from a pocket in her robe. Lucia blinked in surprise. Real surprise. She hadn't foreseen this part of the conversation, thinking her old journal was where she'd left it at her bedside.

"How did you get that?" she demanded, moving to snatch it when Gwendolyn opened it to an entry toward the back.

"I will return it when you explain this," she said, pointing at the cypher that covered the page.

Wrath creased Lucia's face. *How dare she steal from me!*
Repay her in kind!

She took a deep breath, knowing her fury betrayed that she had something to hide in that cypher. "I developed that just in case my findings fall into the wrong hands. If you'd simply asked instead of stealing it, I would've told you the same."

"You see why this seems suspicious?" Gwendolyn didn't look like she accepted that explanation, her eyes narrowed in distrust.

Let her wonder, Lucia thought, tugging the journal from her grip and securing it in her lap.

"Regardless, you need me for something," Lucia said,

crossing her arms. "You come before the only true practitioner of Fell magic. What do you need help with?"

Abruptly, the other woman stood, looming over her. "I need you to swear something on your blood first. Whatever's gotten into you has to stop, Lucia. You have to stop acting suspicious." She met Lucia's stare, unblinking and intense.

"I can do that. Did you bring a knife with you, too?" Lucia said dryly, unsurprised when Gwendolyn unsheathed one at her boot and offered it. "What am I to swear?"

"Swear that you will use everything in your power to help me retrieve the second half of the Portal Key from the Grand Occultarus."

"This is quite unnecessary," she said, coloring the words with her best imitation of bitterness. The knife bit into Lucia's palm, and she repeated those words verbatim. There was no swearing to end her other behavior, which Lucia counted on. This was the kind of oath that she could work around while Gwendolyn seemed mollified by it.

"The Portal Key is no more." Gwendolyn took out the shards of the amethyst that used to grace the Fell Key's band. "Half of its power is in my veins, and half remains in the Grand Occultarus. Since it was destroyed when I closed the portal, my best guess is that its power was split between the two forces that broke it."

Lucia hummed, an electric feeling tickling her fingertips as she beheld the broken Key. It was in her best interest for Gwendolyn to acquire both halves. Later, Lucia could extract the magic from her and make a new Fell Key that could be controlled more easily. She wasn't sure how such a spell would go—only that it was necessary. No one should carry the power of a Key in such a way.

Kill her! Take the power!

"I will need to consult my spell books. Which means I need permission to leave my quarters. And my occultarus back." Lucia put a touch of sweetness to the words, waiting out the thoughtful silence as Gwendolyn considered her. "I'm not sure why this is an unreasonable request." As far as the other woman knew, her only crime was killing that Fell.

"It is not," Gwendolyn sighed at last. "I look forward to working with you on solving this problem."

She swept out of the room, consulting the guards at the door. Both saluted and walked from the threshold, and Gwendolyn nodded to Lucia. "See you in the laboratory?"

"Be right there," Lucia said, letting her close the door. She smiled to herself as she took the poisoned potion from its hiding place, holding it to her side within a fold of cloth.

Her victory was so close. A vicious, too-big smile split her face as she imagined Nyixa's moonstone crown perched upon her brow. It was a difficult wait, but she let ten minutes slip by, only leaving her quarters as the bells called the hour.

As her sight predicted, she was close when Elandros left his quarters. "Lady Lucia." He bowed politely. "You are out of your chambers."

"Gwendolyn and I have resolved our misunderstanding." She gestured with her free hand. "Come, walk with me."

He shadowed her like a loyal hound, his eagerness quite apparent. "It is time you repaid me," she said, lifting the vial of potion to gleam golden in the light of a passing torch.

11

GWENDOLYN

A thousand possibilities converge on this moment. I see clearly what I must do next.

-From Lucia's Journal

Gwendolyn and Lucia stood before the Grand Occultarus the next day, watching soldiers flood into the city square and line up to form a solid wall of steel and muscle around the unearthly tool. These men and women were the next generation of Fell hunters, trained up from common soldiers and volunteers.

The weight of their gazes rested on Gwendolyn. Word had spread quickly of how she'd caused the Grand Occultarus to spin just by touching it. Now she stood with the Sorceress that had been sequestered and then freed with no public explanation. She knew how quickly one lost trust. Her own experience in its absence stood next to her in the form of Lucia consulting a Fell text and her own notes.

Somewhere behind the line of Fell hunters would be Nyah, under guard by Neala and Chandra as both her closest friends and the Blood Princes who believed strongest in her peace mission. Adrius held court in their absence, stating that he would cut down the first Fell who attempted to approach them in peace, leaving his brother Sirius in command instead.

"Prepare yourself mentally. You are fighting a magic-infused tool for its right to make portals." Lucia drew her attention back to the present. "It will lash back at you, as you well know."

She'd shared with Lucia the angelic reflection it'd shown her yesterday. It was a manifestation of its power, the Sorceress had said. It could read the deepest desires in those who attempted to wield its power and mocked and taunted with what it saw.

"They are only taunts, yes?" Gwendolyn asked, needing to hear some reassurance.

"It is so. The Grand Occultarus tempts you to madness the longer you stare into it. It shows you what you want so you forget what you came to it for." Lucia spoke grimly, her eyes shadowing. Of anyone, she had the most experience manipulating the tool's magic.

"We will do our business quickly then."

With Lucia lending her magic, it would be possible for Gwendolyn to pry free the rest of the Portal Key's power and take it into herself. But in the process, the Grand Occultarus would spin. There was no way to stop a portal forming over a battle for portal magic. They could only mitigate how large and strong it would be by taking what they needed quickly.

"Are you ready?"

Gwendolyn took one last look at their defenses, rubbing clammy palms on the bodice of her gown. The task would not grow more pleasant from her hesitation. "I am prepared."

They turned together toward the darkened surface of the orb suspended above them. Lucia linked their fingers together, holding the box containing their remaining Fell Keys in her other hand. An uncomfortable tingle coursed over Gwendolyn's spine, spreading over her skin like the sting of static.

She reached with her free hand, trying to hold the base of the Grand Occultarus. This time, her palm touched cool metal and stuck.

Gwendolyn felt the hum of its magic resonating within her at the same frequency. It vibrated her fingertips, drawn with a hard tug from Lucia's magic. She could not watch to see if her fingers were to be shook from their sockets by the violence of the growing stream of magic, as her gaze was transfixed on her mirror image once more.

The orb reflected her back, blazing with light. Not as an angel —not yet—but as a nephilim with palms and eyes full of heaven's light. It showed her what she used to be, reaching into her heart and drawing out a memory that erased the reflection of Lucia and the soldiers waiting tensely behind them.

Instead, she saw bodies littering the ground around her. Fallen vampires and twisted corpses of Fell. Her eyes stung, knowing where in time it'd taken her. She recognized Adrius, protecting her with a sword sheeted in black blood as she raised her hands, discharging her light in one blinding blast.

The Grand Occultarus wanted her to flinch and look away. If she did, it kept its half of the Portal Key and continued to terrorize them.

She gritted her teeth. *No. You cannot have it.* It'd reminded her where she'd fallen as her life faded from her, unable to continue without the light that blazed through her veins like a second pulse.

But instead of Adrius offering his blood and a second life as a vampire as he had mere yards from where she stood now, she watched her body die as the fight raged on.

Her soul emerged, a ghostly double rising and shining like pure light. Angel wings unfolded as she looked around at the battlefield. This version of her muttered a silent prayer for her fallen men.

Then she held up her hands, thumb and index fingers forming a circle. She stared at the real Gwendolyn in defiance. Tears welled up in Gwendolyn's eyes as she beheld what she could've been had she decided to pass on. An angel, an immortal warrior, just like her father.

The Grand Occultarus tugged back on its magic, almost expecting her to turn away from the reminder.

"Oh, look what you could've been." The voice that entered her head was no manifestation of the otherworldly tool but instead a soft purr from Lucia.

"If only you'd let yourself die. Is this what an angel looks like? Your words hardly do them justice."

Gwendolyn hesitated. Her nerve was shot—she heard danger in Lucia's words. Her heart beat against her breast like a caged sparrow as Lucia's magic locked down and kept her focused on the vision in front of her. The vibrations were coursing up her arm now, numbing her from below the elbow.

"Think of who was waiting for you on the other side," Lucia continued. As if she'd summoned him, another angel descended from the sky on a beam of sunlight. His feathers glittered as if it were day instead of Nyixa's permanent gloom.

The sight of him hit Gwendolyn like a punch to the gut. He was back in his prime, her Gabriel, his hair golden as wheat in a field, smile white and full as he rested an arm over her reflection's shoulders. With his free hand, he beckoned to her, flexing powerful muscles honed from decades of fighting. Wet trails streaked her face as her own fingers twitched, wanting to reach forward and touch him once more.

"You could still go to him. No one would question it," Lucia said. Indeed, the reflection of him called for just that—for her to leave this life behind and come to him instead.

"W-why are you doing this? This isn't part of the plan," Gwendolyn protested. She saw her heart's desire in front of her, tempting her like a demon's pact. For that was what it was—only hell compelled one to step into the abyss. Nothing good and whole in this world would ever ask for a life in such a way.

The vibrations ran further up her arm and into her shoulder, flowing into the cage of her chest where they faded to a dull hum. She wept, but she watched, imagining devil horns sprouting from the two reflections looking back at her. There was no way she would succumb to their evil.

The pull of magic slowed, something of Lucia's doing. Each second grew torturous, a constant flow of pain up her arm and into her core. *"You're getting exactly what you asked for,"* Lucia said, holding her in place for every moment of it. *"Consider this a thank you for locking me away and tarnishing my reputation."*

Cold shock thrilled through her in sharp contrast to the transfer of magic. *"We agreed—"*

"Only that I would help you retrieve this magic. You never specified how quickly." It sounded as if Lucia was smirking, smug as a noble after a feast.

Meanwhile, the Grand Occultarus reflected pure light back at Gwendolyn as if sensing its taunts were not working. A guttural cry sounded in the air like that of a wounded animal. As it grew louder and higher, she realized it came from her as her eyes seared. The intelligence in the otherworldly tool sought to remove her ability to look directly at it in the most literal way, through blinding.

"Hurry, hurry," she begged Lucia. *"I will forgive you your taunting if only you end this torture."*

"Hmm...I think not." Darkness enclosed over Gwendolyn like the grasp of oblivion to the cadence of Lucia's mocking laughter.

12

ADRIUS

I made Elandros swear on his blood that it was Gwendolyn who asked him to deliver the potion. In every vision, he panics, watching its intended victim die without calling for help.

-From Lucia's Journal

Adrius held court for as long as he could stand, knowing his wife was down in the city, waiting with half of their able-bodied soldiers and recruits for another portal to open. His hand would twitch to the blade at his side, a bad habit when speaking to the civilians and mortals lining up for a few moments of his time.

His patience didn't break when the air charged with magical static, raising every hair on his body. He had to remain calm, knowing he'd put good men and women in charge. If all went well, there would be minimal bloodshed and the possibility of peaceful accord. He would ruin it in an instant if he saw a Fell anywhere near Nyah.

So instead, he sat military straight on his throne, his smile stiff and fake as he beckoned to the next person in line. An elderly woman hobbled forward, leaning on a walking stick and an escort of Elandros, the only Blood Prince who'd volunteered to assist Adrius in his monarch duties.

Elandros flashed him a look of sympathy, taking in the extended fangs that Adrius could hardly hide. Adrius hungered for battle with the hum of a portal right on the verge of his hearing. He needed the taste of Fell blood once more…

"Your Majesty," the elderly woman cut into his thoughts as she bowed stiffly.

"Greetings, citizen. How may the crown help you this day?" he asked.

As she stood and looked him straight in the eye, something even his soldiers were finding harder to do, he had the feeling he wouldn't appreciate what she was about to say. Her lips were set in a mulish line, chin lifted proudly. "Your Majesty, I wish to tell you that you're looking in the wrong place for your portal problem."

"Oh?" he asked, glancing to Elandros and lifting his hand in a silent signal.

Nerves stole over Elandros's expression, his gaze darting from the woman and back to Adrius as she continued speaking. Curious, as he hadn't hesitated to remove anyone else from the throne room.

"Yes. I saw with my own eyes that Lady Gwendolyn almost opened a portal yesterday," she said. "You must do something about her, Your Majesty. Word is spreading—"

"That is enough," he cut her off, gesturing a second time with a scowl pinching his brow. He had full faith in his mother-in-law and wasn't about to go entertaining anything to the contrary.

Elandros sighed as he stepped forward, putting a gentle palm on her shoulder. She tried to shrug him away. "Think about it! No one else has physically opened a portal before," she shouted, kicking as Elandros picked her up to hasten her away.

Pinching the bridge of his nose, he rested his eyes until the Blood Prince returned alone. "I would rather be doing peace talks with Fell than listen to everyone else's opinions. Does that make me a bad king?"

"Just a new one, I think. You are a king, so you may do what you like, and the people must obey," Elandros said.

Adrius uttered a derisive laugh. "Obey? The people are going back where they came from carrying stories of desperate vampires who can't control the Fell even now."

"I imagine it's not that bad." There was sympathy in his tone and bearing.

They weren't doing enough to keep mortals around when death lingered just behind a portal that could open at any time. "No mortals means no vampires." Adrius spoke mostly to himself. He muttered a prayer beseeching that Nyah succeeded in her task today.

"Before Gwendolyn left, she gave me this." Elandros pulled a vial of golden potion from a pocket in his breeches. Moisture flooded Adrius's mouth at the very sight of it, an elixir to cleanse the bloodlust and dark thoughts that hounded him from his extra generous absorption of Fell magic.

He stepped off of the throne to accept the vial. "Generous for her to think of me." Heavens knew that Gwendolyn had more pressing matters than his health, but she'd still ensured he had his medicine on time. So, he didn't think twice as he drank every drop of the syrupy potion.

His stomach turned immediately, bile rushing his throat in a burning rush. His legs collapsed beneath him as his chest heaved, tossing up the thick contents of his stomach. As cold sweat gathered all over his skin, he turned slowly to Elandros, who had turned ghostly white.

"Adrius?" he whispered, more still than a rabbit on a game trail.

It felt like Adrius's face was aflame, the feeling spreading out from his head, down his limbs, and into his chest cavity. He struggled for breath as his heart slowed from a constant drum to a painful seize.

Tha-thump. Tha-thump.

Poison, said his last coherent thought.

Thump…thump…

He reached out for Elandros as his body tipped forward,

sprawling as he struggled mightily for one last breath that just wouldn't come.

His heart went silent as his lids fell for the last time.

13

NEALA

"I wish I had the empathy to pity monsters as you do, Nyah."
-Neala

Neala shifted with unease as she stood behind a line of soldiers. Her job for this mission was to guard Nyah even though she felt she'd better serving up front as one of the trained Fell hunters readying themselves for battle.

Nyah rested a gentle hand on her bicep. "Remember, we're not here to fight. Mother is gaining her power, and we're talking to the first leader we can find of the Fell."

It was as if she'd read Neala's emotions brewing tumultuously under the surface. With no voice to express them, she kept them bottled within, ready to explode with fist and blade to convey her meaning. She relaxed, turning a reluctant smile down toward her friend. "I believe in your plan," she whispered, muffling a cough as damaged vocal cords rasped.

She turned away before she could see the pity cross Nyah's face, instead focusing on what she could see of Gwendolyn and Lucia over the shoulder of a shorter soldier. They'd begun the

ritual, and the Grand Occultarus's great orb started to spin. At
first, it was like watching a giant marble inch forward from the
nudge of an ant, but the gleaming surface picked up speed with
unusual agitation.

Shields raised for soldiers to break the gale that kicked up.
Neala shouldered in front of Nyah, sparing a glance toward
Chandra, who took cover on the rooftop she'd claimed, amongst
the other archers who clustered behind the queen in a second line
of defense should things go poorly.

The portal didn't open right away. It was heralded by streaks
of lightning across the surface of the spinning orb before it flat-
tened out into a black sheet that rippled like water. A gaping hole
between worlds, its opening caused a wave of goosebumps over
Neala's flesh. She held her breath as the first Fell hopped through
and looked around.

It was the most emaciated specimen she'd seen yet, rags
hanging loosely off a skeletal frame. Bearing twin rows of fangs
with a hiss, it fixated on the closest person—Gwendolyn staring
up at the open portal.

Sirius rushed forward, grasping it by the neck before it could
leap. He held the creature aloft at an arm's length as it thrashed
and snapped its fangs at him. "Please work, please work," Nyah
said under her breath, clasping her hands as Sirius spoke to the
Fell briefly and tossed it back through the rippling portal.

Silence.

Neala swallowed hard, nervous sweat beading on her forehead and spine. As they waited, Gwendolyn fell into Lucia's
arms at a full faint. A pair of soldiers hustled forward out of position to support her and listen to something the Sorceress whispered to them. They glanced at one another but took her away,
leaving Lucia to exchange words with Sirius as they waited.

Neala held hope that her warden had claimed every drop of
portal magic from the infernal Grand Occultarus. It meant they
could make portals on their own terms—if they so chose.

"There will either be one Fell," she whispered, taking a deep
breath, "or another flood of them."

"Please Lord, let it be one." Nyah quivered with nerves as the
portal continued spinning.

A single Fell emerged, obscured as the line of Fell hunters closed ranks, weapons bristling outward. It held up a tarnished metal rod with a scrap of cloth fluttering atop it. Nyah raised her hand as the creature paused, looking around at them anxiously as it sat back on its haunches.

"Don't shoot," Nyah called, chancing a glance at Chandra, who had an arrow nocked and ready, along with a few other archers flanking her. "It's surrendering! Don't shoot!"

Neala took that as her cue to move forward, shouldering her way past the line of defenders and flanking the queen as she stepped forward. Sirius and Korin joined them, surrounding Nyah in muscle and menace.

Sirius tightened his grip on his sword's hilt until the leather creaked in protest as he stopped several yards short of the Fell. Hostility radiated off of him in waves as he stared it down. "We are honorable people. We do not strike at those who surrender." Nyah spoke directly to him.

"It's a ruse. When it smells your blood, it will attack you," he said.

"That is not true." A man's voice entered Neala's mind, rough as a cat's barbed tongue. They all turned back to the Fell, who regarded them with its mouth firmly closed to hide those rows of sharp teeth.

Seeing their attention, he sat up straighter. *"Greetings. I come in peace as you've requested,"* he continued. *"I am Caladorn, last remaining son of Calinhes, late Emperor of Fell."*

Neala's brow rose. A curiosity to know the Fell Emperor's name but a moot point with his passing. "Does that make you Emperor then?" Nyah asked.

"It is a possibility. I come as the most likely candidate."

Sirius and Korin exchanged a dubious glance over Nyah's head.

"I want to hear what he has to say. That is why we're here," she said, meeting either male Blood Princes' gazes in turn. They watched in wary silence, staring daggers at the single Fell as the other defenders clustered around and watched this creature who'd come under a more peaceful banner. One wrong twitch, and he would be skewered by several weapons at once.

Neala looked him over more closely as he sized up the situation around them. The last Emperor had silver eyes, but this Fell was fully corrupted, as were most, with bottomless pits for eyes and visible black veins right under the skin. In theory, he wouldn't have control of a Fell Sorcerer's devastating magic. She wondered if that would put him at a disadvantage for the throne from any silver-blooded creatures still living on their side of the portal.

"I have come to request mercy," the Fell continued, spreading spindly, clawed hands. *"You have defeated my father, the greatest Sorcerer of my kind. Our Keys grace your fingers. Our magic runs through your veins. We have nothing left."*

Judging by the emaciated frames on him and the other Fell that'd come through the portal, she believed that whatever lay beyond the portal, it was not a pretty situation for most of their race. It could be a ruse—this creature could be lying and simply a starved whelp of their lower caste sent to attempt a trap.

"We don't want to fight your kind anymore either," Nyah said. "We've never wanted you here."

He bobbed his head in understanding. *"We would not need to come here if we had life in our land. If you are capable of wielding such life, perhaps you can help us come to a peaceful solution for both sides."* He gestured to Nyah's hands where the Spring and Autumn Keys sat next to each other on her fingers.

"No," Sirius muttered.

"I would be happy to grant you such a gift as long as you can, in turn, promise me that any who pass through the portal will be safe from corruption and death." The vampires around her shifted uncomfortably as she squared her shoulders. The other side of this portal was a big blank, an unknown only painted in hearsay. If they were to head through, their safety would be on the wording of a promise.

Sirius turned to her, incredulous. "We cannot make a deal with this creature. Your safety is paramount," he hissed.

Neala spoke up as well, forcing her voice as loud as it went despite the pain that seized her lungs. "We did not agree to go beyond the portal. It is unsafe."

The Fell before her tilted his head thoughtfully. *"I swear that you will come to no harm for the duration it takes to cast your spell and return. My people will protect you."* Heading forward on overlong legs, he kept low to the ground and inched his way toward her as swords unsheathed. He stretched out his hand for a handshake.

"Stand down. It's fine," Nyah ordered Korin and Sirius as they boxed the Fell between them, a solid wall of muscle that kept all but his hand out of touching distance from her. She shook it, surrounded by gasps from astonished vampires.

"All of you, with me," she said to the defenders. Some hundred vampires exchanged glances, surprised at the sudden decision.

Equally shocked, Neala turned to Sirius, whose jaw was grinding. It looked like his eyes would pop from his skull at any moment. She felt a chill of fear for Nyah. She recognized this for what it was, a plan Nyah had held close to her chest until it was too late to stop her.

Her sweet friend wanted more than just to barter an end to their conflict with the Fell. She wanted to save them by any means necessary despite what they'd done to countless human victims.

"This is a mistake," Neala whispered, wishing she could take her friend by the shoulder and shake her.

Nyah met her gaze, head raised. She looked truly royal, not about to back down based off of what others thought. "Either you follow and protect me, or you stay behind. Which will it be?"

Sirius muttered an angry stream of curses before turning to his soldiers. "Protect your queen! Form up!" he hollered. The Fell loped back toward the portal, waiting on the very edge. She lost track of him amongst the crush of bodies as she pressed close to Nyah's side while being surrounded by reluctant soldiers.

They marched forward at Nyah's nod, pushing into the darkness of the portal.

14

LUCIA

Butterflies have their seasons. Ephemeral, just like most beautiful things. It was fitting Nyah chose them to represent herself.
  -From Lucia's Journal

L ucia savored her victory from the moment Gwendolyn fainted, knowing Adrius would be dead while Nyah was in the Fell Lands where she wouldn't feel the sudden severing of their connection. Time moved slower for the Fell. Seconds stretched to minutes. Hours turned to days. A minute in Nyixa was three minutes in the Fell Lands, and the sand ran thin in Nyah's hourglass. All she had to do was give fate one last nudge in the right direction.

The area around the portal was full of movement as vampires came and went. Korin was coordinating their fighting force and chasing off civilians, as many a curious man or vampire wanted to see what was beyond now that it was proven safe. Lucia scoffed to herself. Those fools would be lost if they weren't careful.

If she were ruling, she'd order a stronger guard in front of the portal rather than take them all with her. But she wasn't queen, at least not yet. If she didn't set her feet down in the right places, she would never attain her goal. A thousand possibilities, and only one led to that crown gracing her head.

Nyah was the queen, a gentle soul willing to help their most dire of enemies. She was the kind of leader the people needed, one who made butterflies instead of new war.

But Lucia would see her dead. A part of her struggled not to take the next step, the most important one.

I must have her power.

But it isn't too late! she thought in a voice that sounded more like her own.

She shook her head, trying to dislodge the doubt taking root within her. She merely took the steps that would lead her to her throne, and if it cost her Nyah, well, the other woman was standing in the way.

She didn't go far into the Fell Lands, lingering next to the rippling portal that had led them here. Her sandals dug into ashen sand. As she'd expected, the portal was in a random place midair rather than established from an identical Grand Occultarus on the other side. It was how she'd found enough Fell to attack Nyixa each time, catching different groups of the monsters unawares for them to pile through in a hopeful free-for-all.

This time, the portal was atop a heap of ash like a sand dune, similar hills sloping far into the distance. The closest civilization, made of the same white stone as Nyixa, was simple spires on the horizon. Any Fell found here would be wild and starved, hunting each other like animals now that there was no other life in their barren home.

That kind of situation would speak to Nyah. Lucia followed tracks in the ash, admiring the pop of color that new grass made as it spread. Life flooded from one central point, and that point was Nyah, her head bowed and hands clasped together as she murmured to herself. She drew and drew on the power of the two Keys she wielded, performing her miracle as a ragtag group of Fell watched.

She would not be able to sustain this magic for much longer, but she was fulfilling her side of her pact. Create life, earn safety.

Lucia smiled to herself, placing the pads of her fingers on the Mind Key slipped around her finger like a wedding band.

"Call the retreat. Send our people back," she whispered mentally, projecting those thoughts into the mind of the vampire standing closest to Nyah as he observed her magic with his arms crossed. With the power of the Mind Key, Sirius would think those thoughts were his own. Much as he annoyed Lucia as the spitting image of his brother, he was useful. The soldiers here would listen to him and so would the civilians. Though he wouldn't act right away, once news reached him of his brother's untimely death, he wouldn't think; he would simply move.

Sirius glanced around, holding his temple from a sudden headache. Ducking out of sight, Lucia continued to whisper, putting thoughts into Nyah's head next. *"Mention your alchemy. Ask about their people. Relax."* All else followed.

Lucia turned on her heel, sure of her timing. She wasn't needed here. Standing once more before the portal back to Nyixa, she saw it now—there was no turning back once she did this. Nyah was a good queen, wasn't she?

Lucia would be better.

Gwendolyn was her friend, wasn't she?

Not anymore.

And Adrius...Adrius would be dead and discovered by now. It would be too damaging to leave this measure half-done, so she reached into the portal's edge, one hand clasped to her personal occultarus. The portal quivered as she removed a piece of it, wobbling like ripples in a pond. She headed back through it, ready for the final act as she started to scream for mortal and vampire alike to stay back lest they get trapped on the other side as the portal started to collapse.

15

NEALA

"Nyah, you're making a foolish mistake. You cannot fix the Fell, no matter how much magic you pour into their dead land."
  -Sirius

Neala guarded her queen as Nyah swayed on her feet after a long session of magic. New greenery shot out all around her, transforming the land with new shoots. Insects grew rapidly, starting to build a foundation of life. Caladorn, the Fell who'd lead them to this barren place, had mentioned that there was water somewhere, and it could be used to maintain this slice of land.

"Perhaps we can offer you a place to rest for a moment," he suggested, eyeing the three Blood Princes that continued to flank Nyah as he took a step forward. He and the other Fell watched from a safe distance, empty eyes on the many blades unsheathed and ready should they attempt anything.

"I would like that, thank you," she said, shooting Sirius an irritated look as he shouldered before her, his arms crossed and an angry scowl aimed her way. He gestured for the Fell to lead the way, boxing her in with him in front and Chandra and Neala behind her. When they moved, it was as one unit, a Blood Prince's steel guarding her in every direction.

For a moment, Neala thought she saw a feminine figure bustling through the portal still open within sprinting distance. It could've been another civilian since several had already come and gone, muttering about the ashy sand and the reek of sulfur, barren nothingness stretching as far as the eye could see.

Seeing how the other side lived was a powerful thing even to an original Fell hunter like Neala. It was hard to imagine thriving on a planet without so much as a blade of grass or the sweet chirping of crickets as evening fell. The only thing she found even a drop of envy for was the sky which glittered brilliantly overhead like countless diamonds stitched in blue-black velvet. A full moon hung directly overhead while a second, merely a sliver, peered down at them from the westernmost horizon.

The Fell led her farther from the portal and its reassuring hum to a tent city as silent as a crypt. A few emaciated creatures peered from the confines of their homes. Most were small and feeble compared to the Fell they'd fought in the last few weeks. She had no doubt these were survivors or those unable to fight.

However, she hardly pitied them as much as Nyah did. These creatures were still monsters that would eat a victim down to bones if they had the chance. She hadn't fought them for years just to throw away her caution on one visit to their homeland.

Nostrils flared as a few leered, but their faces were gone in a split second when Sirius or Neala turned to stare in return. "*Do not worry. I have warned them that you are all under my protection,*" Caladorn told them. He shadowed the outskirts of this encampment, which kept Sirius following, though his shoulders were ratcheted high with tension.

Eventually, the Fell stopped before a circle of rocks worn smooth like bench-tops, and that was where Caladorn sat, breathing out a tense sigh of his own. "*Thank you for what you've done for us so far.*" Nyah seated herself across from him as her guard remained standing and alert.

Sirius turned to Chandra, muttering in her ear. "As you wish," she said, heading into the encampment. Neala heard her start organizing soldiers, dividing them up. Some stayed behind to help guard the queen while the majority went to patrol the Fell camp.

Turning her focus fully on Caladorn, Nyah nodded. "It will not be an easy or quick process, but if you have clean water, it should be doable."

He chuckled bitterly, a watery sound in his alien throat. *"Water is the only thing we have an abundance of. It falls from the rest of our land."* Receiving only confused, dubious glances from the vampires, he shook his head. *"I suppose no one has had a chance to tell you where we come from."*

"We know some," she said, leaning forward slightly as she shared openly what they knew—mostly facts about the Fell Keys and the actions of their Archfae, Izell, who had led them straight to their banished, cursed state. Neala shifted uncomfortably, but she didn't interrupt. As her queen had proven, she was running this show now, and all Neala should do was fall in line.

Caladorn listened and stared, acknowledging occasionally with a dip of his head. *"Whomever you spoke with told you true. That is how we became Fell."*

"Do you have Izell? Can we speak with her, too?" she asked.

He considered her with an unblinking stare. *"We do not have Izell. After most of us were killed, the Faerie King retrieved her to do with as he pleased."*

Neala breathed out a sigh. It was a shame but not a huge loss for their purposes.

"Once, we lived above. There is a whole continent above us," he said, gesturing upward. *"Below, this land is barren of all but the worst criminals and murderous creatures. The Fell Lands is a place of eternal punishment. It was said that any who live here will never die but suffer from starvation until the end of time. We know that to be true as well."*

She thought that a terrible existence and one that explained why the Fell seemed so emaciated now that Gwendolyn had closed their permanent connection to Nyixa. And also why they seemed to die within hours of being captured. Whatever magic extended over them in the Fell Lands to sustain their lives ended once they were on the other side.

"We were once Exalted Ones. In your tongue...fae." He tripped over the word even with the magic of translation that was undoubtedly at work between them. *"We were the Exalted Ones of the Astral Court. My father ruled us as best he could with desperation at our lack of resources to sate our appetites. I was once fae, but most Fell still alive were born with the affliction."*

Sympathy fluttered over Nyah's expression. She turned to Sirius as if expecting some level of the same before doing the same with Neala, who met her gaze with a grim look. Though she harbored nothing but disgust for the creatures, she had to admit to herself that it was a terrible fate to be born into.

"I want to offer you something. It works for my friends when the curse is too much for them," Nyah said. She turned to Sirius and held out her hand, wiggling her fingers with a little smile, cheerful in the face of his palpable anger. "Could I get that purifying potion I gave you? I know you always carry an extra." For a few moments, she touched her forehead as if stricken by a bout of dizziness.

"Adrius will be very displeased when he hears of this," Sirius muttered, slapping a vial into her palm.

Nyah turned to Caladorn and offered him the vial of golden potion. Her face seemed blank of all thought for that moment, as if all coherent thought had fled, even the good sense not to mention her alchemy to a Fell.

Said Fell uncorked it, breathing in the golden fumes that rose from its glass lip. "It's very helpful for keeping the hunger at bay —" Nyah cut herself off when he tipped up the potion and swallowed it down in moments without any hesitation.

All eyes were on him as he coughed behind a clawed hand, hard spasms rocking his emaciated form. That potion was a miracle worker for Adrius and the other Blood Princes, clearing away their driving hunger so they could exist free of the cursed blood they'd ingested. But this Fell coughed and coughed, his hands coming away coated in sticky, black blood.

He smiled, revealing blood-smeared teeth—flat, square teeth —in the shifting frame of a face with high cheekbones and a regal hook for a nose. The ink in his veins bled into his skin rapidly, turning it as blue-black as the sky above him. Bones cracked, shifting as he stood to a man's height, free of the bunched, frog-like leg structure.

Neala exchanged glances with her friend, their mouths drop-ping open in sync as he finally opened his eyes. Those flat, black orbs sparkled from within as if he'd captured the constellations and displayed them from his personal night sky. Astral Court indeed. Though terribly emaciated, he was striking and *different* in a way no human man could ever achieve. Stringy sheets of unwashed, white hair seemed to glimmer with muddled pinpricks of light as well.

"At last," Caladorn sighed, glancing down at himself and tightening his loincloth before it could fall off his slim hips. "You are a true miracle for my people. I am loathed to ask it, but I have one last, urgent request." Capable of speaking aloud to them now, his voice was a smooth roll, speaking their tongue without accent.

However, then he tilted his head and met Nyah's gaze. What-ever passed between them was personal, a mental request. "If you have something to say, we all would hear it," Sirius demanded, his hand flying back to the pommel of his sword.

"We are working out another deal. Calm yourself," Nyah said in her gentle way but spoke aloud for their benefit as she addressed Caladorn. "You will explain all of fae culture in exchange for us saving two babes from the Fell curse next?"

"And fostering them in a place with life and wilderness, yes," the fae said.

"I see nothing—"

Sirius clamped a large hand over her shoulder. "Please excuse us for a moment." His politeness was spoken through gritted teeth. Nyah took one look at his stormy expression and stood, both of them heading further into the ashen wastes and leaving Neala and Caladorn alone for the moment. She flashed an uncomfortable half-smile as he inspected her with narrowed eyes.

16

NEALA

> *"To think we had the cure for the Fell curse all along! I'm glad we made these first diplomatic steps."*
>
> *-Nyah*

"I recognize you," the fae said, conviction in his tone.

Neala raised a brow in disbelief. She hardly wanted to waste words, but she may as well warn him away. "Do not bother me with such foolishness," she said, gritting her teeth at how harsh her voice sounded compared to his melodic fae tones.

"Some of us can see the future, Lady Neala," he continued, unperturbed. Now it was her turn to bristle, no better in her reactions than Sirius. "You may practice your mental communications with me. There is no need to tax your voice."

Fixing him with a scowl, she focused to speak mind to mind with him. It brought a mild headache from concentration. *"You will tell me how you know my name."*

"Of course," he answered in kind. *"In truth, your queen told me your name. And of the angry one, Prince Sirius. And herself, Queen Nyah. Curious that your names do not compel you as they do the*

Unseelie. Despite the Fell blood in your veins, you are not Unseelie creatures."

She shook her head in irritation, watching Sirius and Nyah argue in hushed tones instead of continuing this connection. There were several wide gestures and accusing fingers being pointed. *"He will bow to her will,"* Caladorn continued, startling her.

"You sound very sure of this," she replied, wondering if he'd hear her. She'd never spoken to someone mentally without eye contact.

"This is a very important moment that I've scried over and over, Lady Neala." Was he really still talking? She turned to fix him with a glare to find him holding a bundle in a threadbare blanket. A Fell had snuck up while she'd had her back turned, sending a thrill of alarm up her spine.

"Last night, my mate gave me a daughter." His voice dropped to a tender murmur as he gazed down at the bundle. If she weren't imagining it, glimmering moisture gathered at the corners of his eyes. *"She passed away moments after this one took her first breath."*

"I'm sorry for your loss." Though her words were a reflex, she couldn't imagine bringing another life into a land so desolate. Raising a small monster to know the pain and emptiness of an empty stomach.

The child was born a beggar, and that was something Neala could intimately understand. Fate handed out such lives with unkind generosity. If it weren't for Gwendolyn's charity, Neala may never have escaped a premature death clutching an empty stomach.

She knew why he'd brought the child. The grief twisting his expression was explanation enough. *"It is too late for me to leave. The others here need me,"* he said, rocking his daughter slowly. *"I would ask you to give my girl a better life."*

Though she understood, she schooled her face into a blank expression and offered only a noncommittal grunt. She did not want to take responsibility for his child nor for the second one another Fell carried to them. The second babe appeared a toddler's age and was already showing signs of corruption in tiny, sharp baby teeth and black veins pulsing just underneath his paper-thin skin.

Seeing a toddler Fell struck her revulsion just right. It looked like the spawn of a monster, which made her question what kind of creature was hidden within the bundle in Caladorn's arms.

Nyah rejoined them while Sirius went stomping past the fire pit, barking orders to his men. "We have an agreement," Nyah said, reaching over to shake Caladorn's hand. "Neala, would you give half of your vial to the two children?"

Neala turned toward her, focusing hard. Speaking mentally to her friend was nowhere near as easy a task as speaking to Caladorn. *"Was this agreement worth his ire?"* She raised a brow in judgement, full of unsaid chastisements. She simply didn't have the words to express them, and it seemed that Sirius had given up trying to do the same.

"I know this is the right thing to do." Nyah's expression seemed blank again before it hardened a moment later with determination.

Shaking her head, Neala took out her hidden vial of golden potion and uncorked it. She knelt before the boy first, tilting his chin up and pushing the glass into his mouth before he could nip her with his baby monster fangs. *"I suppose you also want help smuggling them through the portal?"*

She turned back to Nyah as she spoke. "I was thinking you could do that while I speak to Caladorn. We'll figure it all out on the other side." With Neala's power over illusions, she was the obvious choice for it, but her movements were stiff with the idea of leaving her friend here.

Neala grunted again as she took the vial away from the boy and approached the would-be Fell Emperor. He drew back the cloth over the babe's head. As she approached, she expected to see an even smaller, twisted reflection of a Fell in babe form.

What she saw was a little, drooling child, nearly identical to a human baby save for the gently pointed ears and overlarge eyes which glinted up at her as if full of stars.

Her eyes were silver. One day, she would be a Fell Sorceress, dangerous beyond measure. Fell Sorcerers had the most enticing and powerful blood, something the hunters like her had taken pains to find.

Such thoughts were wrong when applied to a babe, and she pushed them away as thus. Neala inspected her with a scrunched brow. She was a warrior, her hands too roughened for the tender work of handling a child. The vial trembled in her grip as she tipped the last of the golden liquid into the infant's open, pink mouth.

As she watched, the corruption lingering in the child faded, and her skin darkened to the star-flecked sky like that of her father. A tuft of white hair fluffed up from her head. *"Her fae name is Elianna, but you may also give her a human name for protection. Someday, please tell her of her parents, Caladorn and Anora Nightweaver,"* he told her as he pushed the babe into her hold. Neala imagined he was moments from losing his nerve as he took a step away from her. *"Thank you, Lady Neala. I hope one day I may be able to return the favor."*

She sighed as she laid an illusion over the fae babe, making her disappear. *"And the boy?"*

Caladorn turned his gaze to the toddler. *"He is a special boy, destined to protect my daughter. Tell him he is Rorak Firebrand, a distant descendant of Archfae Izell."* He paused for a moment, considering his words. *"That is a high honor in our society."*

She beckoned to the boy, who approached with a serious expression far older than his couple years in this land. He'd transformed while they spoke, now a night-dark child with matted gray hair and overlarge eyes glimmering with more stars than darkness. He eyed Neala with distrust but allowed her to pick him up, and from there, he disappeared under another illusion.

"Stars shine upon you," Caladorn said by way of farewell, nodding stiffly to her while Nyah gathered new guards to protect her.

"See you on the other side," Nyah said, offering a tense smile when Neala observed her stonily.

"You will be the one to explain this to Adrius."

Little did she know, those would be the last words she'd

speak to the queen who watched her carry her two new charges to another, kinder land.

Neala returned to the portal once the fae children were secured with a wet nurse who'd sworn a blood oath of secrecy and protection on Neala's prompting. That duty taken care of, she watched a flood of soldiers charge through as the Grand Occultarus squealed to a halt.

Neala thought Nyah would be safe with Sirius, Chandra, and an honor guard. She didn't spot her milling with the others, but she did meet the silver gaze of Lady Lucia moving toward her through the crowd. Those eerie eyes lingered a moment at Neala's arms, as if she could see the illusion she'd recently had there. She wouldn't be surprised if so, but a part of her was uneasy at the continued stare of their Sorceress.

"Where's Queen Nyah?" she heard Sirius call, startling back to herself as the crowd shifted and murmured. He approached Lucia and Neala, breathing like a bull about to charge.

Lucia spoke in low tones, leaning in as she scanned the crowd. "I don't see Chandra either."

Groaning low in his throat like a wounded animal, he pivoted and punched the dial of the Grand Occultarus with a dull *thunk!* "I knew she couldn't trust him." He clutched at his hair, uttering a string of curses that would make a sailor blush.

"Who? What do you mean?" Lucia asked, resting a hand on his shoulder before he jerked away.

"That Fell she healed. He must've tricked us," he said, turning burning eyes toward her. "Can you open the way? We have to go back! Where's Gwendolyn?"

Neala felt like she was submerged underwater, turning toward the dormant Fell structure behind them. If this was true, her two closest friends were a world apart from her—and she hadn't been there to save them. She would've gladly held the same fate had she not been tasked with saving the children. Her stomach heaved as talons of guilt buried themselves in her chest.

She hadn't done her most basic duty, keeping Nyah safe.

Undoubtedly, she and Chandra would die, stranded and doomed with those Fell refuges. "As we agreed upon when creating our nation, I was second in line for the throne," Lucia was saying as she pulled her awareness back to the conversation held with barely a glance toward her. She was used to it, never asking for feedback with her mute voice.

"We have to have a meeting," Sirius injected, his face the picture of grief. "It's what Adrius would've wanted."

"I understand your pain," she continued in a gentler tone, "but we cannot dally. Let us leave it to a vote if we must."

Neala wondered what she'd missed, when the other woman's voice entered her thoughts. "*Adrius was poisoned by your warden an hour ago. We must decide a leader.*" Those talons clenched tighter around her heart as she thought selfishly that at least Adrius wouldn't know of her failure. If their souls could reach the same heaven, they could still be together.

"Yes, we will vote. Let's go," Sirius mumbled through numb lips. He started trudging toward the palace.

"*I will, of course, require your complete support. Else some unpleasant things will come to light, won't they? Someone wasn't with her queen when she needed help the most,*" Lucia's voice continued, silken, in her mind.

Neala gritted her teeth, which helped keep the moisture welling in her eyes from spilling out. Without Nyah to explain the fae children's adoption, it could mean an execution for treason. Sirius may not be believed, having been on this side of the portal as well. "*You have my support.*"

"*Then soon you will have a pardon,*" the other woman promised. Neala accepted her fate with a weary nod, feeling as though she were sidestepping the executioner's axe as they spoke. All it cost was the heartsickness that twisted and cracked her heart.

She focused on Sirius, making mental contact with him even with his back to her. "*How could you leave Nyah behind? Letting your temper rule your sense.*"

"*You left her first,*" he replied, as sullen as a child.

"*As per her agreement with Caladorn.*"

He turned back toward her, grief painted over his face. She

imagined her face was not much better. *"You have the children."*
He inclined his head. *"Do you wish Lucia to know of them?"*

Neala shook her head slowly. She thought of all the grotesque
experiments she'd caught Lucia performing on Fell cadavers. Her
world was turned on its head, but there was one thing she was
certain of. Those children would have better lives, free of any
kind of experimentation.

17

LUCIA

I will lead our people to prosperity. The world will learn to kneel for vampires, their true masters. From horizon to horizon, everything the darkness touches shall be mine.

-From Lucia's Journal

L ucia's coronation was a rushed affair, taking place in the throne room with the remaining Blood Princes, other ranking personnel from the vampire court, and mortal politicians. The vote had been sharply in her favor with Adrius's remaining family and friends broken by the twin deaths of their beloved monarchs and the news about Gwendolyn.

The former nephilim waited for judgement in the dungeon, framed neatly for quite a number of Lucia's sins, including Adrius's poisoning with Elandros posing as witness. And with her power over portal magic, who would the public believe was opening portals? Lucia had never shown a soul that she was capable of commanding the Grand Occultarus from afar, let alone make it bridge the gap between their land and the Fell's.

Neala had voted for her, wearing her defeat and fear like a

shroud. She had no idea that Lucia couldn't see past her illusions and thus didn't know what exactly she'd taken from the Fell Lands. For all her scrying, it was like her mind's eye bent away from that moment, seeking to focus on anything else.

Such as what would happen next. She sent away most of the court to recess and anticipated passing judgement for the first time as the vampire queen. Her subjects would be congregating soon, waiting for her to explain what happened and guide them to a new, better age. But first, she had unfinished business.

Still seated on the throne, she admired the intricate dome of cut glass that arched high above. There was a tiny window at its apex, which she found responded to her magical will. If there was light above, it would shine directly downward into a pit not unlike where gladiators fought. *High entertainment for the Fell Emperor*, she figured.

Multi-tiered seating surrounded the pit, enough to fit thousands of bystanders. She imagined their cheering and feet stomping all for her. Adoration and screaming, a massive court there to lavish her with attention.

Her too-wide smile faded as the doors to this grand place flung open. It was a long walk to her throne, but she sat back and waited it out in silence, watching Taryn drag Gwendolyn to her. Barely moving, her shins trailed the ground as he carried her by the chains linking her arms together. He threw the former nephilim at the foot of her throne, standing back with a hand on his weapon.

"Gwendolyn Firetree, you are hereby sentenced for the murder of former King Adrius," she said, practicing her lofty, queenly tones as she tapped the arm of her throne. Gwendolyn barely stirred, her face obscured by a thick fall of her disheveled hair. It didn't matter if she looked up anyway. Her eyes were dull and milky, burned too intensely for vampire regeneration to fix.

Gwendolyn inhaled sharply as if waking from a deep sleep. "These chains. I made them myself." She drew herself to her knees, pulling at the manacles. It was true—before she'd lost her powers, she'd fashioned several sets of nephilim chains. To slap a pair on their creator was a curiosity alone, seeing if its magic affected her like the beasts they hunted and studied. It seemed successful so far, though it was difficult to tell when Gwendolyn was so weak a vampire to begin with.

"Have you any last words before I decide your fate?" she intoned, a little bored already. This wasn't the confrontation she was expecting. She hadn't scried this moment, wanting to savor it the first time as it was meant to be savored, like the juicy victory it was.

"Nothing?" she breathed at last, lounging back in her seat. *Pathetic*, she thought. Just like that, she took this trial in a new direction. No one was there to complain, only Taryn, who waited with a blank expression for her next order. He would not breathe a word of this to another.

If Gwendolyn lived, she would have to live with her pain. *Yes! Show her who's the queen. Punish her!*

The vicious whispers swirled in her head, suggesting different cruelties to make the fallen nephilim speak. "From this day on, you are hereby banished from Nyixa. You are required to swear a blood oath to me now."

"How ironic," Gwendolyn spoke at last, "that you would see fit to judge me when you were the one opening those portals."

Lucia froze, raising a brow thoughtfully and allowing her to speak. "I held the Grand Occultarus's power only for a moment, but in it, I saw everything you've commanded of it. Opening portals from afar. Now you would use my name to say I killed Adrius?" Her voice broke, a sob interrupting her. "*Why?* Why have you done this to me?"

"You were in my way," Lucia said, inspecting her nails.

She nodded to Taryn, instructing him to make the incision. He drew a dagger from his boot and slit Gwendolyn's forearm from wrist to elbow. The other woman screamed as blood spattered at the base of the throne. Such a gruesome injury would kill her if her vampire regeneration wasn't already healing it over. "Repeat after me," Lucia said harshly.

Gwendolyn spoke in a bland monotone, giving her no trouble. "I have committed treason. I will not speak of what truly happened, in word or in writing. I will not return to Nyixa. I will uphold the terms of my banishment until the day you release me from my vow. I swear it on my blood."

"Take her away, and send in Prince Wraith," she sighed to Taryn once Gwendolyn went silent once more, her head bowed in defeat. Only in her dreams would she see the flash of temper over her face as the other woman was marched stiffly away and the circle she made with her fingers. She'd only realize it later, when Gwendolyn was long gone, that Lucia's journal went with her.

Lucia began to bore further as she waited on her throne, wondering if Taryn was having trouble finding the mute Blood Prince. It felt like hours when he finally returned, the massive redhead trailing after him. Grief did little for her features. If Lucia found her ugly before, the reddened face and swollen eyes made her downright repugnant. *"Queen Lucia,"* she said mentally, making a proper masculine bow.

"Neala. How are our people?" She watched keenly as the Blood Prince shifted, scratching the back of her neck. There was no way she'd been in the city watching over her people. Talking was not her strong point.

Lucia saw wisps of the future gathering at the corner of her sight. A future where Neala was infinitely useful, coming to Nyixa's shores at the head of a new army. By her side was a man as handsome as any vampire, with a face of chiseled perfection shadowed by a crisp blond beard. He would be unremarkable to Lucia except something about him compelled her to look further. There were many, many futures with this man in her life, and most involved them entangled in Lucia's bedsheets.

Maybe he was her lifemate as Adrius had Nyah. A smile tugged at her lips as she tucked away those thoughts to examine on a later date.

"Our people are restless, my queen. They desire some reassurance after losing both their rulers so suddenly." That, Lucia imagined, was a surface-level assumption. Neala was too preoccupied with her grief to look outside.

Lucia considered her punishment. "I shall address them after addressing you. As your new ruler, I must express my disappointment that you did not protect our old queen. That is nearly treason in my eyes."

"I apologize. You must know that no one has lost more than me this day."

"Be that as it may, I must issue you a punishment. You are to leave. Do not return until you lead a new army for me to command. Then, and only then, will I officially pardon you of your part in Queen Nyah's death," she said, her mouth watering at the snippets of the blond man. How defined his muscles were, made thick on his frame.

"I accept this as my due. May I have a day to pack and make ready?" she asked, bobbing her head in supplication.

"Yes. Take two, actually." She spoke as if she were giving a great generosity when in reality, she would be delaying so she would not cross paths with Gwendolyn.

"May I ask one other thing?" Neala hedged.

Lucia turned back to her sharply in the middle of making a dismissive motion. "Yes?"

"Gwendolyn could re-open the portal to the Fell Lands. Nyah is probably still alive right now. And our men, too. Waiting for rescue."

It was a notion she would need to fight for a while that the old queen could be saved. As far as Lucia would say from then on, the portal could not be opened again. She savored Neala's crushed expression as she said, "Gwendolyn is dead. Portal magic is gone. The Grand Occultarus budges no longer." She grinned, affecting a carefree air. "You should rejoice, Blood Prince! The Fell are no more."

"I shall attempt to rejoice," Neala muttered, bowing her way from Lucia's presence.

That matter finished, Lucia freshened herself up and watched her personal occultarus spin around her shoulders. She channeled a spell through it, bouncing it to the Grand Occultarus, to settle over the island like a blanket. Soon, the inhabitants would be calming, waiting with a curious, new eagerness to hear and accept the decrees of their new queen.

They would forget Nyah, thinking her lost and dead in an unforgiving land. And why would they want a weak queen back anyway? They had Lucia now.

18

ADRIUS

"I had reunions with many friends while I was dead. But she wasn't there with them."
  -Adrius

When he first returned from death, Adrius could barely lift his eyelids. It was like everything in him rejected being alive again. His heart, sluggish. His limbs, unresponsive. His head, numb.

Oblivion felt like the descent of a well-needed rest. He'd slept. He'd seen old friends who barely had time to welcome him before he was back to life, trying to twitch his fingertips and shake off the weakness that invaded his body.

He was lying on a cold slab, somewhere silent and dry. His arms were crossed over his chest, clutching the smooth leather of his sword hilt. A shiver worked through him, body cold from the lack of its own temperature. But one place on him was burning hot to compensate—the Shield Key, where it was welded to his ring finger. It was also the first finger he could move, sensation returning as it coursed up his left arm.

By the time he opened his eyes on a heavy gasp of air, he realized something was missing. He couldn't feel his connection to Nyah anymore, and the lack of constant feedback of shared emotions and thoughts felt like the absence of a phantom limb. Worry gnawed at him, though he reasoned that their mating bond could be reformed if his death had severed it.

Looking down at himself, he couldn't help a chuckle. It appeared he was to be buried in the newest, finest thing he owned, a suit of royal purple velvet that the palace tailors had whispered excitedly of when they thought he wasn't listening. It was hideous and overwrought, exactly the kind of lavish trapping he would never wear. He would say that he wouldn't be caught dead in it, but...

He secured his sword back on his belt, realizing he had no idea where he was. Someone had moved his body to a chapel of sorts with a stone slab at the back for a body to be viewed. The other object on the slab was a small, bronze-bound occultarus, glimmering without the help of ambient light. Wooden pews lined the elongated room in two rows.

Moving to sit up, he was hit by a wave of dizziness the moment his head lifted from its cushioned rest. Darkness crept in at the corners of his vision as his heart stuttered. It felt like death loomed over him, waiting for his body to give out once more instead of thriving with the new thread of life it'd seized.

A door flung open, admitting someone as Adrius groaned his agony. The other man screamed on sight of him moving on his slab. He'd recognize that voice any time, even crying out in an unmanly fashion. "Sirius. It's just me," he said. Rather, he tried. His voice rasped as badly as Neala's, parched for blood.

His brother eyed him, rushing forward to take his hand. "You're alive!" He loomed to take a closer look at his face. "But...how?"

Adrius held up a shaking hand, wiggling his ring finger. It took a moment for Sirius to understand and reach out to touch the Shield Key. He withdrew his fingers with a hiss as if burned.

"Where is Nyah?" Adrius asked, needing to see her face before any others.

Just like that, the happiness fell from Sirius's face. It was like someone had come along and snuffed it like a candle. Worry squirmed in his gut, unfettered from how quickly the change came along and how his brother wouldn't meet his eye. "Well?" he rasped.

"Nyah is…gone. I'm sorry." Sirius spoke to his feet, trembling.

He repeated it to himself, uncomprehending. Gone? How could she be gone? He'd just seen her, before…

"Tell me she wasn't poisoned, too!" he reached for his brother, wanting to give him a good shake. "Did you find who did it?"

"Yes…n-no. No, she wasn't poisoned," Sirius stammered. It was with great reluctance that he lifted his head and explained how she'd been left behind in the Fell Lands as a portal had collapsed on her and an expedition she'd taken beyond. They'd lost forty soldiers but more tragically, his mate as well.

Adrius shook his head slowly. This couldn't happen. She wouldn't be so headstrong as to go through a portal without him. She wouldn't be *stupid* like that. The Nyah he knew would wait for him so he could protect her. No Fell would dare to touch her even on the turf of their homeland.

"I'm sorry. Really. We thought we lost you both." His brother's voice sounded a world away as if he too was beyond a portal, beyond saving.

"Gwendolyn. She can still open a portal back," Adrius said, desperation clawing at him. When his strength returned, he'd go through a portal to the Fell Lands alone if he had to. But he wouldn't leave Nyah alone, not when there was a chance she was still alive.

The same guilty, ill look came over his brother. "Gwendolyn is gone, too. Executed for treason. It was Lucia's first decree as queen because she was linked both to your murder and to opening the way to the Fell Lands with her access to the Portal Key. With her death, that magic is no more." No wonder Sirius looked like he'd swallowed rancid blood. Adrius registered nausea in the middle of his pain, his heart stuttering in his chest. Not just Nyah, but Gwendolyn, too…

Darkness swept in.

Adrius drifted in that darkness, wondering when he'd fall back into the sleep of death. It stayed just out of his reach, leaving him to fade back to the waking world.

First, there were voices speaking in a hush above him. Grunts and creaking wood broke up their conversation.

"Think for a moment. Gwendolyn would never reopen a portal to the Fell Lands."

"I know."

"It's Lucia's doing. All of this has to be her doing. Who else benefits from all of this?"

The ground rocked below Adrius, accompanied by the slap of water. Salty brine coated his tongue as he tried to swallow.

"But where will we go?" He recognized his friend Korin's voice, touched with despair.

"Far," Sirius answered. "Somewhere Lucia can't reach until our true king is ready to make his return."

19

NEALA

"Here, we honor our fallen. The brave and the lost. We live due to their sacrifices. Never forget."
-Neala

Time was supposed to heal all wounds, or so it was said. Neala put no faith in that even twenty years later. She travelled the world looking for a place to belong and found it by the ocean far, far from Nyixa. She swore she would never return there.

What was there to return to? Gabriel Legion had fallen long ago to Fell, Gwendolyn to her madness, Adrius to treachery, and Nyah and Chandra to her own inattentiveness. So, she put one foot in front of the other, wandering. Her new purpose was showing two young fae how to survive on Earth and ensure that she hadn't made a grave mistake bringing them here.

Not that she believed she had anymore. Both children grew slowly compared to their human counterparts, but Keegan now seemed as large and mature as a fifteen-year-old boy as he strode by her side while Sorsha skipped ahead of them, the picture of a carefree girl of almost fourteen in appearance, though she acted younger most days. Neala smiled to herself as the girl found and chased a fluttering moth.

Neala had renamed them both as if they'd come from her home country rather than one sealed away by sheer necessity. When they were very young, they'd laid in the grass with her and watched the stars shine over their home. She would turn to see the same lights in her children's skin before telling them how lucky they were.

Rorak Firebrand and Elianna Nightweaver.

The only fae saved from the Fell Lands.

She told them of their heritage. What little of the positive she remembered. How young Sorsha had a birth father who loved her so dearly that he sent her to a better life. Her silver eyes meant she held great magic within her. How they would shimmer with awe as Neala spoke, the work of a bright imagination within.

Keegan was not aloof to stories of his past either, though his were mired with a need to know Izell, his ancestor. He puffed with pride nonetheless as they grew older and into an understanding of what Fell were and the role and the Fell hunters had had in saving the land they lived in. Both Keegan and Sorsha showed a great appreciation and affinity for the wilderness they'd grown up around.

Neala knew these woods well from her youth. Honfleur, France was a port town, a landing ground for the little Irish orphan. Her wardens never stayed in Honfleur long, seeking out their next adventure on distant shores. But it was a home for Gabriel, and now it was the closest thing for Neala, who still enjoyed how the night insects sang during her many long walks in the woods.

Often, her two fae children would come with her and soak up the night as well. Neither, she found, could venture out when the sun rose, their skin burning more quickly than hers. It was the type of fae they were, she guessed, when they both had dark skin that seemed fashioned from night itself. They lived on her schedule, taking their morning walk before a busy day of education and training under her watchful eye.

She would ready herself to draw her sword at anything unusual, but there was never anything malicious afoot that needed Prince Wraith. Instead, she found her services needed as mother instead. Like when Keegan sneezed fire and set their breakfast table alight as a young boy. Harsh words wouldn't help the table nor the swollen, burned flesh around his mouth, so she settled for rubbing balm on his face and holding his nose when he went to sneeze again a few minutes later.

Sorsha was more special still. She drew wild animals to her with some kind of magnetism and seemed to speak with them. Her skills fell in communication as far as Neala could tell. Anyone she met, she could find something to chatter about, not even seeming to register that she was different even when she had the brainpower—or more likely some kind of communication magic—to speak several languages fluently.

Both fae existed under a thick layer of Neala's illusions to hide their unusual starry eyes and pointed ears. She covered their night-sky skin and made them as pale as she so they could pass as her blood children and not draw undue attention. But she would drop those illusions when they were alone, quietly admiring the sparkle in their skin like the glitter of crushed diamonds just below the surface.

One day, she had to admit they grew on her. She may not have known what to do when Keegan breathed fire and shaped the stream like a loop or when Sorsha skipped by with an entire swarm of butterflies following her, but that was okay. They weren't human children, and so they didn't have human development.

Keegan chose to be nonverbal, acting much like Neala, even though he had a working voice. She worried for his future in particular. He held little interest in anything beyond his next sparring session. Once she entrusted him with a blade, she watched him excel and turn swordsmanship into a fine dance. It was the kind of thing he lived for. That and quiet nights with her and Sorsha.

"I found another one!" the girl called, her voice as sweet as music. She carried an impressive bundle of wildflowers, some still showering dirt from their roots. Neala and Keegan had tame, trim bouquets from a florist, but the girl had scoffed at a matching set of flowers and decided she would bring her own.

Neala smiled and nodded, chuckling at the enthusiasm. They made this trip often enough, visiting a place she'd marked off for a special purpose. A tiny footpath branched off from their trail and delved deeper into the moonlit night. Sorsha skipped ahead, happily humming to herself as she started to part the rich dirt around a tree's branching roots, planting the roots of a wildflower with practiced tenderness.

Neala observed and shrugged to herself. If anyone came across this path, they'd find an inordinate amount of wildflowers arranged in the colors of the rainbow. They'd flourished and spread as the years passed, surrounding five simple grave markers Neala bent to dust off. She'd recognized Gabriel's honor, Adrius's courage, Nyah's love, Gwendolyn's sacrifice, and Chandra's humor, filling their stones with words to immortalize their memory.

She sat and rested her bouquet before them in tribute, bowing her head in prayer. *"What's on your heart, Mother?"* Keegan asked mentally, undoubtedly still upright and watching over Sorsha like a protective shadow.

Neala sighed to herself. *"I just wish they were still here. I have so much I would say to them."*

As the forest sounds settled between them once more, he reached over and covered her hand with his. They sat like that for some time before she lifted her head and found Sorsha gazing at her, her forehead wrinkled in deep thought. *"What is it, mouse?"* She chuckled.

"Just thinking! Do you see what I did with the meadow? I was thinking of how to plant more," she said, speaking as she circled around the back of the clearing.

"Will I need to clear a few trees for you?" Keegan chuckled.

Sorsha gasped. "No way! This tree is a heritage oak, and this one struggled so hard not to drown in the stormy season last year. They work so hard to survive for you to cut down in a couple of hours." She started to wring her hands as Neala turned to stare and inspect the trees she'd indicated.

She already knew their tutor hadn't covered horticulture

recently. This went beyond that, so all she did was shake her head and tamp down the fear growing in her belly. *"Sweetheart, you mustn't speak so casually of your abilities."*

"You...didn't know all that?" she asked sheepishly, blushing as Neala and Keegan both shook their heads. "Sorry. I try to be so careful."

Neala patted the grass next to her in silent invitation, troubled anew. She put her arm around Sorsha, worried that her chattery mouth would reveal herself to the wrong person. Their small coven was used to Sorsha's unusual insights, but they thought her a gifted vampire child. The wrong vampire could take a taste of her out of desire to share those gifts. And Neala knew first-hand how thirsty vampires were for new power.

20

GWENDOLYN

"Forget what you know about me, Boy. My achievements mean naught, and my burdens are great."
    -Gwendolyn

Gwendolyn wandered in wake of her banishment. The Grand Occultarus had yielded its half of the Portal Key but at great cost, stealing away her sight in gruesome trade.

She crutched on her vampire regeneration, expecting it to return her vision. For weeks, her head ached and burned like her body attempted to right itself. During that time, the darkness swam with snippets of what she'd seen within the reflection of the Fell tool—glimpses of her late husband glowing brilliantly with the fire of heaven as a full angel. Reaching, beckoning.

How she wished she'd gone with him when she'd had the chance. Anything was better than the world of darkness she found herself in, guided forward by a young human charmed by Lucia's magic. He was Lucia's mercy, according to the new queen, someone who would ensure she had blood and afford her a measure of dignity in her banishment.

He never said a word to her. Not his name nor where they were. But his small, gentle hands guided her away from stepping in holes or tripping over tree roots. She began thinking of him simply as Boy, allowing him to guide her to resting places safe from the scorching rays of sunshine that could incinerate her. He nudged her along when her thoughts halted her in her tracks.

Her emotions would take over sometimes, overwhelming her body and mind alike in a black wave of heart-rending agony. She felt ready to collapse and curl in on herself as she thought of her family departed from this cruel world. "Do you know who I am, Boy?" she asked during one such episode, needing to hear something other than the breath in her parched throat and the chatter of birdsong.

As expected, he said nothing, though she felt his presence at her elbow. "I was once someone. But...that's not who I am anymore. I am no one, just as we all begin in this world." She spoke more to herself as she rested her palms on her knees to stay steady. "This is my new beginning. God has a plan for me even still. I pray it leads somewhere better than this."

Her new beginning was harassed by memories from the old one. She remembered Lucia's satisfied voice speaking to her from Nyah's throne. The throne she'd *stolen* using Gwendolyn's good name and reputation as a stepping stone. Hatred was a living thing in her chest, nourished by every moment of her suffering.

One morning, as she hid within a shallow cave, huddled as far from the incoming sun as the scoop of earth could allow her, she saw her first glimpse of Boy. Outlined by the wan light of early sunrise, his silhouette was a blob of moving darkness as he settled a blanket over her. When she blinked, her eyes burned from effort, and she allowed them to rest.

Outlines and shapes were all her regeneration gave back to her. Boy remained a dark silhouette next to her, drawing her ever closer to human civilization. She moved slower every day, bloodthirst digging its talons into her with his proximity. She didn't want to drink too much from Boy, not when they'd hiked through wilderness and down mountain slopes for what felt like an eternity of silence and introspection. Who knew how much longer this would continue? There seemed to be little point in plodding on when she had so little to live for, yet each sunset, she still forced herself to stand, to walk.

She'd lost track of the days by the time they found civilization. Farms heralded the edge of a village, quiet in late evening. The stench of domesticated animals flowed over her nose and was strong enough to make her gag. She regretted the heightening of her other working senses, as that scent lingered for miles down a well-trodden dirt road. Gwendolyn hoped for a larger slice of civilization with inns and townsfolk who'd heard of vampires and the great good they'd done for mankind in slaying every last Fell that'd graced the world.

They were stopped when the silhouette of a man stepped out of the shadows and into their path. "State your business, travelers." His tongue was an unfamiliar one but translated with Lucia's magic, a lingering reminder that made bitterness rise to the back of Gwendolyn's throat.

She knew he was a vampire, sensing the air around him. Vampires had an aura of sorts, wearing their heightened mental powers like a shroud. Powerful vampires like Adrius—rest his soul—or the Blood Princes had auras that expressed a sense of weight. The man before her had an aura like tissue, present but ephemeral. Newly turned. "We are searching for a place to rest our heads. We've travelled far."

"Which coven do you hail from?" the other vampire asked. A shifting in his shape suggested crossed arms.

"Coven? We are not witches," she said, puzzled.

"Which coven of vampires?" He sounded impatient with her already, a measure of disbelief there, as if he didn't believe she could be so dense.

"I am from Nyixa." She figured that would be a good enough explanation, and it was—it granted her an audience with his coven master within the village proper that he guarded. There was little way for her to tell what scale of civilization she'd entered. Maybe she and Boy could stay here. If the coven master allowed it, that is.

She continued in her bemusement, wondering if the translation magic was unable to properly categorize *coven* for her own language. It was a good enough term for a group of non-humans, but her negative assumptions colored the word as she was seated before the coven master, another man, in a room lit with generous candlelight. She appreciated more light, able to see more of his angular figure and the beard he'd groomed to an immaculate point.

"I was not expecting such esteemed company. You are Lady Gwendolyn." He stood upon her entering the room and offering a courtly bow, recognizing her despite weeks of travel and little energy or effort to keep herself presentable.

The man, Shen, introduced himself shamefully as a deserter from the Fell hunter army. He'd settled far from battle and started his coven for a measure of companionship. "I must apologize and beg for forgiveness for my desertion. I saw the true odds of survival and—"

She held up a hand, forcing a smile. "You need not apologize. I understand. How many people does your coven number?"

"Eight, counting myself. We are nothing like the city covens to the east," he answered, holding his breath as she considered.

"I think I know of a way for you to repay your desertion," she said.

Weeks alone had stripped away her identity as Gwendolyn, nephilim and advisor. Nature didn't care who you were or what titles you held. Now, calling upon her former authority felt like a sham. Like Shen shouldn't be nodding eagerly, but he was. "I require a place to stay. As does the boy. Perhaps we can join your coven for a time." She gestured to Boy, who stood at her elbow in his customary position.

"That is a girl, Lady Gwendolyn." He sounded puzzled.

A girl. She bit her lip, filling her mouth with the taste of blood. "Describe her to me. I cannot see any longer. It is a long story." One she doubted she would ever tell in full to another person.

Still sounding confused, he did. He described a girl with short red hair and a raised scar to the corner of her lip. Politely, he suggested she was not a handsome youth, with a dribble of drool at the corner of her mouth. "I see." Gwendolyn swallowed thickly.

He'd described a girl like how Neala once appeared, down to

the distinctive scar which prevented her ward from smiling widely. She didn't ask it of him to check the girl's mouth, so she did it later once they were left in a cozy room to sleep away the incoming day.

With a heavy heart, Gwendolyn reached into the girl's mouth and felt for a tongue that wasn't there. "What a nasty soul," she muttered, holding the mute girl to herself and weeping. Lucia had given her one last twist of the knife—a girl just like Neala. Only this time, it was the girl guiding Gwendolyn. How times changed.

———

Gwendolyn stayed with Shen and his coven for years, learning that they resided far from prying eyes on purpose. Somehow, her guide had avoided all other civilizations, leading her to this one instead. She would be suspicious if she had the energy.

She practiced her portal magic when she could muster getting out of bed. Nothing motivated her with the same fire of her youth, not even the excitement of making objects rearrange themselves at her will.

She could send people through portals as well, though it was taxing. Her biggest helper was Quinn, the child who remained by her side. With a dose of vampire blood, she'd regenerated her tongue and control of herself, but she was not a vampire...yet. Gwendolyn suspected she would turn the moment her body matured into adulthood. *Good for her*, she thought, though she felt a knot of guilt at the back of her throat every time Quinn begged her to get out of bed or to feed.

Gwendolyn was the closest thing Quinn had to family, having been stolen away from Nyixa and maimed to serve as a parting shot from Lucia. She didn't have Nyixa's translation magic and struggled with the language of the land. So instead, she stayed by Gwendolyn's side, aiding her, and was sometimes the only one she could talk to.

Quinn knew about the journal and tried her very hardest to crack its cypher. Nothing came of it but frustration for them both. With her magic, Lucia could've used any language before transferring it to a cypher, so its contents continued to elude their understanding. In the meantime, Gwendolyn's tongue stalled on telling its truths aloud. Her oath could not be broken.

No one but her knew how evil Lucia truly was.

But someday, if she persisted, someone would translate that journal. They could read for themselves the thoughts Lucia jotted down.

It was just a matter of time.

And that thought kept Gwendolyn going in her half-life of portals and darkness. Somehow, some way, she would repay Lucia for every scrap of her suffering.

21

GWENDOLYN

If we intercept her here, I will get my research back. Otherwise, I see no future with it in my hands.
  -From Lucia's New Journal

"Lady Gwendolyn, please wake up," whispered Quinn's voice one night, accompanied by a jostling of her shoulder.

Aches bloomed over her whole body as she woke to the twilight gloom of another day with young Quinn's form a dark shape above her. "Not today," she murmured, shuffling to turn her back to the girl.

"It is urgent." This time, it was Shen's voice, enough of a shock in her bedroom that she opened her eyes once more. It must be for the man to barge into her private quarters.

"I'll be up once you leave." She spoke primly; even after a few years together, he allowed her that trapping of her former nobility. Bowing his head, he left the room, leaving Quinn to help Gwendolyn's old bones from bed and into presentable clothing.

She had a moment to gaze into a mirror, seeing only the outline of a gaunt figure with cloth hanging limply over her.

Unlike the rumors circulated amongst mortals, vampires could see their reflection—if they could see, that is. She didn't need her own sight to know she was fading away.

Quinn tucked a walking stick into Gwendolyn's hand, its surface familiar and worn. Accepting it and the guiding arm on her other elbow, they left the room, which was situated on the ground floor of an inn. The tavern was silent as they passed into it, unusual for this time of night. Quinn guided her to a seat.

Blood scented the air, and murmurs followed in its wake from a few familiar voices. Other vampires she shared this space with. "Lady Gwendolyn, we have a situation." Shen sounded close by. "It, ah, concerns you rather directly."

Her hands laced together on the sticky wooden table before her. "Go on," she said, a sick feeling in the pit of her stomach. *Lucia?* she thought. Surely the future-seeing queen knew where she'd ended up. What new suffering was the woman to inflict upon her?

"Zhi intercepted a pair of vampires in military dress at sundown," Shen said, sounding grim. "They kept him alive to send a message back to us."

Alarm tickled at the back of her throat. "Is he all right?"

"For now. We've sent for Miss Li to see to him." He spoke of a woman who held the same healing power as Prince Jaromir. Gwendolyn knew the woman to be gentle and well-meaning, but her Gift was a weak one and incapable of returning her sight. Still, she was highly sought after in several villages as the only Gifted healer and often spent her time travelling between them to spread her services.

"The message?" Gwendolyn prompted, swallowing her nerves.

Shen's feet scuffed against the wooden floor. He seemed almost as nervous as she. "Those two men were representatives of an alliance of covens in service to Queen Lucia. They came to demand we join them...and relinquish you to the crown."

It *was* Lucia. Gwendolyn grew still in horror. What lies had they also told the coven that'd taken her in and kept her going this long? "We have tonight to do as they demand, or they'll execute us all for treason," Shen added.

It felt like all the air was punched from her chest at once. She gasped like a dying fish. "You should do as they demand and join them," she said, licking dry lips and lingering on the cracks in the corners. "I will find my own way."

Dubious murmurs surrounded her as the small coven reacted. "She wouldn't make it on her own..."

"...Skin and bones already..."

She continued, trying to ignore the whispered stings. "But whatever you do, do not return me to Lucia."

"I've seen your struggles for myself, Lady Gwendolyn. Whatever happened to you on Nyixa is not something I would ever wish you to return to." Shen spoke gently, resting a hand on her shoulder. "And...I do not serve a queen I have never met. She is an ocean away and reaches too far. Where you go, I will follow."

Deafening silence followed from the rest of the coven. Gwendolyn waited for one of them to disparage, but if they felt negatively, they held their tongues. "Then come with me. We will take a portal to a safe place," she said.

Within hours, she and her small group had their essentials packed. She fed from Quinn and cursed her weakness as she struggled to form a portal large enough for a person to fit through. If they survived this, she told herself she would keep up her strength instead of rotting away in bed.

She relocated her coven to a location further inland, far from the reach of any of Lucia's military. The effort took everything from her. Sweet darkness set in the moment her feet hit new ground.

Gwendolyn awoke feeling like thousands of needles were stuck into her scalp. Upon opening her eyes, she screamed at the sudden assault of noise. Colors. Shapes. Her eyes burned.

Gentle hands pushed her shoulders back into a bed. It was a nice one, better than the straw mat she'd grown accustomed to, but she still thrashed in animal panic and scratched at the strong arms holding her down. "Unhand me! Don't you know not to hassle a lady!" she hollered from a clear throat.

A familiar voice accompanied a gentle shake, quieting her after a gasp of surprise. Her eyes flew open for a fleeting glimpse of Jaromir, his Blood Prince maroon eyes standing out stark against an exhausted face. She screwed them closed again from the spike of pain that followed. "Stop. Stop this," he said, and she did. She laid back, capturing his hands when he moved to release her.

"*Jaromir.*" She put every ounce of her pain and loneliness into that one word. He was one of many she thought she'd never see again. Tears threatened to spill as she trembled from the sheer overwhelming relief of seeing him once more.

But did he think of her as a murderer as Lucia had painted her? Her grip slackened with a sigh, her energy wilting at the thought. "I'm glad to see you, too." He took on his usual, soft-spoken tone. "Consider my surprise when you're said to be deceased."

"Not yet." She found she could say little more since her banishment itself was part of her oath. Not a word alluding to it could escape her lips.

"Though you were well on your way to that fate. I repaired what I could," he continued, giving her hands a squeeze.

"My sight." She marveled at the idea of having it back even if it caused her pain.

"And your bloodthirst. That's the good news." He pulled gently from her hold, rearranging pillows and moving her to sit up.

"I don't want to know the bad news yet," she said, keeping her eyes closed throughout.

"Very well."

"How are you here?" she asked more quietly.

A cool glass pressed to her lips. She opened dutifully, taking a sip of water as he tipped it into her mouth. "My Gift compels me to go where it's needed most. For the first time, I sensed your need and came to you."

"Hmm. Fascinating." For a moment, she thought of the miracle his magic was, wondering how it came from the same source as the diseases Prince Elandros could make on a whim. "I've missed you."

"And I, you. Seeing you gives me hope that other miracles may be on their way."

She chuckled bitterly. "What miracles remain in this world?"

Jaromir set the glass of water aside, pausing in his thoughtful way. "Sirius and Korin disappeared the night Lucia was crowned." A chair scraped, and he sighed as it creaked under his weight. "Neither of them were there for the royal funeral, but I was."

Her breathing took a sharp turn. "What of it?" she whispered.

"Lucia asked me to say last rites over two empty coffins." An expectant silence followed during which Gwendolyn thought of the moment despite herself.

An empty coffin for a king killed by poison. Lucia had orchestrated it somehow, removing both royals from her path during the same day. But if he were dead, why not make a spectacle it? Lucia would only gain to display the bloated corpse, proving she was truly their queen.

But if she didn't *have* the body, well…

"You think he's still alive," she gasped.

"I am sure of it." He rested a hand over hers as her shoulders shook with a quiet sob. "Maybe you can help me search for him once you're recovered."

"Once I am and not a moment later," she said, her reality crashing down around her. She'd neglected her body for years, and now she expected herself to jump out of this bed and go straight to a more active role of searching and maybe using the portal magic she'd barely trained.

It was no surprise when Jaromir sighed, the sound colored with the weariness of a trial to come. "We had best get started."

22

NEALA

"I hate to come to your peaceful home with a heart full of war and revenge."

   -Gwendolyn

I t was a rainy evening when one of Neala's coven members burst into her sitting room, interrupting a private etiquette lesson. Sorsha dropped a bundle of silverware with a surprised yelp.

"Out," Neala gritted in her sandpapery voice, taking in the man's expression. He was soaked through with rain and was as pale as if he'd seen a ghost.

Usually, she had affection for this man. His wife was the wet nurse who'd fed Sorsha in the tender, youngest years of her life. The couple were the only people she'd confided Sorsha and Keegan's true heritage to. So, she waited while he gathered himself. "There's a new vampire in the city," he began, licking his lips nervously. "She, ah, wanted to speak with you. Quite insistently."

Raising a brow, she switched to mental speech for ease. *"And you sought to interrupt me on the whims of this person?"*

"Well, yes. You won't believe it until you see her."

"This had better be good." She followed after him and stopped short at the receiving room. Her coven inhabited one of the largest houses in Honfleur, but the figure before her seemed to suck the air right out of it.

It turned out he *had* seen a ghost. For Gwendolyn Firetree stood at her door, leaning on a walking stick. The years had not been kind to the former nephilim who'd wizened up like a grape in the sun. A pair of spectacles graced her nose. If they were passing on the street, she would hardly recognize her save for the proud bearing and steady gaze that was familiar and grounding in a reminder of her childhood.

"Impossible. She had you executed." Immediately, the words felt lame. The first she'd chosen to speak to her warden in almost two decades.

"And yet, I'm still here," Gwendolyn replied. A tearful laugh hiccupped from her throat as Neala rushed forward, pulling her into a fierce hug, which only lessened when she felt how frail the other woman had become.

"Have you been feeding?" Concern crossed her brow as she held her.

"Regularly now. This is better than I was."

"I hope you have fought off what madness held you in its grasp," she said more quietly, releasing Gwendolyn at last. A frown tugged at her lips as the pleasant buzz of her reappearance faded. This was still the woman who'd killed Adrius and was supposedly put to death for regicide.

Doubt niggled at her belly, an uncomfortable feeling when she'd rebuilt her life on a foundation of that betrayal being in the past. Gwendolyn was alive, and so something in the past was a lie. That much was apparent. "I've never gone mad," the older woman said in a serious tone that allowed for no argument. "There is much I need to tell you."

She produced a leather-bound journal from nothing. The hair prickled on the back of Neala's neck from a familiar feeling.

Magic. Keegan and Sorsha could both induce the same sensation with their own tricks.

Paper stuck out from the journal, various notes all jammed within its pages. She had a feeling she wouldn't like what was written there.

Neala set a steaming mug of tea before shaky, elderly Gwendolyn, listening to the patter of rain against her parlor windows. She'd sent her fae children off, not wanting someone so well-versed in the supernatural anywhere near them until she knew what to make of the situation.

They sat in silence. Gwendolyn sipped, and Neala read.

It was Lucia's journal, full of diagrams, spells, and potion recipes. Detailed retellings of how her days had gone. Completely normal until she skimmed to a page containing illegible symbols. The notes began on that page, written in Jaromir's slanted script.

The mug containing her own tea cracked in her hand as she read and read, growing tenser as the words undid all of her certainties. She felt a pit open in her stomach as Lucia detailed how she'd opened portals to the Fell Lands from a distance, moving around where they appeared in the Fell Lands in blind certainty that they'd find a desperate pocket of starving Fell to rush through and attack.

It made sense. Far more sense than a former nephilim losing her stones and doing it from some connection forged by the broken Portal Key.

She could hardly understand the journal further in. It was full of random scribbles and diagrams that led nowhere. Thoughts and directions that didn't link up. The work of a mad mind that would orchestrate the deaths of everyone Neala held dear.

Instead of ripping the journal, she closed it and slid it back over to Gwendolyn, who waited patiently for her response. *"You cannot speak of any of this, can you?"* Neala asked. If she could, Gwendolyn would've shouted it to every corner of the known world by now.

"My oath prevents it," Gwendolyn said.

Neala's fingers clenched in and out of fists as her breathing quickened. *"I will go back and kill her myself. How dare that miserable excuse of a Sorceress do this to me? To us?"*

Her vision swam with her fury as it mounted and took grasp of her like a living thing. She punched right through the table, bowing it inward as her knuckles filled with splinters. It felt good, reminding her that she was alive and capable of exacting revenge for those who were not.

Gwendolyn sipped her tea, still perfect in her calm as she used her palm to rest her mug when the table collapsed a moment later. "Patience. She currently has some things we don't. Men. An army. A crown. Years of uncontested rule."

"I can get close to her as a Blood Prince. Except I, too, had to swear an oath to her," she said, deflating as she picked splinters out of her hand. She told Gwendolyn of her banishment and how her return to Nyixa was contingent on her bringing Lucia an army.

The elderly woman's eyes gleamed with a hint of her old cunning. "I see a way around that, but first, an army would need to be raised."

"And I haven't tried to assemble one in all this time. I've been... distracted." As if to prove her point, a young voice called from upstairs. It was another of the coven's children, running from his bath. She'd pooled resources with her coven members, and they'd purchased the house together, living peacefully at the outskirts of town. She'd made her coven from scratch, one member at a time, before ending up with the small group she now lived with. They were like family to her.

"You've found your place at last." Gwendolyn's tone was wistful as she gazed into the depths of her mug. "Have you children now? A husband?"

"Children. By a twist of fate, I've adopted two."

A smile brightened her warden's face. "May I meet them?"

Hesitation took hold of Neala as she plucked the last splinters from her hand. She knew she didn't have the guts to lie to Gwendolyn, but Keegan and Sorsha were the last link in the chain of bad judgement that'd cost Nyah her life. At the same time, didn't she deserve to know them? Perhaps they could offer her a modicum of peace as they had for Neala.

"They are very special. A secret I've guarded all this time." She stood from the ruined table with a sigh and privately spoke the story of what she'd seen in the Fell Lands, including the miraculous transformation of Fell back into fae and that fae leader's emotional request to save his daughter and another child first.

"And thus, you have the children," Gwendolyn said, her face an unreadable mask.

"They are odd souls, but they are still mine. Fully adopted members of my family." Unlike Neala and Gwendolyn, who always had the gulf of ward and warden to separate them. Gwendolyn had never claimed her as full family, a thought that still ached like an old bruise.

Gwendolyn's shrewd gaze seemed to read this off of her. She probably already knew, truth be told. Neala had asked before, in her youth. Back when Gabriel was a celebrated knight, there was a matter of dowries and inheritances for them to worry about. But now, he was gone, as was Nyah.

The older woman bowed her head. "Everyone should have a family, and you and I are all we have left. Won't you be my daughter at last? So I may meet my grandchildren?"

Neala paused in a hallway, feeling how big this moment was to the person she used to be. It wasn't an offer for her anymore but for Keegan and Sorsha, but it caught the breath in her throat all the same. *"Yes, I accept."*

She tried on the name like a well-worn boot, once too big for her feet. Neala Firetree. It carried the legacy of a nephilim's righteousness and a knight's honor, and she would wear it with pride. *"Sorsha, meet your grandmother,"* she called from the girl's door as she knocked.

When she opened the door, Sorsha was still wearing illusions over her true self, appearing as close as Neala's daughter with a head of thick blonde hair and highlands-pale skin streaked with freckles. She turned a curious look up at Gwendolyn. "You're full of magic, like me."

When they were all safely in the girl's room, Neala dropped the illusion hiding Sorsha's true self. A gasp left Gwendolyn's mouth as she beheld the girl's star-speckled skin and glimmering silver eyes. "I may have magic, but it was borrowed. *You*, my dear, are true magic," she said, stroking her starry hair with trembling fingers.

She turned to Neala. "Does she have a mentor for her magic?"

"No. Who would mentor her? Only one person has magic like hers."
At first, she didn't want Sorsha to become one of Lucia's experiments. Now, with an understanding of Lucia's true madness, it was the best decision she'd ever made, even if Sorsha's magic was never refined.

Gwendolyn hefted Lucia's old journal, cracking a smile. "Maybe we can borrow a few spells."

23

GWENDOLYN

Fennel tea sharpens the sight. With the right magic, a Sorceress's eyes can pierce the veil and see what lies beyond the present. Combine with a strong will to guide the visions, and the future becomes another useful tool.

-From Lucia's Journal

Gwendolyn borrowed far more than a few spells from the journal, all told. Sorsha's magic exploded in potency with the opportunity to cast true magic with the proper tools. For a magical focus, they used a geode to channel and magnify Sorsha's power properly. Unlike Gwendolyn, she could cast spells without hand gestures.

Magic came to Sorsha effortlessly. It humbled Gwendolyn anew to witness. Much of the magic she controlled was a blend of Nyah and Lucia's powers, marking her as a budding force in their dark world. It was a blessing in disguise that Lucia took such meticulous notes.

Gwendolyn still spent hours worrying about such power in the hands of a child. Someday her childish sweetness would wash away, and they would see what kind of woman she would become. Would the Fell's destructive nature still emerge in her as a full-blooded fae? She couldn't imagine.

While she trained with Sorsha for over a year's span, honing her magic, she discovered some unique quirks to the girl. "Try to tell me a lie," she said one foggy evening while they walked the woods searching for rare materials. Gwendolyn held the basket, and Sorsha did the foraging, working around the older woman's slower gait.

Sorsha turned to her, her lips pursing. It looked as if she were holding in a cough, her brow furrowing with strain. "Okay, tell me this morel is blue," she said, holding up one of the rare mushrooms from their basket.

The girl relaxed, saying, "It is blue if you believe it to be."

Not quite a lie, but close enough. She shrugged and stashed the morel away, leading them home. Neala's coven members were a peaceful people. Gwendolyn liked them, spending less and less time with Shen and his coven where they'd settled on the northern outskirts of China. Even Quinn, a full woman and new bride, had less need of her as she started her own family.

They moved on, and so did Gwendolyn, holding her gratitude in check with her new expectations. She and Neala were going to war. There were a few things they needed first to make it possible.

One such thing skipped ahead of her, attracting a following of glowing fireflies. With enough training, Sorsha had the magic to counter anything Lucia could throw at them. It was worth waiting for her to grow older and more confident in her abilities.

Gwendolyn scoured the journal daily for any spells she'd missed that pertained to searching or seeing the future. She held onto the hope that Adrius was alive despite her closest council of Jaromir and Neala putting out fruitless inquiries to his whereabouts. They would try a new spell tonight to serve just that purpose, in seeking out a heart's desire.

Sorsha stopped short at the door to their coven's residence, looking back at her. Another quirk. While Gwendolyn turned the iron doorknob effortlessly, just a touch would burn the fae's skin like an open flame. "Think it'll work?" Sorsha asked, smiling without an ounce of worry as they went up to her second-story room. Neither of them spoke openly of spells until they were behind a closed door.

Setting aside a highly polished hand mirror, Gwendolyn checked with the journal and took a measure of fennel from their basket. "I certainly hope so," she said to herself, leaving Sorsha to prepare her magic as she went down to the kitchen to brew a fennel tea.

Outside came the clash and shriek of striking swords. Gwendolyn glanced out the window to witness who would be dueling at this time of night. Her lips thinned with disapproval at the sight of unsheathed steel flashing so close to another fae's sensitive skin.

At this distance, she couldn't hear Neala's mental voice, but it was apparent she was testing and challenging Keegan to fight for all he was worth. Despite commissioning a special sword with hilt and pommel made of a neutral metal so he could hold it, Neala had never coddled him once he showed an aptitude for swordplay.

"Each nick is twice as painful for him," she'd told Gwendolyn. Yet, he didn't let that stop him. If anything, he practiced longer and harder than any boy his age. He fought like a man with twice his experience, and she couldn't assume that was all practice.

Keegan was built to fight. A tall and lean whip of a boy, he wore a glamor that made him appear a as teenager with his adopted mother's red hair and serious bearing. If Gwendolyn didn't know better, he could pass as Neala's full-blooded son. He had a bright future as a knight or bodyguard. Someday, Neala would lead him into battle.

Muttering a prayer for that day, Gwendolyn took piping hot fennel tea up to Sorsha. The girl had prepped the mirror with wax and herbs, leaving its formerly pristine surface caked with a thick white paste. "Why must I dirty up a mirror to look through it, Grandmother?"

She turned a curious, twinkling gaze over at her, having dropped her illusion in the safety of her own room. "If you were looking at yourself, it wouldn't make sense," Gwendolyn said, setting the tea before her. "But you're gazing into the mirror and asking it to show you something far from here. This tea will help you see the spell's results clearly."

Sorsha took the steaming mug and opened her palm. Ice crystals formed like falling snow at her whim, which she directed into the tea. The hair on Gwendolyn's arms raised at the influx of magical energy even though it was a simple trick of freezing air.

Simple for Sorsha.

She sipped the cooled tea and pulled a face. "Drink it down. Fennel is good for you." Gwendolyn chuckled.

"There's no sugar in this," she complained, pinching her nose and gulping in quite the unladylike manner. There should've been a scolding for that, but Gwendolyn was too eager to see the spell's results.

Once the fennel tea was gone, the actual spell was an anticlimactic affair of Sorsha staring intently into the mirror. Night insects intruded on the silence of the room.

"I see…a lot," Sorsha murmured. "Snow and ice mostly. Curtains of it."

"What about people? Do you see anyone?" Gwendolyn wanted to jump for her eagerness but contained it under a tight façade of calm.

"Men. A lot of men," she said, blinking rapidly. "I see…an army. An army and a man that will be Mother's. And an alive king who has been dead."

A gasp escaped her throat. "Adrius? You see Adrius?"

"I think so," she said, turning away from the mirror and clutching her head. "A dark, sad man who is both alive and dead. He wears a ring of fae power on his hand."

It sounded like him. Gwendolyn hugged her close as her heart felt fit to burst from her chest. "Where is he?"

Sorsha smiled brightly from a job well done. "I'll point it out on a map for you."

24

NEALA

---

*"We've tried to piece him back together for decades. You think
you'll fare any better?"*
   -Korin

After so long thinking he was dead, Neala tingled with
anticipation to see Adrius again. She hoped that he would
be similarly eager when he laid eyes on her. Losing a lifemate
was serious business. He'd lost his soulmate the day she'd saved
Sorsha and Keegan and thus an important part of himself.

No wonder he'd fled Nyixa, whose very name would remind
him of what he'd lost. But where he'd ended up…it interested
her. A port, just like where she'd inevitably settled with her
family and coven. For her, it was transience. A part of her
yearned for the crash and roll of waves singing the promise of
freedom. She could always escape with the sea at her back. She
wondered if, for Adrius, it was the same promise that led him
here.

Gwendolyn stood beside her as they looked around. She was
shaky from the use of her magic, leaning on Keegan as color

slowly returned to her cheeks. The fae were both eager to see portal magic at work, and that was mostly why they'd followed. *"Our first location to check is a tavern,"* Neala said, knowing Adrius and his friends.

"Carousing. That's more Korin's style," Gwendolyn remarked, clucking in disapproval. "I will walk the town with Sorsha to see if she recognizes any other places."

Anxiety re-clenched its fist in her belly. *"I don't trust this place. What if you ran into a bad sort?"* She hadn't left Honfleur in many long years and didn't realize how much that'd closed her off until she was in a new, unfamiliar location.

"Keegan will come, too! It'll be fine," Sorsha said brightly. "Besides, we have...other stuff." Magic, she would've said. She had magic, and thus no mugger or drunkard could truly touch her.

"I just worry for you," she sighed, lifting a shoulder in defeat. *"I will check in with you mentally if I find anything."*

She was reliving news of Adrius's assassination as she found the tavern by the drunken singing echoing in the street. How he'd died by poison, killed instantly from a potion he thought he could trust. Sorsha called him "alive and dead" when scrying for him. What manner of man were they about to see?

This late at night, only the die-hards and the vampires remained at the tavern. She entered and scanned the room, taking in overturned tables and a scattering of wooden stools. It was mostly empty. A disgruntled woman was righting the furniture, barely sparing Neala a glance. "We're closed for the night."

Unable to respond to a mortal woman in the way she'd become accustomed, she cleared her throat and allowed a rasp to escape. "I'm looking for someone."

"Aye, aren't we all?" She grunted as she hefted a table and set it on its feet with a solid thud. She watched Neala's back as she headed to the bar and the lone man still nursing a drink in a shadowed corner.

Korin glanced up, sporting a tangled mane of dark hair and a full, uncombed beard. His eyes glowed crimson, unusually bright even for a Blood Prince. At first, it seemed he didn't recognize her, returning his gaze to the glass in his hands.

She slid in next to him, hearing the woman return to her cleaning in the pause that followed. The only way she wouldn't recognize the oddity of Korin would be from mesmerization, so he could sit around in peace.

He knocked back the last of his drink and then reached over the bar, pouring himself another shot. "So you've found me." His breath blew out a cloud of sour alcohol.

Nose wrinkling, she judged him a mess from those four words. *"You're not the one I was looking for."*

"He's dead. You can stop looking." He took this shot, his glowing eyes practically pulsing his agitation. She stared, shock warring with disbelief that she could come so far just for Adrius to be dead…again. He shook his head in a few jerks. "I had to kill him this time."

"You what?" She gasped, wondering what he meant by "this time".

Implying Adrius had died multiple times. "He doesn't exist anymore, not really," he continued, rolling his glass between his palms. A heavy slur marked the words. "You should just go away."

"Explain yourself before I force it from your tongue," she demanded, looming over him as she pushed away from the bar. Her stool clattered on the ground, drawing a vaguely annoyed sigh from the barmaid.

Korin stared up at her, immediately seeming tired and defeated. "You want to see it for yourself then?" She nodded curtly and ended up supporting him for a trek across town as he stumbled and weaved. In this state, she was lucky he was still walking. He led her to a ramshackle house in an impoverished district.

They found Sirius inside, similarly unkempt, sobbing quietly as he embraced Gwendolyn. Sorsha smiled to herself and waited to the side while Keegan shot a relieved glance at Neala as their entrance startled the two apart. "They want to see Adrius," Sirius said, rubbing the back of his neck.

While Korin seemed feverish in his drunken state, Sirius was fading away, his form dwindling and aging, much like what'd happened to Gwendolyn. He wasn't getting enough blood to sustain himself, she thought, frowning in concern. Sirius wore his years like a yoke, seeming fatigued and dragging on a level that went beyond mere exhaustion.

"Think he's up yet?" Korin sighed, stumbling back out the door. "Might as well check."

The others followed him as he circled around to a cellar. He removed a lock from its door with a fumble of mental influence, tossing it aside as he descended the stairs and almost fell if not for Neala's clenched fist on the back of his shirt. The circle of space below their house was enough room for a coffin along the back wall. Its wood was secured shut by two more locks.

Korin reached out and knocked on the lid. A muffled groan answered him, followed by a parched whisper keening for blood.

Neala exchanged a glance with Sirius, whose smile was wan. "He's awake."

25

ADRIUS

"There is no happy ending for him unless he gets a cure."
   -Sorsha

Adrius was back in the twilight gloom between life and death. His newest wounds burned along with the Shield Key, serving as hot reminders that he could not escape to the sweet, permanent darkness of the afterlife.

This time, the deathblow was a strike to the heart, a clean kill. His heart struggled to mend itself. After suffering several deaths, Adrius learned that one part of his body always lagged behind. Once that part was mended, he would "awaken" ready to do it all over again.

Waiting to resume his life was the worst part of the process. The initial death sent his soul onward for a brief but pleasant reunion with his old friends in that place beyond life. Each time he was there, he searched for any sign or sight of Nyah. She wasn't there this time. *She might still be alive*, he thought, *or spending time in the Fell's version of an afterlife*. He hoped for the former so hard, his cold skin flushed anew with the need.

Heat, he craved heat. He hated the cold in-between where he had to lay and think, trapped in his unmoving body. Thoughts of Nyah buzzed in a torturous circle, pushing away the other reality he didn't want to acknowledge.

Korin had driven his sword through Adrius's back, killing him this time. And his friend was a hero for it. Adrius could still see her, the dirty street scamp whom he'd fixated on. A girl with buck teeth and a girlish giggle, she was one of many who swarmed sailors begging for coin.

She was easy prey. And to someone constantly and literally dying of bloodthirst, easy prey was exactly what he needed.

Killing him was a way to turn the hourglass over for Adrius's bloodlust. He retained the wounds that'd killed him in his last life, healed to a state he could live with, while old injuries faded and scabbed. Without a glamor over himself, he was peppered with countless scars, as it seemed the magic was indiscriminate in how it healed him.

The wounds he woke with were the worst kind—healing slower than a mortal's body. Their slow dribble of precious blood was what weakened him into desperate need time and time again.

Voices intruded into his rest. His heart kicked as it registered familiar tones, drawing a pained moan from his dry throat as molten heat traced its way through his whole body.

"Please, blood," he whispered, attempting to swallow with a mouth that felt stuffed with cotton.

"This isn't how I expected to see my son-in-law." His heart threatened to stop for a second time as he heard Gwendolyn's voice infused with all the prim ferocity of a highborn lady.

"Sorry," Sirius said on the tail of a sad sigh. His brother sounded exhausted already. Guilt took up residence in Adrius as he imagined why that was.

"Wait." Neala's voice, another shock as he registered her gruff rasp. *"Just...wait. This is all very shocking. I want to know why he needed to be killed and locked away like this before we release him."*

"He's waiting for us—" Sirius hedged.

"You want me to tell 'em? I'll tell 'em," Korin said at the same time. "It's not actually a long story. We lost Nyah, and Adrius's heart could barely keep him alive. We took the first ship out that we could find to save him."

"That doesn't tell us how he ended up in a box," Gwendolyn interrupted from between gritted teeth.

Korin laughed hysterically. "I was getting there! Can't a guy tell a story? You're never patient with me and..." he trailed off. Adrius imagined murder in her expression and smiled faintly to himself.

"Take Sorsha and go upstairs," Neala interrupted, instructing someone. She breathed a troubled sigh after a few moments. *"So why kill him yourself, Korin?"*

"What?" Gwendolyn sputtered.

"To stop him from killing others. He comes back a little better within a few days." Korin sounded apologetic.

"I would see him. He is still my son-in-law..." Gwendolyn drifted off, clearing her throat and sniffing.

Someone removed the locks from his prison. He sprung free from its confines, hissing like a cornered animal. He could help it no more than he could change the way his feverish gaze sought out the most vulnerable target to drink from. Gwendolyn gasped, her aged face filling with pity upon seeing him.

"Easy now," she murmured, watching his mouth.

Sirius shoved her aside without preamble, bearing his neck. They'd been through this—he knew what his brother needed most. Adrius grabbed hold of his shoulders and took enough blood to bring him back to his senses but not a drop more.

Still, his brother slumped with fatigue. Neala caught him, shaking her head in disapproval as she offered her wrist. *"You are too weak to offer him sustenance. Think of yourself, too,"* she chastened.

Adrius turned to the last person in the room, unshed tears wavering in her eyes. "Gwendolyn. You're alive." His voice was the barest whisper as he stifled a sob to match hers. She embraced him, rubbing his back and letting the emotion run its course as if she were his true mother.

"And you are, too. I had my suspicions, but...I never expected this." She held him at arms' length, inspecting his whole body. With how he'd traded healthy muscle for an emaciated frame, he expected disappointment and even judgment. She flashed him a sad smile instead. "Let's go somewhere more comfortable, hmm?"

He nodded in agreement, leaving the cellar. One look at his closest friends told him that they weren't ready for more excitement tonight. Sirius was looking pale even after a blood donation from Neala, and Korin was stumbling drunkenly. Fatigue pulled at his own frame. Waking from the dead felt like he'd gotten no rest.

Still, he put on a strong front as Gwendolyn and Neala seemed rested and intensely displeased. He sent Korin to bed and Sirius out to feed, leaving only himself to answer the questions the women undoubtedly had.

He sat at his rickety table with them. Wind whistled over the house's foundation, drawing a line of goosebumps over his chilled arms. "I suppose you have questions," he offered once they looked to him expectantly.

"Sirius and Korin didn't fully explain what's going on. How are you alive?" Gwendolyn had a reverent hush to her voice.

He held up his left hand where the Shield Key rested like a permanent wedding band. "It won't let me die."

"*Let* you die. Like a living thing," she said, eyes narrowing behind a pair of spectacles.

He shook his head. "The magic is tethered to my soul. If I die and my soul tries to leave…the ring yanks it back." No matter his wishes, it felt like he was doomed to remain in his body forever. He began to sweat at the thought of an eternity living like this.

"*And your body heals off what killed it?*" Neala asked.

"Of a sort." His fingers hesitated on the hem of his tunic, but he drew it up so they could understand what he meant. Gwendolyn's fingers flew to her mouth on a gasp.

Blood wept slowly from a wound on his chest that hadn't quite healed. The steady drip of essence wasn't noticeable now, but without constant sustenance, it would drive his body to bloodlust to replace what it'd lost. Around that wound were several other scars, healed reminders of past lives. "If I stay alive long enough, it heals itself. It takes years," he continued, covering it up once they'd gotten their look.

"You haven't made it years without dying?" Gwendolyn asked, reaching over to rest her hand over his. He cupped her palm, feeling dry skin and fragile bone.

"No. After I was poisoned, my heart couldn't take the stress of travel. That was my second death on the way here. We met up with Korin's sellsword friends and rejoined their company." The former nephilim made a sound of derision, which he expected. For her, fighting needed a purpose; but for those who weren't so pure in their ideals, the coin was good, and it kept him on the move.

"I've died...a lot. Either from fighting or from Korin doing the deed. Sirius never has," he continued, feeling a grateful twinge for his brother. He didn't think either of them could live with it if Sirius had to put him out of his misery.

"*Why would Korin kill you though?*" Neala frowned. Both women grew grim. He couldn't fault them for their judgement.

"With the open wounds...I need blood daily, and sometimes that's impossible." He felt the skin over his heart throbbing at the reminder. "He kills me before I am pushed to bloodlust. Unfortunately, I never developed your sense of control." He spoke directly to Gwendolyn.

"I am not as you remember me. My body degraded ten years from me drinking the bare minimum. Now I'm a proper vampire to fix that damage," she said with a dash of bitterness.

Neala spoke up again as he struggled to think of how to answer that. "*So you've been hiding away from Lucia this whole time.*"

"It's less hiding and more trying again and again to rebuild my strength." The attempts wore on him and felt like running through water. Perhaps one day he'd make it to Nyixa's shores by churning his legs, but it was more likely he'd make a futile mess. "In theory...someday, I can go back and reclaim the throne as my right."

"*Every moment you wait, Lucia grows stronger.*" Neala frowned, looking him over as if expecting the old version of him, the king. He hoped she still saw some glimmer of potential.

"I'm not ready yet," he said, taken by surprise when she pushed a leather-bound journal into his hands. He recognized it once he opened to a random page and found Lucia's scrawl inside.

"Read the notes in this, and you will be. We need you." They needed a king, Adrius thought, not who he'd become. He just hoped that person still existed within him as he opened to one of the first pages of translations from Lucia's cypher and began to read.

26

NEALA

Adrius in particular takes little notice of my activities. He assumes I am as pure and focused as Gwendolyn or Nyah, with no ambitions for myself. The fool.

-From Lucia's Journal

Neala sat across from Adrius the next evening, waiting for the first stars to speckle the sky after sunset. Fatigue rimmed his dark, bloodshot eyes. *"You haven't slept, have you?"*

He jerked his head in a sharp *no*, seeming to stare right through her. "I trusted Lucia too much. She mocked how gullible and blind I was and for good reason." He slid the journal back to her. Though the leather wouldn't lay flat, as if crumpled by a strong hand, it was remarkably intact after spending time in Adrius's care.

"We all did." She took a deep breath, tamping down the anger that burned at the back of her throat. *"But all is not lost—you are alive. So is Gwendolyn."*

"Some help we are," he muttered, startling back when she

slammed her fist into the table before her. This time, she checked her strength, leaving it intact.

"Keep up that attitude, and our mission is over before it started."

"Excuse me? Our mission?" He pushed out of his seat and began to pace, heat entering his own voice. *"Our* mission. I must've missed something. When did I have a mission with you? Where have *you* been all this time?"

A smile touched her lips as he shed his sadness like discarding a cloak, looking down his nose at her with some of the same fire as her former commander and king. *"If you agree that Lucia must die, then we have the same mission."* She put her palms up.

"Right," he sighed, running a hand through his overlong hair. "How do you intend to do that?"

"Lucia banished me, expecting me to bring an army to her. Where have I been? Honfleur, France, thinking I would never go back to Nyixa at all." She stood, too, crossing to the room's window which overlooked a shabby patch of yard. Outside, Korin sparred with Keegan, their swords shrieking and clashing. *"I started a family instead. They are adopted, my son and daughter."*

She hadn't told her friends of her children's fae heritage, knowing what rabbit hole that led to. They were her constant reminder that she hadn't been there when Nyah needed her most.

He nodded, completely unsurprised. "I knew you would adopt."

A fleeting smile passed between them. She could talk about her children to any vaguely interested party for hours, but with him, it was different. The self-pity he shrouded himself in was so intense she doubted he'd hear more than a few words. He joined her at the window, watching the sparring match.

"I intend to find an army and go back to Nyixa," she continued. *"I'll raise up a band myself if I have to."*

Adrius glanced to her, frowning. "I don't think that'll be necessary."

She hoped he was about to say he'd do it himself. As strong as she was, she needed a man to recruit his fellow men. Neala simply wouldn't be able to command the same level of respect.

"This land is Korin's stomping grounds. You remember how we joined up with his old sellsword company?"

"You've already amassed an army?" she asked hopefully.

"Not personally," he said, dashing her hopes. "We've ended up spreading our bloodlines. Korin has a particularly strong coven going amongst the Hartson Company. That's about ninety men."

"Personally?" She'd hardly had the same amount of luck in finding interested candidates. Perhaps Korin wasn't as weak as she'd thought last night. Perhaps *he* was leader of this company and capable of recruiting more people to create a viable army.

"All first or second generation. They have little need for us though." With a sigh, he ducked his head in quiet guilt. "If Korin asks it, their leader may agree to join up with us."

She pulled out her crude seafarer's map as he named a location some thirty miles inland, a small stretch of land between townships that the Hartson Company settled in when not on contract. Skilled killers indeed to have a base of operations on the scale he described. *They would make a good start to our army,* she thought.

There was one thing that was apparent: Adrius could not stay here. He could not remain in one place, eternally trying to stack himself back up like a house made of flimsy cards. If he wouldn't be the leader they needed, perhaps others would take up the mantle. Neala herself would try. Not just to remove Lucia from her ill-gotten throne but also to honor Nyah's memory.

"I shall go to see this company myself. Korin and I will convince them to join us," she said.

He turned back to the sparring match. With her son's fae agility, he was almost a match for Korin's experience. Their swords leapt as they danced together in the fluid give-and-take of parry and retreat.

She knew what he saw as he lingered on watching this scene. Her son looked like a virtuoso, his sword the baton and his body the symphony, flowing like a fine melody. "He would do well to go with you."

"He has a brighter future than killing for coin." Neala sighed

aloud. There were few prospects for him though, having such a secret to hide. He still deserved better than becoming a sellsword or fighting in their personal war.

"I didn't mean that he should join the company. The leader, Hartson, has connections. He could get your boy something better," he said, elbowing her and forcing a half-smile. "Anyone who can stand toe-to-toe with Korin should get to show off his skills anyway."

"I suppose he has nothing to lose." Though reluctant, she inclined her head. She could stay with Keegan and meet this Hartson fellow for herself. Her son was nearly a man grown and thus needed to see what was out there for him. A fist had her heart in a vice. It still felt too soon and too dangerous for him to look for prospects that would take him away. He'd have to rely on his own flimsy control of illusions to shroud himself and would be alone in the world without his sister. In truth, Keegan Firetree had a lot to lose if he ended up in the wrong place.

―――――

They arrived the next day by horseback, taking the three steeds the men kept. She'd expected Adrius and his brother to come with them, but they'd declined, letting her and Keegan take their horses instead.

She worried for her children, reminded anew how Gwendolyn wanted to build Sorsha up as their side's Sorceress. Neala would rather hide her and Keegan both, keeping them from the inevitable bloodshed and death that lay ahead.

The encampment came up past the tree line, the journey quick when she was lost in her own thoughts. The trail was pounded clear of greenery from endless parading of boots and hooves. It was pure night above them, with a sliver of moon and the shine of stars to see by, but the camp was as busy for these vampires as a city of mortal men during the daylight hours.

Men chopped and stripped logs, clearing out a larger area as they passed into view. Most nodded politely to Korin upon seeing him, grunts and elbowing following as they spotted the

woman and teen that followed him on their own horses. Neala
clutched her reins as she felt the stares over her stocky, muscular
figure, followed closely by sniggers. Ninety men made up this
company, and she would wager that there was not a woman to
be found amongst them who could fight.

She kept her head held high, not acknowledging a single
chuckle. It wasn't uncommon for strangers to laugh. She knew
she wasn't an ideal beauty—not feminine, slim, or dainty in the
ways men expected. It never grew easier though. Especially not
after years of seclusion with her cozy French coven.

Korin led her past the working men and a tent city where
individuals were going about their business. It looked like they
were packing, getting weapons and personal effects ready.
Nestled against the trees was what she'd describe as a hunting
lodge mixed with a barracks. Immediately, she knew what it was
for. Tents could not promise complete safety from the rays of the
sun. For a company on the move, they'd have to do. Otherwise,
the safety of a full building was far more ideal. Korin led his
mount to a boy waiting by the lodge, who squinted at them like
shadows in the night as he held up a lantern and counted out the
three of them with a nod.

"How many live in the building?" she asked, having marked a
few sunburnt faces amongst the men.

"I believe they have a rotation going until they can construct
another barracks," he said, gesturing to where a foundation was
being laid in another corner of the camp's clearing. He took her
and Keegan into the lodge after their horses were led away. The
inside was bare and stank of mud and unwashed men. It was
built into one spacious room on the lower floor, remnants of habi-
tation in the furs spread across the floor. A wooden staircase led
to an unseen second level, doubling back on itself into two
flights.

Next to her, Keegan gagged from the smell, covering his nose
and mouth daintily with a kerchief. Neala waited as Korin
bellowed for Hartson, and a deep voice responded in an unfamiliar tongue. She recognized that she didn't know what he said
before Lucia's spell of understanding took hold after a few

seconds of foreign language, translating him perfectly. "Is that Korin? Ready to join us again at last?"

A set of boots thudded down the stairs as Korin's face split into a rare, full smile. "Afraid not, old friend. But I did bring you two folks you should meet."

Coming down the stairs was a specimen of a man unlike most Neala had met. She wondered if he were from a dream where her mind had mixed its lonely desires with the name Hartson and created a man she had to stand back and admire. Nearly brushing seven feet tall with the muscle to match, he was in the pinnacle of physical shape. A weak glamor covered his form, the work of a vampire she guessed to be about five years into his new life. She saw through it, replacing the handsome visage he wanted to show with the reality of a rugged face pockmarked by the cold and aged by a full blond beard and mustache neatly kept and braided.

She'd guess him to have been in his late thirties, if not older, upon being turned and immortalized. Finding herself thinking she appreciated a man with experience, she gave herself a mental shake. What was she thinking? Gawking over a stranger's appearance just as she judged others for, especially when it came to herself.

Yet, when his blue eyes found her and roved over her form, she hoped he found her warrior appearance as attractive as she found his. "Well, hello there," he said, also acknowledging Keegan with a dip of his head. His gaze returned to hers, drawn like a magnet. "Marcus Hartson, at your service."

She fought a blush as they shook hands, even their touch electric. Korin stood in to make the introductions. Hers was quite formal as a Blood Prince, though Marcus barely batted an eye. "Why do you call her a Prince? Are you blind?" He laughed.

"It's just a formality. All of us are Princes," Korin chuckled, speaking of the very reason she rolled her eyes at her formal title.

"What about you, do you feel like a Prince?" he asked, turning to her and laughing heartily. It was a deep belly laugh, the kind that was hard to get started but rolled downhill like a snowball on a slope, inviting the same of others as it went.

She offered a shrug in reply, chuckling in a dry rasp. Tapping her forehead, she tentatively reached out to him mentally. It never felt polite to speak in another's head without warning. *"I feel about as Princely as you would in my position."*

"A good answer. I am pleased to make your acquaintance, Prince." He inclined his head. "Are you two here to join my company?"

"My son and I don't sell our swords." A confused frown crossed his face, inspecting her as if she were a puzzle he was determined to solve. *"I am here to make—"*

Korin elbowed her, and she drew off, giving him a warning look. "You should put your best swordsman again him," Korin said, gesturing to her son. "I guarantee you he's the best you've ever seen."

Marcus let his attention waver, turning to inspect him. The illusion over Keegan didn't change much about him, hiding only his nature but not the tall, whip-thin body he held with stiff-backed precision. He grunted to himself, finishing the once-over by staring him in the eye, seeming unimpressed as Keegan fumbled his kerchief back into his pocket. "How old are you, boy?"

To his credit, he didn't hesitate. "Almost sixteen."

"I'll bet good coin that my man can beat him," Marcus said. And thus, Korin met his wager with an eager grin, the two of them heading out to find a worthy opponent.

Keegan hung back once they left the stink of the building behind. "Should I lose?" he murmured. "I don't know about this."

Some part of her agreed that losing would be the prudent choice. A slim boy of sixteen wasn't expected to have the strength or skill he wielded with ease as a fae. *"Don't throw your match, but don't show off. You can reasonably demand half of Korin's winnings as your due."* In a foreign land, having a fistful of the local currency could do wonders for them.

Keegan smiled to himself. He stuck to her word once he was faced off against a big man named Bjorn, who snickered the moment he saw his teenage opponent. For that reason alone, Neala wanted to kick his behind personally but left it to her son's capable hands. She watched Marcus instead, her eyes creasing with amusement as his expression went from self-assured to shocked as Keegan got his three strikes within the first few minutes, emerging without a scratch.

"That's impossible. He got lucky," he said, shaking his head in denial as Korin held his hand out, gesturing for his palm to be filled.

A crowd was starting to form. Men came from across the camp to watch, though the fun was short-lived for that first match. "Show me your moves, boy. I want to see what you've got," Marcus continued. He drew his sword from its sheath, limbering himself with a few warmup swings.

Keegan shot her a desperate glance. This was unexpected, but she shrugged and inclined her head. He couldn't turn down a challenge without all of these men jeering. Though seeming uncertain, he squared off against the mountain of muscle that was Marcus Hartson. It was not over in minutes. The two of them sparred at the same kind of standoff as she'd seen before. Marcus was on level with Korin, which made him quite formidable indeed as a much younger vampire. She found herself watching him and the line of his body, admiring the athleticism even as he got the upper hand and delivered the last cut he needed to win the duel.

"Damn it. He's going to say that he's his best swordsman," Korin grumbled. Defeated, Keegan kicking a rock like a petulant boy. Though he'd heal from his wounds, it'd take longer than normal. He retreated to stand next to Korin, nursing the steel-made cuts sizzling like burns under his glamor. Money exchanged hands around the crowd, but few had bet for him over their leader.

True to his word, Marcus approached with a palm out.

"Double or nothing for one more challenge?" Neala offered, patting the hilt of her own weapon.

The merrymaking around her suddenly drew to a halt. They recognized what the gesture meant even without the words to accompany it. She hadn't projected her voice past Marcus. "I don't back down from a challenge, Prince." A grin swept across his face. They squared off in the middle of the circle of men while her son and friend exchanged glances behind her back.

Neala bet money she didn't have, flooding herself with heart-pulsing urgency as she sized him up. For as much as she admired him, it was something entirely different to stand against him. "There's no shame in backing down." He dropped into a defensive stance. Her move then.

"I would say the same back to you." The crowd gasped as her form began to blur, illusions of herself dancing around her silhouette like double-vision. They hadn't said a word about her abilities.

"Cheater." He was laughing as he braced for impact. Their blades danced faster than the eye could see as they fell into step. The murmurs of awe that surrounded them faded like the susurration of a distant brook. All that mattered was placing her next step right, swinging in tandem with her illusion to strike from two places at once. One hit, two to go.

He came at her more aggressively, striking where he now knew her to be standing. A line of warmth opened over her bicep. *"I want to hire your company."* The two of them struck more quickly still, their weapons shrieking from impact.

"Whatever for, Prince? You're a one-woman army." He gritted his teeth in concentration. "I see where you son gets his skills."

"Something far more important than whatever border skirmishes you're hired for." Sweat beaded on her forehead, finding herself unable to make progress even with her illusions.

"Is the coin good?" he chuckled, scoring a second cut as a sister to the first, this time getting her sword arm.

"You will be paid a handsome salary. You and your men alike," she promised. If they got Adrius back on his throne, they could pay Marcus and his company with crown funds. But payment wasn't something she'd thought hard about, and she thought on that subject a moment too long.

"I'll consider it…if you can beat me," he taunted, his next swing coming dangerously close to her cheek.

She gritted her teeth, delivering her next stab to his sternum. At the speed of the strike, his armor took the blow, but he still bled. He flinched, just long enough for her to finish the duel with a cut to the bicep, just like he'd done to her. "Remind me not to get on your bad side," he remarked, bowing in defeat.

All at once, she became aware of their audience as they jeered and howled. Coin exchanged hands once more, funneling toward Korin and her son, who'd bet on her against steep odds. She turned a pleased smile onto Marcus. *"It seems you must consider it now. Shall we discuss the prospect?"*

Marcus laughed, shaking his head in bemusement. "Let's go for a walk, you and I."

27

NEALA

"I've never met a woman such as you, Prince. I wouldn't mind crossing swords with you again."
    -Marcus

Neala was relieved to have a moment alone with this man as they walked from his camp and into the quiet wilderness. Inspecting the planes of his face, she searched for the reason he'd caught her allure. She realized he was doing much the same, his brow furrowed. "You are a very attractive woman, Prince," he said, once they were alone.

"You may call me Neala."

"Oh, I may, hmm?" A smile tugged at his roughened lips. "Tell me, Neala. Do you often beat men at their own game?"

"If it fancies me." She took in his rising humor with a raised brow.

He shook his head, still smiling in his own private amusement. "It's just, I never expected to be on the business end of a sword owned by a woman, let alone bested by one. You've delivered two firsts in one evening for me. Were you a man,

I'd nurse this ego bruise until the time we met again in a duel."

"But as a woman?" she prompted.

"I liked it." He shared a grin, fangs out in a vicious smile. "I would get my ass kicked by you any day, Prince."

She found herself chuckling with him, intrigued by this man who brushed off his loss so quickly. *"If you come with me, perhaps you will have the opportunity again. I have a proposition to share. I would like you to come with me to the vampire homeland, Nyixa. It is an ocean away, off the coast of China."*

"That is quite a way for a band of sellswords." His eyes narrowed as he calculated. "Besides, we are fighters, not sailors. How do you expect us to make it there?"

"We will charter transport. In a matter of a couple of years, we can make it there. I intend to wage war to reclaim the crown which rightly belongs to Adrius."

"With my company alone?" Now he was quite incredulous.

"I am talking of fighting vampires, and your men are already used to doing just that. Tell me where else in the world I can find a company like yours ready to fight for the highest bidder."

"I'm sure there are some," he said slowly.

"I'm sure. But you're here now, scraping coin when you can have riches on salary. King Adrius would make you an officer. Ninety men under your command on salary to him. And he pays his people quite handsomely." She spoke more to money as she noticed the glimmer of greed lighting his eyes. Sellswords didn't make their way to a company without an eagerness for coin, if not a better life for themselves and those who depended on them. She wondered what had motivated him onto this path. With his skills and size, he could easily find permanent work.

"How much are we talking? What can your promise? I have met the man you speak of, and he seems neither rich nor a king." Sober reality stole his eagerness away a breath later.

When he was king, Adrius started paying with a new standard of white stone coins, backed with artifacts and riches from the Fell treasury filled with currency from several nations and a hodgepodge of other assorted gems and precious items. She may not know much about current-day Nyixa and how it was run, but she assumed there were enough riches that remained to pay these men as handsomely as she suggested.

A sudden headache grasped her head in its talons. *"Neala…"* Her eyes went wide as her head whipped around, looking for the source of the voice.

Marcus reacted quickly, dragging her by the shoulder against a tree so her back was to his solid front. Their armor pressed together awkwardly as they both listened. Wondering if he'd heard it too or merely reacted to her reaction, she nevertheless waited silently, her breathing slowing as she pinpointed various sounds in the night.

Small animals crept in the shadows around them, but otherwise, nothing. No woman around to whisper her voice like a caress. She was apparently going mad herself and prepared to tell him it was nothing when it happened again. *"Neala…"*

A stab of pain accompanied the whisper, but this time, she recognized the voice despite how distant it sounded. *"Lucia?"* she tried to send back, fueled by sheer disbelief.

"You can hear me. Good. I've tried to reach you for a while." Neala didn't have the sense of accomplishment from speaking across continents when it hurt to receive Lucia's words. It was like they were both straining their mental capacities to even have this conversation.

A cold sweat dripped down Neala's back as she wondered if Lucia had already seen all of her plan. Her future sight was her one huge strength, likely seeing the coming tide of war before it was a mere whisper on Nyixa's shore.

"I've watched you when I can. Your image is often fuzzy in my visions, but one thing is clear. You…and Marcus Hartson coming to Nyixa." She sounded excited, far more excited than Neala had ever heard. Was she excited for war? Neala barely twitched as her belly tied in knots.

"Do you hear anything?" Marcus whispered, finally letting his guard drop as the night's silence drew longer.

She shook her head, stepping aside as he let his arm drop. *"I suppose I imagined it,"* she said, feeling it a lame answer but better than explaining her incredibly long-distance conversation.

"Not trying to delay answering my question, are you?" he

asked. For a moment, she froze before realizing he wasn't serious. His icy-blue eyes danced with private amusement.

"That was not my intent. This is a serious offer," she promised, rubbing at the goosebumps that rippled across her flesh despite the ease she affected for him.

Lucia continued to speak in her mind. *"Travel by land. Take my new army to Rome where I have magical means to bring you to Nyixa. Congratulations, Neala. Your banishment is nearly at an end."*

Lucia next promised something she thought impossible. She'd discovered teleportation as a means for them to all use the occultari, which would save months, if not years, on their trip to Nyixa. She wasn't about to look askance at something like that.

Nor did she withhold the sum that Lucia offered to pay Marcus and his company. That money would belong to Adrius soon enough.

They walked in silence for a while while he mulled over her offer. His face gave away nothing, not even a hint of the fancy she thought she'd earned. Despite herself, she found her palms sweating as the moment stretched on. The stakes weren't so high that she couldn't walk away if his response was negative. She would simply continue to exist outside of Nyixa and escort Adrius to the occultarus in Rome personally.

"I require a few things in return for such a risky venture, Prince," he said at last. "First, a blood oath from you."

Going rigid, she eyed him askance, and he seemed to notice and smiled readily. "Just saying that you're speaking the truth to the best of your ability. Can you control what others do? Perhaps not. But I want you to swear that your offer is truth and made in good faith."

She didn't hesitate to score her palm. *"My offer is truth and made in good faith."* There was no hesitation to promise the truth to him.

He waited for a solid minute, stopping to look her over. Though she'd never witnessed someone breaking a blood oath before, she'd heard it was an imminent death sentence, bringing on the horror of Fell madness even in a vampire untouched by the Fell Emperor's blood. When she didn't immediately start to twist and shrivel up into a monster before him, he nodded to himself and accepted her words for the truth that they were. "Second, I will be seeking contracts as we go. That is not negotiable."

"Fair enough."

"We will be finishing our current contract as well. I won't have us leaving behind a poor reputation." She nodded in approval of this demand, seeing how he would want an avenue to return to his burgeoning base of operations if things didn't go as he expected.

"And finally…" he seemed to focus on her, only her. The air between them simmered with his regard and intent. "I need the swordswoman who bested me to ride at my side into every battle we fight."

Her breath left her on a ragged sigh. *"It would be my honor and pleasure."* She broke into a rare smile of her own. It felt like he saw her and admired what he saw. There was not a moment of judgement for being "unwomanly" but instead an acknowledgement of her strengths and pride of place because of them.

"Then we have ourselves a deal. Who knows? Perhaps the company will grow on its way to Nyixa." He exuded confidence as he casually placed his arm around her shoulders. She allowed him to turn her back in the direction of the camp, hoping that was exactly what would happen. They'd need every man they could get.

Her spirits winced as Lucia's voice scythed into her mind. *"I would be happy to pay for any you can recruit. You have done well, Neala."*

Though it took every ounce of her self-control, she did her best to imitate a simper and sound like she wanted to kiss the foul woman's boots. *"Thank you, my queen. Have you news to share of Nyixa?"* She wanted to know exactly what situation she was walking these people into.

"Nyixa prospers as a nation. We have covens spreading from sea to sea." The queen spoke with ultimate pleasure at that fact. Only with heavy influence would the vampire race be able to spread that far, but it was still a shock to imagine how fast it'd happened. Adrius's talk of restraint and withdraw had obviously been put to the wayside.

She gave herself a shake, realizing that Marcus was still speaking, squeezing her shoulder for her attention. "…would appreciate such a big job. The biggest in my company's history."

"Hopefully the largest I am involved in as well." Realizing she sounded distracted, she tried to draw away from this unwanted long-distance connection to Lucia before she spoke to the other woman with utter disgust. Lucia deserved to have her mind full of threats and dread for Neala's homecoming, not to assume Marcus's company was coming to *join* her army.

It felt like their connection went thinner, but something still had its hook in her. Lucia could reel her back in if she wanted.

He let off his hearty belly laugh, smiling at her with full, warm regard. "Why do you not speak aloud, Prince? Afraid I will be spellbound by your lovely voice?"

A part of her said to lie, to tell him her vocal cords were severed by some terrible wound. Surely such things happened. She had never been so intensely embarrassed by her damaged voice before because it meant explaining that she wasn't whole to a man who was the image of perfection. She took a deep breath, anticipating the pity or disgust her spoken voice usually brought. "I don't have much of one actually." Her rasp was like sandpaper, worse from lack of use, and heralded a flurry of coughs.

Marcus didn't look at her like damaged goods. In fact, his good cheer hardly faded. "Our flaws make us stronger. I can't speak more than a sentence at a time mentally." He tapped his temple. "Yet you're completely fluent, and you don't even have to stare to make it happen. That's incredible."

"Thank you." He hadn't allowed her a moment of disgrace and didn't help water the garden of her own doubts. Instead, his warmth filled her, sparkling in her chest like starbursts.

Was this love at first sight? she wondered as they returned to his camp, his arm releasing her and a stern scowl falling over his expression as a few curious men looked their way. It was a silly notion that she would feel drawn to someone so quickly despite other vampires reporting instant love and chemistry with their fated mate, so she shook it off, glancing upward to find the first signs of dawn.

Marcus followed her line of sight. "I can make space for you here," he assured, leading her toward the building where they'd met. Korin stood close to the doorway, surrounded by a crowd of mercenaries that she assumed were his fledgling vampires, all of them looking at him with adoration.

"I would appreciate that." Her gaze alighted on Keegan, who stood at the outskirts of the group. Her boy listened keenly to the discussion while doing idle coin tricks between his fingers. A favorite of his—making a coin disappear and reappear—was *real* magic, but none noticed the simple sleight of hand for anything special.

As she strode past the group, she felt Lucia's presence in her head reach out for a few fleeting moments. *"Neala? Neala, why can't I see you?"*

Keegan turned to her, his brow furrowed. He gave her such a clear look of puzzlement as Lucia faded from her mind completely. There was some connection there, but she merely shrugged. It was simply a relief that the pain of the long-distance connection was fading, leaving her clear-headed as she followed Marcus into his home and up the stairs to a landing with several separate rooms.

One door was ajar, revealing a desk and a few messy stacks of papers. The other doors were closed. "If this is our last night here, we might as well be comfortable." He opened one and revealed a plain room with a single cot in the corner. It was about as small a space as could be, but she imagined he'd planned it that way to fit as many people in this building as possible.

"I'm not displacing someone else, am I?" she asked, seeing no personal affects that would suggest such a thing.

"He'll get over it." He regarded her with dancing blue eyes. "Unless you would like to share a room with someone."

"You look like you have a place in mind."

He'd eased himself closer to her until she could feel the body heat radiating off of his armor. Palms skimming his chest plate, she felt his presence steal away the air around them. He was a force, this young vampire who could almost keep up with her.

If she weren't a Blood Prince, they'd be equals. The thought brought a shiver of pleasure. Her belly quivered with a tango of butterflies as he drew off a glove and ran a calloused thumb over the scar that marked the side of her mouth. They breathed the same air as he leaned in, tipping her chin up to meet him.

As her lips locked with his, it was a precise lightning bolt of pleasure. It felt right, her world falling into place as her worries for the future faded away. She would reorder her affairs to make him fit in with them. But first, they needed to spend time getting to know one another better.

28

ADRIUS

The timelines tangle like a weaver's nightmare. I need my Marcus, but he must come to me, else Nyixa sinks below the waves in my absence. I tire of waiting for Neala to perform her duty.
   -From Lucia's Journal

Adrius went out hunting on his own, unable to stand the hunger needling his stomach. The good news about his port town home was the constant stream of new mortals, most healthy enough to supply a donation of their blood.

He didn't mention to anyone, not even his brother, how fast the thirst returned. The wound on his chest burned with every throb of his heart, a reminder that he wasn't completely healed or whole.

But this was something new, a broken heart on top of a wounded one. As he entered the town tavern, he thought of her mocking words immortalized in Jaromir's handwriting and her gibberish cypher. He would rip her silver eyes straight from her skull for the offense and throw her blind self into the Fell Lands himself. She deserved a slow, terrible death.

He slammed himself into a chair at the bar, joining a few late-night patrons as he passed a coin to the barkeep and accepted a mug of beer he had no intentions of drinking. No, his thirst was much darker. Inspecting the room over the rim of the mug, he counted five men and a few younger maids flirting with hope for some extra coin.

One slid over to him, sitting right into his lap. She may have been pretty, but she'd colored her cheeks with too much rouge. *Blood* was his only thought as she traced her fingers over his jawline and whispered something in his ear that he didn't have the focus to hear.

His gaze was focused on the pulse throbbing at her throat, the veins visible under near-transparent skin. Underneath her cheap perfume was the more intoxicating scent of her fresh blood.

The object of his attention pulled away, brow furrowed as if confused by his lack of response. Her lips parted as they locked eyes. Coy promise faded as her skin turned pale. "What's wrong with your eyes? And your face?" Her voice swam in and out of his hearing as she tried to stand just to find his arm locked tight around her bicep.

He realized she was opening her mouth to scream and silenced it with a bit of vampire influence. With a look directly into her eyes, he commanded her to keep silent. He couldn't feed if she startled everyone away.

"What's wrong with my eyes?" he asked, stroking her too-red cheek and allowing her the presence of mind to answer that one question.

"They're black. All black."

Adrius remembered little of what happened next.

It was like waking from a bad dream, full of screaming and pain. One moment he was sitting, the next standing, something dripping from his chin. He brushed it away, catching a glimpse of crimson on his hand.

"Hmm?" Fresh blood glimmered there. He would've licked it up, but he was full and comfortable for the first time he could remember.

He turned with dread rising in his chest to find the bar silent, tables and chairs overturned with bodies strewn around like discarded dolls. The woman who'd been in his lap lay closest to his feet, empty eyes staring up at him in accusation.

"No. No, no, *no*..." he muttered, taking a step back as he beheld the jagged throat wound that'd sealed her fate. It was sterile, cleaned of blood completely.

He went around the bar and checked every patron and the barkeep, finding similar wounds.

Years ago, he'd come across a similar scene, finding half-chewed and exsanguinated corpses in the remains of a Hungarian village. He'd closed eyes then as he closed the eyes of those in the bar, muttering a prayer against evil over each patron.

Fell hunters followed a strict creed, believing anything that would prey up and kill humans was a monster in need of extermination. If they could not find a better food source, they needed not suffer to live.

He drew his sword. Placed the blade flat over his palms and beheld what reflection lay there.

Black eyes stared back at him, pools of darkness. Dark veins branched out from them, staining his face. *Fell* eyes. *Fell* veins. He'd closed countless eyes with the same hungry stare reflecting back at him from his own face.

"I would not suffer a monster to live," he told that reflection and plunged the blade into his chest.

29

NEALA

"We may not suffer monsters to live, but he's no monster. We will keep a close watch on him and make sure this doesn't happen again."

-Neala

Neala made the return trip with Marcus and Keegan, smiling despite the weather's chilly turn. The late Danish autumn heralded the bite of bitter cold with snow drifting its seasonal blanket over the woods. The horses blew smoke from their nostrils as they travelled at a near-leisurely pace toward the port town where they'd left the remnants of her family.

She couldn't remember a time where she was more content. A private smile flashed between her and Marcus, unabashed with Keegan taking the point several yards ahead of them. She figured her son had gotten tired of the furtive whispers and stolen glances.

Korin had chosen to remain with the company, helping get the men prepared for a much longer trip than usual. They all waited for Neala's friends and family to get their affairs in order before they began their long march south.

She led Marcus straight to Adrius's shabby home. Sirius let them in. Despite his grim expression, he'd improved over the last couple days. A couple of blood meals had obviously improved his constitution. He stood straight, looking like he'd lost fifteen years in age to return to the thirty-something appearance matching his age when he was turned.

Hopefully Adrius had also used his new control to return some of his strength. Heavens knew he needed it, but his physical recovery would take more than a few meals.

Sirius rubbing the back of his head self-consciously. "Neala, there was...an incident while you were gone." He glanced behind him where Jaromir of all people walked out.

"When did you get here?" she asked.

"Not long ago." He sounded distracted, waving a hand dismissively. "Gwendolyn's portals."

Still marveling at his sudden appearance, she made the introductions for them and Marcus. For Jaromir, she also introduced her son, putting a proud arm around his shoulders.

"Why don't you all have a seat?" Jaromir suggested, his tone suggesting he had something to say that would require it.

She seated herself at Adrius's table, right next to where she'd punched it. Flashing her a confused glance, Marcus settled next to her.

"Adrius is dead. Again," Jaromir said without preamble.

"What?" she exclaimed, bouncing back to her feet from an immediate shot of adrenaline. *"Who killed him?"*

Jaromir flashed her a sad look. "He did. We'd just finished containing a panic when mortals found his body along with ten exsanguinated mortals. Gwendolyn called me in to help and see to his body."

Shock turned her numb as she fell right back into her seat. *"Did Adrius..."*

"As far as we can tell, the whole scene was caused by him," he confirmed.

She bowed her head for a moment, mourning the lives of people she didn't know. A sour feeling coursed in her belly that her brother-in-law had lost control to that level. The Fell killed by exsanguination, *not* the noble vampires who'd hunted that corrupted race off the face of their lands.

Marcus tapped his fingers, frowning intensely. "This is the man that would hire my company?"

Sirius flashed her a desperate look. *"No. I'm hiring you, not Adrius. If he is incapable of providing you proper payment, I shall instead,"* she said.

"Can you make that promise?" Marcus asked, raising a brow.

"Regardless of who pays you, the money comes from the same location."

Jaromir cleared his throat, glancing between the two of them. "If I may speak to the lady privately?"

"Yes, please do." Marcus gestured sharply. She swallowed a bundle of nerves and went outside with Jaromir where they could talk more privately.

He still pitched his voice for privacy. "There's not much I can do for him. Adrius needs something only found on Nyixa. I believe a vial of blood purification potion would restore him to his old self."

"One of Nyah's old potions?"

He inclined his head. "Gwendolyn claims she gave several to Lucia and that none of them were consumed."

"After so long, assuming they're still there...that is quite the gamble." She imagined Lucia would destroy something Adrius needed so desperately if she had any future insight to his need. Not to mention, with Nyah dead or worse in the Fell Lands, there would be no new potions created.

"We don't have many options." He sighed, threading his fingers through already disheveled hair. "Do you remember the Fell madness?"

How could she forget Fell madness, she wanted to counter. It was the condition that shook hands with accepting the Fell blood in the first place. Some of the early Fell hunters had succumbed to it, becoming true monsters just like the ones they hunted. They'd given in to the thirst, claiming more and more human lives as the condition worsened.

Fell hunters still in their right minds executed those displaying Fell madness.

"I see. So, without the purification potions, he has the madness." She pressed her lips together tightly. *"Does Gwendolyn know?"*

He nodded stiffly. "She is in mourning."

There was more he wanted to say. The tension between them could be pared with a knife, so she spoke for them both. *"He is unfit to be ruler."*

"At present, yes," he agreed quietly.

"We cannot bring an army to Nyixa to defeat Lucia just to put someone with Fell madness back on the throne." The more she spoke, the more dread coursed into her veins. *"If there are no purification potions left…"*

"Gwendolyn can use the Grand Occultarus to open a portal back to the Fell Lands. Perhaps Nyah is still alive," he suggested to her incredulous look.

"You think she could've survived this long amongst those monsters?"

"Isn't it worth it to check?"

"Perhaps," she said, grudging only of unleashing more Fell upon the city. If Nyah was alive, she wouldn't think twice of opening a portal, but it was a gamble, not a guarantee. *"But if she is dead and there are no potions…"*

"We need another ruler," he finished for her.

"Gwendolyn then."

"By rules of mortal succession, Sirius would be a better choice."

They paused, sizing each other up. She wasn't sure of her assertion, knowing how physically weak Gwendolyn had become. And he didn't sound convinced of Sirius either or looked like he wanted to have an argument about it. *"We have time to decide."* She hoped this was a moot point and there would a potion ready to restore Adrius.

"We have an army to march south. Apparently, there is an occultarus there that can be used for fast transport."

"That's right. I know of it. I'll come with your army and help keep an eye on Adrius."

"Hopefully, that is enough," she said, parting ways with him to find Gwendolyn.

She would drag Adrius in a box all the way to Rome if she had to because the world could not tolerate another unkillable, bloodthirsty monster. The Fell were bad enough.

30

GWENDOLYN

"We have to stay behind, Sorsha. Your mother needs you well-rested and ready should she need your magic."
  -Gwendolyn

The Hartson Company arrived in Rome at the end of a long, bloody march with significantly more men and riches to its name. Marcus rode at the forefront of their army, for a true army they were, with Neala by his side every night. Whispers proceeded them, of a man who fought with all the fury of a storm and the fierce woman who kept him untouchable.

Gwendolyn was proud of Neala for building such a reputation for herself by the side of her lifemate, finally accepting a man into her life on a more intimate level.

Past that, their position was a precarious one. The mercenaries took contract after contract on their march south since Adrius and Neala's promised payment to Marcus was so long delayed. If his lifemate didn't ask it of him, Marcus likely would've led his men away from their inevitable clash with Lucia's army to easier skirmishes.

Lucia did not contact any of them across the continent again, but Neala barely spoke directly of their mission due to fear that the queen was watching her actions with her foresight.

"I hope she is watching," Gwendolyn said to herself as they made camp on the outskirts of Rome.

On the horse next to hers, Adrius stirred from his bored staring into the trees. He rode between her and Jaromir daily, accepting a ration of blood as the Gifted healer monitored him for any future signs of Fell madness. "Hmm?" He glanced to her, dark eyes free of the inky blackness that marked the descent of Fell hunger. But fangs pressed out behind his lips. She feared the moment his control would start to slip again.

"Lucia. Some part of me hopes she sees her death coming." She gestured to the men setting up camp nearby. At the back of the supply train, they were some of the last people to arrive.

In reality, she knew there would be little predicting Lucia's reaction to their arrival. They had five different plans circulating amongst their men so Lucia would see a confusing mash of possibilities with the coming of their army. Some believed they were to go to Nyixa and start indiscriminately killing people, civilian and military alike.

Others believed the real plan was to come under a banner of peace and take the throne in as quick and painless a coup as possible. They didn't know exactly what they would see. Lucia would greet them with open arms or bare steel.

No one could predict what would happen next, but the men would be instructed of the true plan once the time was right.

"You don't believe that," Adrius said, bringing her back to her thoughts as he dismounted to take shelter for the coming sunrise. Since dying by his own hand, he hadn't fought or overexerted himself. As he stretched, he smelled faintly of blood. It was an improvement. In the early days of their march, she could barely ride next to him, for he wore blood scent like a perfume as his old wounds leaked.

"Tell me you don't," she remarked, looking for the command tent. Recognizing it for its red trimming amongst a sea of brown, she walked toward it, trailing Adrius and Jaromir.

"Of course I do. But I want more than her quaking in fear." He slammed a fist into his open palm.

He held the tent flap for her. Inside, young mercenaries were still setting up an arrangement of furs for carpeting and small benches and chairs for their group. Neala was already there, seated with Marcus's arm around her shoulders. Keegan was the other person seated. Even his glamor seemed exhausted when he could appear how he pleased. The young fae participated in few fights, tending to linger with his sister and Gwendolyn instead as they worked on magic.

A gifted fighter, but a gentle soul. Neala had told her that mercenary work wasn't his calling, and she could tell that was the right of things. Yet, she still insisted he sit in on strategy meetings like this one. Neala believed that his presence would ward off Lucia somehow.

Sirius and Korin joined them last, completing their council. Gwendolyn glanced around and counted them like calculating their odds. One king. Four Blood Princes. One general. One former nephilim. One fae.

Good odds, she thought with some humor.

Marcus held up a hand, silencing the underlying murmur in the room. "Tomorrow, we go to Nyixa. Are we still certain of a stealth approach?"

"Lucia has spread vampirism indiscriminately in our absence," Jaromir said. "I've seen Nyixa the most recently of us all, and she sits in a position of strength. We cannot hope to defeat her head-on."

"All I need is a good opening, and I will cleave her head from her shoulders," Adrius muttered.

"Stealth it is then, unless the situation changes," Marcus said.

It was Gwendolyn's plan, and she could see it didn't sit well with most of the men who shifted and murmured in discomfort. They didn't know Lucia like she did. She only wished she could go with them, but her banishment remained in effect until Lucia was gone. She would remain behind with the two fae children.

Lucia expected a gift, or so she said. For Neala to return with an army, to end her banishment groveling at the queen's feet. In truth, Lucia had coated this gift with poison long ago.

"We march at first sign of darkness," Adrius said, fists tight at his side. "Let the men know our true plan not a moment sooner."

31

LUCIA

It was worth it. Every drop. I am queen. Beautiful, powerful, eternal.

-From Lucia's Journal

Lucia knew on some level that she was dreaming. Part of her brain screamed that they'd been here before, seen this same scene. Many times, in fact. But she kept reliving it.

It was the night that changed her forever, when her and her allies defeated the Fell Emperor. They tied him to an iron block and shackled him with nephilim chains to nullify his magic.

The Fell Emperor stared back at her furiously as she passed a lantern in front of his desiccated face. He could not recoil as its glow began to sear his translucent skin, throwing off curls of smoke as if he were held to an open flame. Fascinating, but not what set him apart from other Fell. No, it was the silver rivers of blood that ran under that skin that drew her eye. She ran a gnarled hand over his pulse, her ancient fingers shaking from the task.

Her dreaming mind flexed her hands in disbelief. She was a

mortal, old and frail again. Adrius hovered just over her shoulder, leering at the creature. "What say you, apothecary?"

"Maybe he'll talk if you step back," she said tartly.

The Emperor smiled. To call it a smile was akin to admiring the dentition of a piranha. His grimace put two full lines of fangs on display, ready to feast on human flesh. *"Do you speak for your group?"* He communicated to her as all Fell did, twisting around her own thoughts until she felt she was whispering to herself. They limited most mental speech to happen upon eye contact, which she posited was the limitation of the human brain, not the Fell's. She stared into those soulless pits, completely silver just like his blood.

She could not respond in kind, but she knew he understood her. "I do."

"I wish to bargain." His mental influence started to hurt her head as if each word was a rap on the forehead.

"Of course you do. All Fell wish to bargain," she scoffed. She leaned in, letting him see every wrinkle that lined her time-worn face. "What do you think you can offer me that the rest of your kind could not?"

"Power. Youth. Sight." He raised a gnarled hand, pointing toward the spectacles that perched at the end of her nose.

She scoffed as she righted them on her face. "The same promise every time. And look where it got us. My tools, please." She turned to the waiting Fell hunters. Jaromir passed her case of implements forward. As their doctor, he had his own out, tending to a wound on Qin's forehead at the back of the group.

Pulling out her codex first, she flipped to a dog-eared page and read. Murmuring to herself, she set out a bowl, a bejeweled cup, and a ritual knife while placing the lantern on the ground.

"I have studied your kind all my life," she said to the Fell. "You do evil upon my people because you've drained your own world of its resources and wisdom. Still, you hunger for more. Look at what your power has done to us. Look at how they thirst for you as your kind thirsts for human blood." Indeed, the remaining Fell hunters, those that would become Blood Princes, stared at him with unvarnished hunger behind her.

"I do not drink blood," he remarked, watching her with that

unblinking stare. As a silver-blooded Sorcerer, he was one of the few Fell who didn't.

"I know." She drew a line across his exposed palm with her knife and bled his silver essence into the cup. She watched the blood reduce to a dribble as the scratch healed neatly with Fell regeneration.

The cup was snatched from her hand, wrested away easily as Adrius took it. "I should have his power of all of us. I deserve it," he said, looking into the silver sloshing within the container.

"No, you fool!" she exclaimed, but it was already too late. He tipped it back and swallowed in one gulp. His victorious smile lasted just long enough for the Emperor's power to fill him, and she could see distinctly when it overfilled. Eyes rolling back, he collapsed, seized by wracking convulsions. Black blood seeped from his pores and she thought, *Finally, I will be done with him.*

Behind her, the Emperor made a coughing sound akin to a snicker. Smiling to herself, she was ready and willing to watch him die for how often he interfered with her experiments and made a nuisance of himself. That was, until Nyah knelt next to him, trying to push him to his back. "Lucia, please," she said, turning to her with wide eyes.

"There's nothing I can do. He's not a Fell, so he cannot contain the same power as one," she scoffed, stooping with a grunt of pain as she tore her cup from his rigid hand. But she liked Nyah and hesitated to see her tears.

Nyah was the daughter of her friend, after all. She owed her that. "Actually…" she looked at the silver-stained knife she still held. "Maybe there's a way. If you all agree to it."

Her gaze went upward to the Fell hunters milling around. Jaromir recovered from the shock of the moment first and attempted to restrain Adrius from his thrashing. They flickered uncertain looks her way. "Share the power. Take from Adrius like you take from the Fell." She cut his palm and let his black blood begin to fill the cup. His spasms eased as the blood smoked, curling and stinging her nose with its acrid tang.

"I will help," Jaromir said, holding out his hand for the cup. He drank. One by one, they all did save for Nyah and Lucia herself. All eight of the surviving Fell hunters swelled with dark might while Adrius sighed with relief as his body relaxed.

Lucia turned away from him and the girl who wept happily at his side. Her gaze rested upon to the Fell Emperor. "I would like to offer you a bargain, after all." She took up her bowl and knelt before the creature so they were at eye level.

"Will the boy do anything else entertaining if we agree on something?" he remarked, his lips still peeled in mirth.

"No. This is just for me. I've noticed something about your kind. You have magic that is beneficial. Flight, healing, regeneration, protection, just to name a few. Yet our hunters only take the ones that harm. They can boil blood and control minds." She tilted her head as if in question of the phenomena.

"Such things are only given, never taken," he remarked. *"Except for healing others. Do you wish for information then?"*

"Oh, no. I want to be given that gift." She dropped her tone to a private whisper. "I want to be unique, as you are unique with your silver blood. And in return...I will take you back to the portal to your world. You will leave here safely, and you will close the portal between our worlds so we may all live in peace. Do we have a bargain?"

The Emperor watched her hold out her hand for a shake. At this point, it became a nightmare as her mind thrashed and screamed. No! No, don't shake his hand!

He coughed a laugh, amused at her audacity. *"You have a bargain. Drink deep of my blood. Let it transform you as your friends have not experienced. They take, and you receive."*

Her hand closed around his. A weight closed in on her shoulders as if sealing their deal with magic. It was their way—she knew that. And they were bound to do what they agreed to, just as she was bound to her word to him. So, she bled him once more, admiring the blood as it pooled in the bowl. It glittered in the lantern light like pure silver, a shade deeper and richer than before.

She pulled some herbs from her supplies and mixed them in the blood, creating a tonic to purify what was not safe for humans. Grinning, she tipped the bowl back and drank. It was stinking and foul, but she took it all in and felt his power flow through her veins instantly. Her spine straightened with a series of pops. Strength swelled in her muscles, chasing away years of age and constant usage.

"How do you feel?" the Emperor crooned, watching the changes with a self-satisfied air. He thought he was getting away, saved from the Fell hunters who'd slaughtered countless numbers of his kind.

"Like a new woman," she breathed, flexing her hands and watching the wrinkles vanish. Her skin plumped with health, taking on a youthful glow. It didn't hurt to move. Her body felt light. Lithe, even. She could go run and do cartwheels like she had as a girl.

She turned to Adrius, who was sitting up now, only just noticing the changes in her. He watched her with his jaw slack. "Well, don't just sit there. I got what I needed." She admired the sound of her own voice. No phlegm, no shake. She reasoned she sounded downright *sexy* with a new, smoky purr.

"What did you do? You're…young? Your eyes…they're silver now."

"And yours are black. While you consumed his curse, I consumed his blessing," she said, haughty with her head so full of power. *Foolish man.* Now she would claim her rightful place amongst them.

He stood, kissing Nyah's forehead with a sigh. "How much do you think is left?"

She eyed the Emperor, who turned a narrow look her way. He caught on quickly, she'd give him that. "Two jugs," she said. One of the hunters had brought the containers, setting them beside the Fell as he tugged at his restraints.

"We had a bargain. You will obey the terms!" he shouted. Lucia figured he had been around long enough to know he was about to be harvested. She did the honors, shifting his head over one of the jugs.

"We've already closed the portal." She stroked his cheek. It was a good test of her reflexes, as his sharp teeth tried to close around her fingers like a bear trap.

"The penalty of a broken bargain is the worst thing you can imagine. Open it again, send me back. Do not do this," he snarled. The

nephilim chains strained as he exerted his preternatural strength upon them. The iron links groaned.

Lucia righted herself, nodding to Adrius. He was careful when it was precious silver blood on the line, slitting the Emperor's throat with precision. They watched his essence bleed out in full until he was just another corpse ready for study. *The last one*, Lucia thought, sagging with relief. They were done with the Fell, and with the beneficial magic of their kind flowing in her veins, she'd thought they were done with the madness of these invaders.

32

LUCIA

I cannot see a stable future. Neala comes for peace. Adrius comes for my head. The handsome stranger comes for my heart. Which future is it, and why are there such holes in my sight?
  -From Lucia's Journal

She woke with a gasp, her sheets soaked through with a cold sweat. "Just a dream," she muttered, peeling out of bed and checking her body. Still hers and still youthful. She was not mortal—she was eternal, silver-blooded, and glorious. How she'd treated the Fell Emperor was how they'd treated countless Fell, slaughtering them as they'd tried to massacre the human race with their unnatural hunger. This tiny remnant of him came back trying to stir her feelings, but she would not repent. Not for his sake.

However, she could see clearly in the oppressive darkness of her city. Her heart lurched, but she knew what it meant even before she moved in front of a mirror and inspected her face. Eyes of pure black stared back, ringed by dark, spider web veins. They were the eyes of a Fell. She traced those veins, searching for any points of pain. Like always, the transformation felt like a part of her, though she shuddered to see her old enemy reflected back at her.

Recoiling from her image, she went to a dresser and pulled out a simple veil of silver lace. She kept her head down as she left her room, shivering as a chill breeze wafted over her damp nightgown. It was unlikely she would encounter another person, but if she did, they'd see only her perfect body and not her ruined face. She contented herself with that thought as she passed soundlessly down a set of spiraling stairs, aiming for a few levels down where her personal laboratory lay.

She'd claimed a spacious part of the palace for herself in the absence of Adrius and Nyah. With its sprawling expanse, she could spend years in her own "territory" and see little of the other inhabitants. The palace was a city in and of itself, pearlescent with its white-silver stone. On the rare occasions when the clouds parted and the moonlight shone down, it glowed with a halo like a miniature moon itself. Her magic was at its strongest on such nights.

Glancing out a window, she sighed when she saw tonight would not be such a night. The perpetual gloom of deep night lay over the land.

She met no one on her walk down to the laboratory, which drew a sigh of relief. No one knew how advanced her problem was, only that she'd taken to wearing veils. A fashion statement for her old age, she would say, waving it off with a shrug. Soon the newest vampires coming to pay their respects would not know what she looked like, relying only on hearsay of her beauty and shimmering, silver eyes.

For she was queen, now and forever, the most powerful vampiress to walk this earth. And no so-called curse would hold her down. She bolted the wooden door after her and pushed the veil from her head, letting it float to the ground in her wake. Her laboratory was the size of three rooms, refreshed with multiple work stations stocked with tumblers of herbs and fresh water.

She went to the first station, kneeling and ripping open the third cupboard. Glass clattered as bottles overturned and rolled, all empty. Grabbing a handful of them, she dashed them to the side. They were worthless to her now, emptied of the serum she needed. Their shards lay broken as she reached into the back of the cabinet.

She retrieved the vial she'd been sipping from, half filled with the golden blood purification potion. How she'd scoffed when Gwendolyn tried force-feeding these to her! Now they were her lifeblood, one drop at a time. She uncorked the vial and dipped a dropper into it as it steamed on contact with the air, withdrawing a single drop that she squeezed onto her tongue.

It rolled down her throat like liquid fire, spreading warmth through every limb and burning in her head. She clutched her head with a cry, ecstasy and pain mingling as the corruption in her mind burned away. Present and future visions mingled together in a tangled blur of noise and color. She laughed and cried, tugging out clumps of her hair to *just make it stop.*

Her delirium ended with her lying face down on the ground, her body curled protectively around the steaming vial still clutched in her fist. Peeling weak limbs from each other, she rolled onto her knees and corked the vial to keep any more of it from escaping. She closed her eyes, untangling what she'd just seen and hoping to make some sense of it.

Today was the day. Neala would fulfill her purpose at last, riding in with Lucia's future mate and his army on their heels. But what happened afterward was a tangle of multiple visions, hardly making sense like pieces to separate puzzles. She didn't let it worry her.

Marcus Hartson would look at her and know what it was to gaze upon a lifemate. Giddiness pushed aside the state she was in now, her skin still prickling as corruption burnt away from the inside out. As she got up and took out a hand mirror, she saw her usual reflection. Silver-eyed and beautiful, no hint of a curse or the Fell madness to be found. He wouldn't be able to resist her.

She cast a glance behind her, scoffing quietly. Taryn would need to clean up this mess. He was the only servant she trusted to come into her laboratory because she knew his devotion would require ultimate obedience. There was no chance he would go rummaging through her drawers, looking for the precious potion she needed so badly. She counted what she had left with a sinking heart. Two and a half vials—it would last her a decade, if that. The dream and the corruption appeared more and more often like a burr she couldn't quite comb out.

There had to be another solution. She needed another source of powerful blood to mix into a purifying potion.

Perhaps she would send an expedition past the portal, looking for a Fell Sorcerer. Since her coronation and Gwendolyn's banishment, she'd simply stopped opening portals as if the other woman had truly been the source of them. For the common vampire, the Fell were relegated to war stories told by their elders. *It would be interesting to watch them pitted against a horde of Fell again, see how well they would fight,* she thought.

Yes, that's what she'd do. She would get a Fell Sorcerer, but this time she wouldn't make a deal with him, she would simply chain him up and milk his blood like a dairy cow. She remembered the herbal mixture she used to purify it and make it safe for consumption. This solution would keep the so-called curse from herself as she reigned into eternity.

Marcus Hartson and his company were another stepping stone to her plan. Every year, her army swelled with new recruits, young vampires newly turned and interested in her shadowy crusade. Nyixa traded peacefully with China and Japan for now, their closest neighbors as the island drifted equally between their shores. Someday soon, those countries would bow to her, mortal and vampire alike acknowledging her not as queen of Nyixa but soon-to-be Empress of the known world.

Who would stop her? No one *could* stop the only vampire Sorceress, wielder of all types of Fell magic. A vicious, too-big grin split the face staring back in the mirror before she stashed it away. She returned to her room to freshen up, sending out a mental summons for Taryn, Qin, and Elandros, the only Blood Princes who remained on Nyixa with her. Two of them would hop to her whims like trained retrievers, while Qin…well, he knew what would happen if he disobeyed.

When she was ready, she used her personal occultarus to teleport her. She'd kicked herself for not discovering teleportation sooner, finding reference to attunement to the occultari through one of her spell books. Shedding blood over the surface of the magical orbs made it possible to attune to one so it would respond to the user's whims later.

With her personal occultarus, she could reach any of the orbs planted around the isle and even the few that littered the land beyond Nyixa's shores. However, she'd never gone that far for fear the island would sink with how deeply attuned she was to the Grand Occultarus. She'd read of how closely the magic of that massive orb controlled the island's movements, feeling it for herself the few times she'd ordered the island to move to a new location.

She arrived before that giant orb to find her three Princes already waiting for her. Taryn stood straight, his face as emotionless as always except for the fleeting smile he spared her. He was a good servant, as obedient now as her personal hunting dog.

If he was a dog, then Elandros was a mouse, practically trembling to please her. "How can we help you, Your Majesty?" he asked. Behind him stood Qin, flipping a coin between his fingers with a perpetually bored expression.

"We are greeting some esteemed visitors today," she said, taking a few steps back from the structure where her new army would arrive.

Elandros exchanged a glance with Qin, who shrugged. "Who is visiting, Your Majesty?" he ventured, hands clasped before him. His transformation from knight to simpering courtier couldn't have been quicker upon her ascent to power.

Lucia smiled to herself, gesturing. Her timing was only a few moments off before Neala appeared behind him. Jumping away with a startled cry, he caused her to whip around and grab her sword hilt. It took her a moment to blow out a derisive sigh and relax upon realizing what happened. Around her, men exploded into being as they teleported and looked around in awe. Marcus Hartson was one such man, as slack-jawed as the rest of them.

Neala didn't gape, instead going directly to her and inclining her head. *"Queen Lucia. I've brought the army you seek. Is my banishment at an end?"*

"Yes," Lucia breathed in pleasure, her gaze still upon her man. "You've done well. I couldn't ask for a better gift."

"If I may?" she continued. Why hadn't she moved away yet?

Her usefulness was at an end. *"Why are you wearing a veil?"*

"It's the newest style here, dear Neala. Perhaps you should take it up as a highborn lady of my court?" Her lips peeled back in quiet mirth, glad the other woman couldn't see it. Neala, wearing a dress and veil. It was as laughable as a monkey in a suit. The palace tailors would have to labor to create a dress to make her remotely feminine.

Her nostrils flared as if she already knew what Lucia was thinking. *"I shall pass. I did not come here just for myself. There is another who wanted to see you again."* Turning, she scanned the crowd before gesturing to one of Lucia's least favorite sights. Adrius stood behind a row of men, Sirius close to his side. He looked awful, bruises under his eyes and dark veins in his temples.

Though she knew his Key brought him back in a weakened state, it was still a shock to see him in the flesh. She'd operated for two decades without worry of seeing his face again as she sat in the throne he'd first warmed for her.

"Ah yes, our runaway royal," she remarked, forcing bitterness into her voice. "Why, he looks awful. He made his bed long ago, and now it looks like he reaps the suffering he so richly deserves."

"I've brought him to see his island once more." Her stoic demeanor remained in place, fixing Lucia with a red-eyed gaze. *"And you."*

"It's true then? The Shield Key resurrects him?" She pitched her tone low, thinking of everything she could do with such a ring on her own finger. If only she could pry it from its permanent place on his.

"You have to know what an awkward place this puts me in. What happens when the rest of the island learns that Adrius the Warrior King has returned?" She saw it quite clearly. Adrius *was* king, the position of monarch only defaulting to her in the absence of him and Nyah and most of their founding court.

"I wouldn't worry. He doesn't want it. Let's get your new army situated, shall we?" Neala said, eager to change the subject. *Not one for politics*, Lucia thought.

"It's not what he wants, my dear, but what the people want. If the people want their big, strong king back, well..." she shrugged, palms up.

A wry chuckle escaped Neala's mouth. It was not quite friendly. *"Perhaps you should marry him. That would solve a number of problems, wouldn't it?"*

Lucia would rather die. Bile rose to the back of her throat at the very idea.

But it *would* easily solve her problem should her people want Adrius back. "I hear the wedding bells ringing already," she said dryly. "How about you introduce me to the leader of this fine force?" Now this was a man she'd marry. Seven feet of pure muscle with a face rugged and masculine below his glamor. He waited with arms crossed, the charm of her city already fading as he returned to near-military vigilance.

"Of course. This is Marcus Hartson." She took her over to him. He bowed like a proper gentleman. Of course, she already knew him from countless visions of them together. *"He is leader of the Hartson Company and my lifemate. Marcus, this is Queen Lucia."*

Inside, Lucia went numb. Lifemate? That couldn't be. Marcus was *her* lifemate, her lover to claim. A hand fluttered to her veil as she struggled to keep her composure. How dare Neala lay claim to something that was hers! "A pleasure to meet you," she forced out. The rest of the words spilled from her in a rush, anything to keep his attention. "Thank you for travelling all this way. As promised, your trip is not in vain. I will be rewarding you and your men quite handsomely and giving you a ranking position in my military. Command of a company this large will give you quite the salary, but we can discuss those details in private."

"Indeed, Your Majesty." Good humor tugged at the corner of his lip. It seemed like he was privy to some private joke. "Do you have quarters for my men and me? We are quite tired from our long journey here."

"Of course. You will have to walk to the palace, but once you attune to one of the occultari we have set up there, you can teleport here and back without the long trek." A few soldiers in earshot groaned at the news, seeing how far the massive palace was from the center of the city.

"Let's get going then," Marcus nodded, turning back to his men and shouting orders. He soon had them marching in a regimented line through the city square. Horse-drawn wagons creaked in at the end of the line with numerous women and small children peering out curiously.

Lucia tried to walk with Marcus, gritting her teeth as he turned back to Neala and strode by her side instead. They glanced at one another, doubtlessly sharing a private word. "Before you retire, I would like to take you to my laboratory, Mister Hartson." She infused her voice with politeness to counter the instinct to see Neala struck by lightning. "There's a potion I give every ranking member of my military for extra strength."

He raised a brow, curious but confused. "A potion, you say?"

"I see Neala hasn't told you that I'm an accomplished apothecary. It was my job before becoming a vampire." Old days, old memories. She'd given up much of the job when Nyah and her Alchemyst-gold blood meant she could make and infuse potions she could only dream of making.

His eyes darted to Neala. "I must politely decline. I have yet to defeat Neala in a duel, but when I do, I want it to be based off my own merits." He flashed a smile, all charm, toward Lucia.

"Keep dreaming," Neala said, a smile crossing her usually stoic face. Lucia bit back a scoff, unused to seeing how her smile stretched the scars the other woman didn't bother to hide with a glamor.

She ended up holding her tongue quite hard as she listened to them banter all the way to the palace. Why didn't Marcus see that he clearly belonged to her? She just didn't understand it. But she would make him understand, thinking quickly as to how she would mix a potion to get what she wanted. This was her one chance to make things right and claim him as her own.

While he was bantering with Neala, she took hold of her personal occultarus and laid an illusion over herself and Neala. She went to her own personal rooms while he followed Lucia, thinking he was still trailing Neala. It would take the real Neala a few minutes to notice the trick, but he would be long gone by the time she did.

33

LUCIA

Nyah's potions hold so much power because of her golden blood.
Perhaps I can make something new from the remnants of one of her
strongest potions.

    -From Lucia's Journal

Lucia took Marcus alone to her laboratory, proud of herself as he continued his banter with her instead. She learned some unflattering things about Neala, such as her pet name, but burned with jealousy nonetheless.

Gwendolyn destroyed every bit of the love potion she'd once used on Taryn, citing it too dangerous to be used. The recipe was ash in the fire pit by this point, but Lucia could take an educated guess as to how to create it. She needed to feed him not one, but two potions, and then he would be hers permanently, as he was meant to be.

"This doesn't seem like your quarters," he said in suspicion once he walked into her laboratory.

She took off her veil as she also removed her illusion, meeting his surprised, glacier-blue eyes. She pushed her will on him as the stronger vampire, and his self-control buckled to her whims. "Sit down and wait," she instructed, gesturing to a stool.

He sat, turning a keen gaze on her as she started gathering ingredients. It was like an unseen hand began to guide her, leading to each ingredient in turn. An unopened bottle of red wine, a liquid base used to represent passion and its many facets. Herbs. Her hand wavered between dried rose petals or crushed lavender, but there was a push, making her fingers close around the jar of lavender.

"How does it work?" Marcus asked, standing and taking in the laboratory in long strides. He ran a fingertip over the spine of a Fell text, grunting at the unfamiliar lettering. Fell language was one of the only ones she couldn't translate with her Language Key. It remained a script that only she and a handful of others could read.

She turned an incredulous look over her shoulder. He should've still been under thrall, sitting obediently and waiting. With her preoccupation with her potion, perhaps her hold on him was loose. While he was moving of his own volition, he didn't seem hostile or about to leave.

"Hmm?" she asked, starting to mix and measure without the help of a recipe. She just *knew*. This was the love potion, the exact blend she needed. Potions like this came in stages of potency. The first stage was temporary lust, sated quickly but mindless in the meantime. The second stage approached permanence and devotion, though the imbiber kept their wits about them.

"The potion. How does it work?" he repeated.

She was blending a stage three, the strongest of love potions. Permanent love and obedience, which turned intelligent men to drooling slaves just as she'd already seen. It was too powerful in the wrong hands. Her kingdom could use a ruler with the ability to turn the mind of even the staunchest of enemies.

She might not have the ability to make it again. Her hands moved of their own accord, mixing, pinching, and stirring until she had a dark red potion heating over the fire. It was the same color of dried blood because of red wine...and incomplete. Hands wavering over the pot, she knew what she must do.

Get her precious golden potion and pour in a drop.

No! Those potions were hers and hers alone. She would not share them, not even with Marcus.

There was one close substitute. She pricked the pad of her thumb with a nearby scalpel, squeezing out four drops into the sweet-smelling liquid. A single bubble rose to the surface, popping with a thick glop. There. It had magical blood now. Maybe not the reagent of an Alchemyst, but surely a Sorceress's would do instead. More magic coursed through her veins anyway.

Heart racing, she stirred the thickening mixture as it began to boil in earnest. Glancing to Marcus, she noticed his senses further returning.

His unimpressed face was far harsher than the Marcus she knew from her visions. Where was the man who doted on her, refusing to flinch as he looked her in the eye and took in every truth he saw? They'd just met, she forced herself to acknowledge. He would have plenty of time to adore her once he drank this potion.

"You wouldn't mind showing me it's safe?" He watched her pour a thick serving into a spare glass and inclined his head to the pot where some extra glistened on the sides.

Drinking a love potion would be anathema to her if she hadn't already seen the life they'd lead together. "Why not? I'll do it first even," she said, scraping the sides of the pot and encouraging the last dribble in another glass. It filled up about a third, enough to make a significant difference.

Aware that he was keenly watching, she tipped the glass up and shook it hard, swallowing a mouthful of wretchedly sweet goo. It took every hint of her self-control not to gag and vomit it right back up. Instead, she turned to him, wiggling the empty glass between her fingers. "See? Safe...*drink it.*" She infused the end with an order as she looked him in the eye.

"Thank you. That's all I needed to see." Curious, she'd noticed this potion affect Taryn instantly, but she waited without so much a stirring of her old heart as he started struggling with downing his own dose. "This is worse than medicine," he muttered.

Lucia remembered Marcus downing medicine the rare times

he was injured in battle. She would bring it to him personally and sit by his bedside as he downed it reluctantly, either on its own or in a broth. They held hands, whispering of his bravery but what foolish thing that'd led to his injury in the first place.

She blinked, rubbing her forehead, but the visions weren't done. She saw them together on a starlit beach, watching a little girl frolic amongst the sand. The girl was their child, she figured, a little miniature of her father. While she played, Lucia and Marcus held hands and counted stars. He knew his constellations, pointing them out to her while she laughed and made up her own.

Other visions came and went, speeding up as her future sight tended to do. She caught a snippet here, a flash there. His smile, his kiss, his more private talents…

The last vision jarred her. He was in the palace—the first time she'd seen him there, in fact—looking around for her. He wasn't his usual self, uncertain as he came up to her. "What kind of place have you taken us to?" he whispered, leaning in as she lifted her head, hoping for a tender kiss. Searching her face, he shuddered as she wrapped her arms around him but didn't return the gesture. "I don't like it here, Neala. I want to leave."

Crash!

Lucia blinked away a fog, her fingers trembling as if she stood out in a blizzard unprotected. Her vial lay shattered on the ground before her. Pinkish shards were embedded into the hem of her dress. She cursed her clumsiness, but it was no matter. Marcus had finished drinking his potion, his expression curiously blank as he looked her over.

She looked up, letting him behold the truth of her. He would *love* her. He would. "You…your face…" he said, his eyes dilating fully.

She straightened her spine more confidently, knowing his brain was associating itself with its sudden, crushing devotion to her. "The loveliest thing you've seen, no?"

Gaping, he drew in his next breath shallowly. He clawed at his throat and then his cheeks, rending furrows in his flesh. "Marcus? Marcus!" she gasped, lunging forward and grasping his wrists before he could do serious harm to himself. A groan issued from his lips. His eyes rolled back before he collapsed at her feet.

She stooped and checked his pulse, breathing a sigh of relief as it ticked against her fingertips. He was out cold, but at least he was alive after that fit. It had her at a loss, as she'd mimicked several Alchemyst potions before—the ones that hadn't called for special, golden blood. None of them had caused a negative reaction to this degree.

Her mind drifted back to her visions, a soft cackle issuing from her throat. It wasn't her laughing—and suddenly a cold sweat enveloped her as she tried to imagine who, or what, was laughing for her. The Emperor's betrayed face flashed in her mind, one apparition amongst many as she stood there, reliving her every vision with Marcus. Except now she heard the one word her visions had avoided.

Neala.

Neala had sat at his bedside, coaxing him to take his medicine.

She'd made up constellations in the night sky just to see him laugh.

Their little cherub played on the beach alone, bringing back a living hermit crab with a beseeching expression.

Countless other moments flashed before her eyes. Their wedding, performed in secret with a handful of guests. *Gwendolyn included.* She seethed the moment she saw the other woman.

Lucia screamed, throwing the still-hot mixing pot across the room. It took out the bottle of wine, smashing a starburst of blood red across the floor.

"No!" she yelled, grabbing at anything within reach. A poker, its tip still glowing red-hot. She melted it to slag with a muttered word of power, throwing the ruined metal into the fire. Her skin didn't burn, but her hair did, not immune to her spell craft.

"This isn't right! This isn't fair." She clutched her middle on a sudden wave of nausea. Bitter tears dripped from her eyes, smoking just like her beloved golden potion. She sniffed, bending double as she waited for a dizzy spell to pass. "It's not... not fair. He's mine. He's been mine."

Why would her visions betray her so? Someone else's memories of this man danced in her head, waltzing together through years of devotion and love. They pirouetted together into the future, one that went blank to her future sight. Blackness swam before her. Nothingness was the future? It couldn't be.

He told me I would be sorry, she admitted in the darkness, her thoughts echoing back to her.

Sorry. Sorry. Sorry.

I knew that power had a price. But still she'd drunk his blood, breaking her word the moment she'd made it. Why worry about a bargain with a doomed creature?

Price. Price. Price.

I am cursed. She'd lost so many on her path here. Nyah and Chandra, dead. Gwendolyn, Adrius, Sirius, Korin…now Neala. They weren't here to see her. They had to be here to kill her.

She opened her eyes, curled up in a ball on her laboratory floor, alone. Red wine saturated her hair in a wet, crusty mess. "Cursed," she repeated to herself, touching the place where Marcus had rested. It was cold. He was likely off begging Neala for them to leave.

Her heart lurched as she forced herself to her feet, crunching through broken glass as she made her way to her work station. Throwing open the right drawer, she took out her hand mirror, gasping as she beheld her expression.

A Fell's face stared back. Black, soulless eyes framed by black veins which spider-webbed deeper into her forehead and cheeks. Her ears were developing a point, and they weren't the only ones. As she opened her mouth wider, she beheld them. Teeth like a bear trap, ready to rend and consume flesh as well as blood.

She had the foresight to put the mirror away before she started screaming.

34

NEALA

Every book says the same thing. The only cure to a Fell curse is undoing the act that caused a break in an oath. But I cannot do the impossible and bring him back. Surely there's another way.
    -From Lucia's Journal

Neala waited in the foyer, tapping her foot as minutes trickled by. Most of her men were safely relaxing in spare rooms by this point, occupying two untouched levels of the palace's sleeping quarters. That wing went up some fifteen stories, each room eerily similar, top to bottom. She'd avoided those rooms, but perhaps in the time she'd been away, Lucia had ordered changes to the décor and furnishings.

Marcus had promised to meet her here through a brief mental conversation. He seemed…confused. Dread made a hard knot in her stomach as she wondered how they'd been separated. The bond that'd formed between them the moment they'd become mates was dull. No hint of his usual jolly presence blazed on the other end of her awareness. That was what truly worried her.

Not to mention Adrius was already drawing attention. Old

courtiers surrounded him on the other side of the foyer, chattering like sparrows as they gathered up a crowd. These people had thought he was dead just like she had. A mix of emotions stirred in her heart as they bowed and surrounded him like a personal flock.

It was the same admiration he'd once earned as king and leader of the Fell hunters. They could use that to more easily get him on the throne. At the same time, any one of these people could be spies looking for a slip of information to leak to Lucia.

She noticed someone coming toward her. "*Marcus,*" she said with relief, rushing forward to close the gap between them. As soon as she saw his face, she knew something was wrong. Pale skinned and wild eyed, he grasped her by the shoulders to stop her short.

"What kind of place have you taken us to?" he whispered, leaning in as she lifted her head, expecting a kiss. Searching her face, he shuddered all over. "I don't like it here, Neala. I want to leave."

"*Nonsense,*" she said, shocked. "*What happened? Why are you so frightened?*"

He shook his head rapidly, pushing off from her. "Nothing. You should've seen what I saw…"

"*Are there Fell here?*" Her hand flew to her sword by reflex.

Chest heaving, he took another couple of steps back from her. "It had nothing to do with Fell. Just me." A smile spread across his face, wider than usual. Chills bristled over her arms, for she couldn't feel what was causing such a reaction in him. Their mating bond was blank, as if he were asleep.

"You know what? You're right. There's nothing to be worried about. Let's go to your quarters."

Her brows rose, and she was at a loss for words. His mood was different in the space of a blink. "*Explain what's happening because I must've missed something. What did you see? Why are you acting like this?*"

Following his impatient gesture, she started leading him toward her rooms situated further into the first floor. She assumed they'd be there and untouched, else they'd be sleeping in one of those Fell rooms all designed by the same decorator.

As she passed Adrius, she flashed him a questioning look. He shrugged in return, a smile tugging at his lips. It was the happiest she'd seen him in a long while. Inclining her head, she strode quicker to match Marcus's wide steps. "I think I saw the future," he said after a quick glance to make sure they were alone.

"That's impossible," she remarked, wondering if he'd taken leave of his wits.

"Is it? How could it be when the queen is known for it?"

Biting her lip, she considered him. *"First off, she is not to be our queen for long. You are of Korin's bloodline, and he does not see the future. Nor will you, at any point, with his blood in your veins. So, how could you have seen anything of your future?"*

He gritted his teeth hard enough she could hear them grinding on each other. "I know what I saw, woman," he said waspishly.

Bristling immediately, she turned to him with the expression that spoke volumes of what she'd do to him if he spoke like that to her again. *"And what did you see then?"*

Unlike when she'd looked so cross previously, her angry face seemed to steam him up more. "What does it matter?"

"If you're going to mouth off about the future, it matters a lot," she snapped.

They arrived at her room, the door ajar. A quick glance inside showed what she remembered—sparse furnishings but all loved pieces she'd help craft by hand. Someone had added a fresh bowl of fruit on the coffee table, the sweet scent stinging her nose as she headed inside.

Marcus smelled overly sweet, she realized as he brushed past her. Between his cloying scent and the fruit a few paces away, she couldn't get enough air. *"You need a wash,"* she muttered, dumping the fruit bowl outside.

"So do you." The corner of his lip lifted with a half-hearted chuckle. "Maybe we'll cool off with one?" He offered his callused palm like an olive branch, and she took it, figuring they could talk about this strangeness later.

She hoped he would snap out of it and talk to her about the plan and what had caused him to wander off without her.

But Marcus stared at her like she was a stranger after a wash, his eyes twin shards of ice. "I'm going out," he said, leaving on an abrupt turn of his heel.

"Marcus, wait?" It came out as a question.

The nothingness of their bond made her chest hurt more than anything. She shoved her way out of the room after him, watching him march further into the palace.

She didn't follow, her brow creased as she thought.

"Lucia," she said to herself.

If Marcus was going to be like this, she'd talk to Lucia to see what she'd done, and that would be a much less pleasant conversation. They wouldn't need an army for a coup, just Neala's fists.

35

LUCIA

Adrius cannot die but wishes to. What if I could harness that power for myself? An end for him and eternal rule for myself—we both emerge victorious.

-From Lucia's Journal

Lucia couldn't get Marcus out of her mind. He'd left her instead of tending to her unconscious form. Had the potion worked?

She knew she was horrendously late. Her closest advisor, a mouse of a man named Timothy Floros, was waiting for her in the throne room, pacing nervously. If anyone suffered from her fits of pique, it was Timothy, who looked like he had especially sour news for her today.

"What is it?" she sighed, sitting and jerking her chin so Taryn would step from her shadow to his place by her throne as she took her seat.

She had her guesses as to what Timothy was preparing to say. He hemmed and stroked his beard. "Are you aware that your predecessor is alive?" he asked, his tone surprisingly delicate.

"Adrius?" She faked shock even though she'd seen him mere hours earlier. "Why, I put him to rest myself. You were there for the funeral, weren't you? Quite the lovely affair. We said goodbye to the old monarchs together." They'd honored Adrius and Nyah's memories as she'd gloated inside at her double victory so sweetly won.

"Yes, I saw him myself." Stars seemed to glimmer in the older man's eyes. A fan then. She knew Adrius had many from his days as the famed slayer of Fell and first vampire.

It seemed that adoration hadn't faded. If it had Timothy in its clutches, a man who'd served her faithfully from the moment she became queen, it would spread like wildfire in the hearts of others. She clutched her hands together and took a deep breath to keep any venom from her tone. "That's all well and good, but did he tell you why he abdicated his position for so long?"

A little of the sparkle faded from his expression. "Well, certainly not. He was too busy talking to everyone." He wrung his hands.

"Everyone? Who's everyone?" she asked, turning a sharp look his way.

He started listing names, and her teeth gritted down harder and harder with each one. A fine group of gossips and rumor-mongers had descended upon him the moment she'd disappeared with Marcus. "Everyone," she repeated, burying her face in her palms with a soft groan.

She knew what this meant and why Timothy was so nervous as he waited for her reaction and next move. "I am the rightful queen, Timothy." With practiced hands, she adjusted the veil over her head and the moonstone crown perched atop it.

"Your Majesty, I'm not debating that," he said quickly, bowing his head in submission to her. "It's just…it's King Adrius. Should he choose to make a claim for the throne, he may be able to rally a formidable force against you. Many civilizations older and greater than ours have crumbled from civil war."

He had a point, and she spent a minute chewing on her lip, staring out into the massive arena that made up her throne room. After another drop of the golden potion, her teeth were blunt once more, but it'd had an unexpected side effect. Her skin felt hypersensitive under her dress and veil, chafing with every minute movement. It felt like she'd had a brush with the sun when there was no sun on Nyixa.

With a sigh, she focused on the matter at hand. "There will be no civil war. We will assemble our people here in these very seats." She gestured to the full arena and laughed quietly to herself. It would be perfectly humiliating for Adrius. "He will deliver a speech to the masses. He'll tell them why he abdicated the throne and reaffirm before them that he doesn't want it back."

Timothy cleared his throat politely. "Have you foreseen him doing this, Your Majesty?"

Scowling, she made a dismissing motion. "I'll put scrying for it on my to-do list. We've kept the subjects waiting enough, don't you think?"

He scrambled to bow and back away from her throne. "Of course, Your Majesty…" he may have said more, but she was no longer listening.

Mind hurtling miles away in moments, she guided her future sight as much as it could be guided. *Show me my victory. Show me Adrius's humiliation.*

Her magic obliged with images, but her stomach turned sour as she took them in. Fair Nyixa in flames, with men and vampires alike slaughtering one another until the streets ran red with blood. She heard Adrius's voice, all right, but not explaining his sorrows to a docile crowd. "Slay them all! Show no quarter!" he shouted above the din of battle. "I'll make a rich man of the one who brings me her head."

She came back to herself knowing whose head he wanted— her own. It was as certain as the bile rising in her throat. "Your Majesty?" Timothy's meek voice pierced her thoughts. He cleared his throat, saying it louder. "Your Majesty? Are you quite all right?"

"It's all right. She's struck by the sight of me," a deeper voice spoke up. She snapped to attention, recognizing the massive form next to her mousy advisor.

"I'm sorry, Your Majesty. He refused to wait," Timothy said.

Sighing, she dismissed him with a gesture and stepped down from her throne.

Marcus waited for the advisor's footsteps to fade before ripping the veil from her head and kissing her so fiercely she nearly swooned on the spot. "I understand it clearly now," he murmured, looking into her eyes with devotion so fierce it was as if they'd been together decades instead of moments. "I spent time with *her* and realized where I belong."

Pleasure hummed a heavy frequency in her breast as she stroked a hand through his short hair. The potion had worked on him, after all. *And not only for him,* she realized, clutching him closer with a laugh of sheer relief. He was perfection given form, her heart fluttering as he stroked her cheek with a roughed thumb. "By my side," she said, eager as a shark circling blooded prey.

When he smiled, it was in the too-wide way she often caught herself doing right before an episode of Fell madness. Her heart faltered in its soar, teetering on the verge of plummeting back down to earth. She saw a different man in that smile. A Fell Emperor, cackling at her expense.

"By your side," he agreed, bending to dust his lips over her forehead.

"Marcus," she said. A little laugh left her lips. He was *hers* now, their bond formed by potion but no less potent for it.

"Yes, my love?" He looked at her with adoration. It was a blank expression compared to what she'd seen in visions. The passion of choice was gone, replaced by blind devotion.

"Let's go to my private quarters," she offered. A yelp of surprise left her as he scooped her up bridal style and carried her there. The queen's quarters were a set of rooms behind the throne, so it was a short walk to the passionate tryst that followed.

Sometime during it, she admitted to herself that she would never let go of Marcus Hartson now that she had him.

36

NEALA

"This feels personal. I know she was jeering at me earlier, but taking my lifemate is the lowest blow she could go for."
    -Neala

Neala found a massive crowd milling about outside of the throne room. Discontented mutters passed from one to another as she shouldered past them. "The queen has canceled her weekly audience," someone called from the head of the line.

Her sharp hearing picked up on curses and something else much more curious as the crowd began to shuffle off. These people spoke of Adrius. They'd been there for less than a day, but already, the common folk, human and vampire alike, whispered of his name and past deeds. They could use this to their advantage indeed. Lucia was on thin ice, and she felt ready to push the woman into the cold personally.

Standing at the doors to the throne room was a near-elderly vampire adjusting a pair of spectacles perched low on his nose. "Oh!" He startled away as he saw her Blood Prince-red eyes focused on him with hot intensity while she crowded his space. "C-can I help you?"

"Where is she?" she demanded.

To his credit, he didn't waffle on her. "The queen is currently indisposed. If you would like, I can add you to her schedule—"

"No! I will speak to her now," she practically shouted. He winced, her voice undoubtedly echoing in his head.

"S-she's not taking visitors." He cringed away.

Her hands flexed, but she realized she had no right to take out her frustrations on this stranger. *"Fine."* She turned away from him sharply before she did anything she may regret. *"Give her a message for me. Prince Wraith is invoking her rights as a founding Fell hunter and calling a council meeting at the earliest convenience."*

"I'll be sure to tell her, Prince Wraith," he murmured, bowing his head with genuine respect. "My son fought with you to take our fair city. Do you remember my boy, Dorian?"

"Floros?" she supplied, taking a closer look at him. *"Yes. He was a good man."* A pang hit her as she recalled how he'd died, cut down just yards from her by a swarm of Fell.

"He spoke highly of you." He stood straighter as he noticed the change in her expression.

"That is an honor. We cannot forget his sacrifice as we shape our new, Fell-free world." She hesitated, wondering if he would entertain a few questions from her. *"What was your role in the war?"*

"Logistics, ma'am. Can't march without us," he chuckled.

"How did a logistics man become a hired hand for Lucia?" She gestured to his fine clothes.

"I'm her advisor now. Hand-selected to serve her." The man's chest puffed out. Despite his pride, she'd seen the quick way he cowered to a sharp word.

"Hand-selected, hmm? And how does she treat you?" She thought him an odd choice for advisor when she still had access to Elandros, Taryn, and Qin if she wanted a Blood Prince by her side. There had to be something more to the selection.

"Treat me?" he echoed uncertainly. "Well, I have all the coin I need to have a vacation home in Rome. That's why there's an occultarus there, you know." A touch of nerves entered his voice as he spoke quicker. It was all the answer she really needed.

She forced a tight smile. "*How nice. Where is Lucia now, exactly? It really is important that I speak to her right away.*"

"I understand, ma'am. My first loyalty is to Her Royal Majesty, I'm afraid. I cannot share such details without compromising her trust in me." He spread his palms in a helpless shrug.

"*Hmm. How about my fellow Princes? Do you know where they are?*" She hadn't yet laid eyes on the three of them. Not that she had a close attachment, but they were a family of sorts by their shared history. She really only needed to be sure they weren't in one specific location, which Timothy confirmed for her. She nodded to him and left with little further pleasantry.

With Lucia tied up and the other Princes elsewhere, she had a unique opportunity that she intended to take full advantage of. Lucia was a public personality and could not avoid her forever. The moment they met again, she would answer for Marcus's strange behavior, right before she answered for everything she'd personally done.

But first, she would take a visit to the palace laboratory. Soon she was at the door, cautiously trying the knob and pushing. Unlocked, it opened on silent hinges.

She did a double take, wondering if she'd found the wrong room by mistake. But this was definitely the laboratory, built large enough to house several Alchemysts at their craft concurrently. The ground around the first station was a ruin of glass shards and something that looked suspiciously like blood. Neala cursed to herself as she closed the door behind her, barring it from the inside.

The personal windstorm that'd swept through this section did her little favors. She'd leave tracks if she wasn't careful, though she saw her destination from where she stood. Gwendolyn shared where she'd found Lucia's stash of blood purification potions long ago. If she were lucky, they'd still be in there, untouched.

She brushed aside the worst of the mess with the tip of her boot, intending to spread the shards back out when she was done. Opening the drawer, a few vials rolled from the back. Two full and one half-drained and sealed with a dropper. Head full of uncharitable thoughts, she secreted one vial away in the folds of her cloak.

Gwendolyn had implied that she would find more than two and a half vials though. Missing even one of these three would be apparent immediately. Such was war, she thought, taking the second full vial and holding the third up to the light. A potion just like this one had killed Adrius the first time…what had Lucia done to it? What twisted experiments did she build with the last remnants of Nyah's blood?

Any of the three vials could be poisoned or tampered with, but every drop of the thick liquid within was still priceless. *Lucia won't need this for long,* she thought, taking it too.

Adrius deserved this cure, and there would be no better time to take it than now. *"Where are you?"* she projected out to Adrius, hiding her tracks haphazardly as she backed away and left the laboratory almost as she'd found it.

37

ADRIUS

"Two and a half vials of salvation, and I must drink one now. How am I to continue in twenty years if I find myself in the same predicament? And the next twenty? And the next? I hesitate to speak of our hollow victory."

-Adrius

Adrius met with Neala in secret, taking one of the unoccupied residences high in the guest wing. His good humor at seeing old, friendly faces was fading rapidly as he sat across from her, taking in the two and a half vials of blood purification potion she held. "That's all that was left?" He felt his hands shake. It was so little to save him.

Only a few feet away was what remained of his mate and wife. Until Gwendolyn returned to the island, there was no way to visit the Fell Lands and find any last remnants of her, alive or otherwise in that inhospitable land. *"Yes. And you are in desperate need of one."* Neala extended one of the intact vials to him, her grim frown digging her scars deeper into the side of her cheek.

Though he agreed completely, he held the vial as if it were a venomous snake about to rear and bite. He grasped its fluted tip between two fingers, inspecting its color and the fine layer of dust that'd accumulated on the glass. Age made it less brilliant and gold, or some other tampering. Lucia could see the future— maybe she'd poisoned this vial, too, waiting for the day that another Blood Prince would deliver his death unexpectedly.

Still, he tried the cork next, feeling the seal within crack as he dragged it free. Golden fumes wafted from the glass, pungent in its perfume of blood and a cocktail of healing herbs. "Oh, Nyah," he whispered, his eyes stinging as he forgot his caution and tipped the whole vial into his mouth, one viscous drop at a time.

It tasted like home, the only home he'd found after his village was consumed by the Fell. That bubble of time and space where he'd had Nyah beside him, keeping him safe and whole. With his eyes squeezed shut, he could still hear her twinkling laughter and the huskier whispers she'd saved just for him.

Those memories were fading, he realized. He hadn't heard Nyah's voice in two decades, and the pain that followed was like his heart rending in two. He clutched his chest on a gasp of air, falling from his chair onto plush carpeting as heat seared through every inch of him, borne on burning veins.

"Adrius!" Neala pushed him onto his side. Her strong hands checked his pulse and held him steady.

Poison, he thought. He'd hastily downed another version of death. But he didn't feel himself growing weaker.

Quite the opposite, in fact. He pushed Neala's hands away as the burning subsided from extremities and into his core, where it lingered over his heart. Threading a hand under his tunic, he brushed tender, new flesh where the wounds lingering from his last death were healed over. He laid himself flat again with a breathy laugh.

"She saved me. Even when she's not here, she's my strength," he said, sharing a sad smile with Neala. As his adopted sister-in-law, he saw the same wistfulness within her.

"Maybe she is still alive." She offered him a hand up. She made a quiet gasp when he folded her in a hug, but after a moment, she returned it.

"Thank you for believing in me," he said, looking into her

maroon eyes. Her faith for him started much sooner than stealing a blood purification potion. Taking in a portion of the magic he'd tried to steal from the Fell Emperor had caused her eyes to turn the color of blood and her powers over illusion to come to fruition. But more importantly, sharing that power kept him alive.

Just like she'd helped march an army into Nyixa when he was unable to fight without succumbing to his bloodlust. *No more,* he thought. "I'm going to make you proud, as king."

She nodded, patting his shoulder as she pulled away. She seemed more distracted than impressed with him, which he supposed was his due. His realization that he needed to earn her respect once more stung. *"There's much to discuss on that note,"* she said, sitting down. He did the same.

"Lucia holds a banquet after her public audience every week. A show of lavishness since she has accumulated much wealth for the crown while we've been gone."

"Wealth she is then wasting," he frowned, leaning his chair back as he considered. "Lucia has a superior army to us, doesn't she?"

"Of course she does."

"If it came to a full war, many of the people here from the old days still remember and support me." He knew he could call on old friends who would convince more to turn to his side.

Neala shook her head slowly. *"If we fight a war, there's no guarantee that you'll win in the end, old allies or not. Lucia's side looks stronger in many ways, and not just in the number of men."* She turned a look on him, so furious he thought the red in her eyes would go ablaze any moment. *"Much as I want her to suffer, the only way we can defeat her is if she is beheaded. We can do it at the banquet tonight. You'll be on the throne tomorrow, where you can prove yourself a strong king this time. Free of corruption."* She gestured to the empty vial laying on the ground.

"You're right. That goes along with our plan."

"And if the chance doesn't arrive to kill her tonight, I've called for a council meeting where you have a second chance to kill her."

His hands balled into fists, a low growl rumbling in his throat. "I won't hesitate."

They parted ways, him to return to his old quarters where his suits, so finely tailored, gathered dust where they hung. The whole place was a relic of another time, abandoned with so much open space in the palace. His gaze lingered on his bed, bright with a comforter of golds and browns lovingly sewn for his wedding. Nyah had loved it.

Giving himself a good shake, he donned a suit. It fit his height but not his frame, hanging looser from the muscle he'd lost. He would work hard to reclaim every ounce of strength. Placing his sword at his hip, he navigated through the palace to the dining hall, startling men and vampires alike as they did double takes and gawked as he walked by. He kept his bearing military straight, walking like a king and general and not like the blood-lusting wretch he'd allowed himself to become.

38

ADRIUS

"Full of hot air and empty promises. You'll never take what's mine."

   -Lucia

The hall was mostly empty when Adrius marched right to the high table, having a seat at the high-backed chair lifted like a throne. Undoubtedly, this place was for Lucia—no longer. The high table was empty otherwise except for place settings and silverware. A few humans whispered and pointed at him from where they sat, and he lifted a hand in greeting.

One by one, his men trickled in, taking up spaces at every bench. Sirius sat beside him, tenser than a drawn bowstring. "I was beginning to worry we weren't doing this," he muttered to Adrius.

"Just needed the right moment," he replied, his own tension rising as he picked up on his brother's nervous energy.

Sirius turned, eyeing him critically. "You're better." It wasn't a question. Adrius had seen the same thing in the mirror—his eyes and veins were clear of darkness, and he no longer bled endlessly from a wound that wouldn't heal. He wasn't a walking corpse with its skin pulled taut over what muscle remained. He was Adrius, the Warrior King.

With a shock of cold down his spine, he saw the same ills in Sirius. A hungry gleam in his eyes, a quiver in his muscles. Skin stretched too tightly. Had he been too focused on himself to not notice his brother suffering too?

"There's more for you, too," he promised.

They both quieted as Elandros slunk by them. Dressed in a freshly ironed suit with a pungent rose in the breast pocket, he looked every inch a fine courtier if it weren't for the red gleaming in his eyes that marked him as a Blood Prince. "I'm so glad you're back, Adrius." He spoke with an insincere simper as he eyed the seat Adrius had claimed. He sent a servant in search for a second high-backed chair.

"I'm sure you are, after delivering poison straight to me," Adrius said, smiling just enough to bare his fangs as Elandros passed, sitting further down the table.

"I didn't know," the other man muttered, studiously ignoring Adrius and his brother as his leg bounced anxiously.

Neala came next, claiming the seat next to Sirius and glancing toward Adrius. *"Don't hesitate,"* she repeated to him privately.

He patted the hilt of his sword in reply, earning an approving nod.

"I wonder what's taking our esteemed ruler so long," Sirius said with generous sarcasm as the minutes trickled by. A distant bell tolled the hour.

With every new courtier and Prince that joined them at the high table, Adrius started wondering the same. He imagined something was wrong—that Lucia had foreseen this trap and anticipated it with a nasty surprise of her own. But what?

He halfheartedly chewed on a salad, its greens fresh and crisp. When he'd ruled Nyixa, serving food to a vampire was prohibited. Every scrap and morsel had to go toward a human mouth when vampires could subsist on a blood-only diet. They couldn't afford anything more. Now, he saw similar bowls being served to everyone, vampire and human alike. The sheer cost of such a feast was staggering, but to have it weekly was an obvious show.

Ending the weekly feasts was first on his agenda. All thoughts of that vanished as the captain of the guard snapped to attention at the back of the room. "All hail Queen Lucia of Nyixa!"

Silence fell over the room in a wave. Chairs scraped as man, woman, and child stood, but not everyone. Many who remained seated were his army, watching him refuse to stand at the high table. Murmurs spread like wildfire.

Adrius's sight ran red as he looked over the feminine figure, her face shrouded in a silver veil, a moonstone crown perched on her brow. *Nyah's* crown. She no more deserved that crown than a common pig who dined nightly on slop and leavings.

It took him a moment too long to realize who was standing there with his arm around Lucia until his booming voice rang out. "You heard him! Stand for your queen!" Marcus barked, startling some of his men into doing just that.

"What is he doing?" Sirius muttered, his eyes narrowing to angry, animal slits as his shapeshifter magic brought his inner beast to the surface. The growl of a savage predator emanated from him.

For his part, Adrius felt rooted to the spot. Despite his promise, he hesitated and glanced to Neala, whose expression held all the fury of a woman scorned. This wasn't according to plan and neither was the way she pushed to her feet, mouth opening to shout over the hushed crowd.

Adrius stood as Lucia reached for the occultarus that spun over her shoulder. Panic seized him when Neala's eyes rolled back, leaving her to collapse back into her chair. Her limbs lolled like a ragdoll, a trickle of crimson streaking from either nostril.

"Neala, no!" He ducked from his chair to support her as her body started to slide from its seat. She slumped in his arms.

Sirius nudged him, hard. "Kill her. You have to kill her. This is your chance," he hissed.

He looked up at his brother, recoiling from the fury in his expression. His mouth was open to suggest Sirius take care of Neala, but those words dried up. Sirius's eyes—black bloomed across the iris, hiding the animal slit in a lake of pure black. "Never mind. I'll do it myself!" Fur sprouted from his pores as his skeleton gave an ominous crack, body twisting in the first stage of a transformation.

This can't be happening, Adrius thought. Lucia had Marcus and Taryn with her for protection. A transformed, Fell-mad Sirius would be cut down like a rabid dog. "Forget about it. Stop it. We can do it later." Adrius grabbed onto him instead as Sirius's clothes ripped further into the transformation. The wrestled their way under the table, where he pinned the wolf his brother had become.

He dodged the snap of a sharp-toothed mouth, going off balance. Sirius shook him off. Hatred rolled off of him, even from the inflexible muzzle of a wolf. "You're still weak. Soft," he snarled. "You don't deserve to be king."

"Stop, think a moment," Adrius pleaded, the wind knocked from him as Sirius put his full weight into a side tackle. As a shapeshifter, he was even larger and bulkier than a real wolf, sending Adrius skidding directly into the high-backed chair he'd been sitting at and knocking it on its back.

"Of what? How I should be king, not you? Wretch," the wolf spat, coming at his throat with sharp maw ready to rend.

His teeth closed around a sword. Korin's deep voice followed. "That's quite enough," he said, scruffing Sirius as he recoiled and spat blood. Someone else nudged Adrius out of the way— Jaromir, who laid his hands over Sirius's snout.

The wolf snarled and struggled with his fervor fading until he too slipped into unconsciousness. The sting of his words remained as Adrius brushed himself off. *You don't deserve to be king.*

His own brother, the man who'd been by his side for every moment of his deaths and rebirths, spoke his deepest fear. Sirius had seen him at his worst and was most capable of anyone in judging whether Adrius's best was enough to reclaim his place as king of vampires.

His gaze turned to Neala, who was just stirring. Her expression was blank, eyes bloodshot as she swiped at her nose. How disappointed in him would she be when she realized what happened?

A melodic laugh drifted over them as Lucia drew back her chair, sitting behind him. "Pathetic. Truly."

Marcus maneuvered the other high-backed chair, putting his bulk between Adrius and Lucia. "I thought Neala was your life-mate," Adrius said to him, lip curling with disgust.

Lucia waved dismissively, answering for him as Marcus smiled at him blankly. "He was mistaken, because he's my life-mate. Don't you remember how strong that pull is? Don't you still mourn for your beloved mate?"

He set his teeth in an unfriendly grimace. "Your cruelty knows no bounds, Lucia."

She simpered, lifting an elegant hand. "I'm not the one who made a scene before the whole court. Do you want my throne, Adrius? You'll have to work a lot harder than this."

A hot punch of anger thrilled through him, lighting every vein. He couldn't act now. They both knew it. "Neala called a council meeting earlier." He was repulsed by his proximity to her and Marcus, who still seemed blank. *Ensorcelled.*

"So I've heard. However, I do not hold to those ways anymore. There is no council, only myself and my close advisors," she sniffed.

"You thumb your nose at rules that us Fell hunters have stuck to since our founding. I, too, would like a council meeting," he said, loud enough to be heard across the table.

"As would I," Korin said.

Adrius stood, realizing he had the attention of everyone in earshot, both at the high table and the commoners who'd witnessed his brawl earlier. "Elandros, wouldn't you like to have a council meeting?" He gave the other man a pointed stare.

Elandros glanced nervously to Lucia before folding, just as he suspected. "I would, actually."

Qin, the quiet and thoughtful Blood Prince from China, spoke up in agreement, as did Jaromir from where he attempted to heal Neala.

"It would be unwise to refuse council with all of us," Jaromir said in his gentle way.

Lucia crossed her arms, making an unimpressed sound from under her veil. "Very well. We'll meet over breakfast tomorrow. I believe that's the earliest convenience for Neala's sake. But Adrius? No weapons allowed."

That was all right, he thought. He was more than willing to punch her smug face into a pulp instead. If he didn't fear for going straight into his old cycle of death and rebirth, he would do it at that moment and risk the ensorcelled Marcus killing him, too.

"One more thing," she said as he gathered up his brother, ready for the walk of shame out of this hall and the rumors that would undoubtedly follow him. "I know you stole something from me. I want it back."

The blood purification potions. He realized it and glanced to Neala, who was standing with Jaromir's assistance. *"Did you bring them?"* he asked her privately. *"I need the half-filled one."*

From a pocket in her breeches, she produced the vial he wanted. He smirked over at Lucia. "This? This is all we have left," he lied, flicking the dropper from its lid. Intoxicating fumes rose from it. His fangs crowded his mouth, but he opened Sirius's wolf jaws and poured it down his throat instead. Lucia made a choked sound of dismay, unwilling to embarrass herself in front of the court.

He threw the remnants of the vial at her, which she caught in a flash of reflexes. "You'll pay for this," she hissed.

He gestured to his friends to leave as he settled Sirius's unconscious weight over one shoulder. "No, Lucia. You will."

39

LUCIA

"Now he is truly mine, just as my visions intended."
   -Lucia

Lucia left her own banquet early, rolling the nearly empty vial between her hands and seething. She may have thwarted one of the many futures she'd seen her life going down, but Adrius paid her a blow harder than he realized in return.

She had the last of a cure in her hands when she could feel the Fell madness returning to her, turning her teeth sharp under the veil. It had never progressed this fast before—but she also hadn't had to use such a huge amount of power at once since he'd left the island. Neala would recover...maybe.

It was no matter if she didn't, however. Neala would not remember her life with Marcus or being by his side as his life-mate. She would not think to convince Marcus to come back to her, which was all Lucia cared about.

Neala's mind was tough as a walnut, but it eventually had caved to the overwhelming power of the Mind Key she turned on her finger. Such a surge of power had turned it cold and unresponsive. She hoped it was merely recharging.

Lucia made sure she was present as the power in the room, only leaving with Marcus when she felt she'd spent enough time at the high table. "We need to make a detour, my love," she crooned to Marcus, who wore his mesmerized half-smile and followed her without complaint as she made her way to the laboratory.

She barged in and took a thorough inventory of her most valuable reagents, making her way around the mess she'd left at her work station. It seemed that everything was untouched, from the shards of wine-stained glass to her other goods. Whomever had come in here had gone straight to her blood purification potions and hidden their tracks well.

Her first thought was of Nyah, who'd so insistently brewed these potions. Gwendolyn had exploded with rage when she'd found them hidden away in an unused drawer. No one else had been so invested in them. But it couldn't be Gwendolyn who'd stolen one of the ones which remained. She was banished by a blood oath and unable to return without Lucia's good will.

Shaking her head, she grabbed her personal occultarus and checked the spells over the room. *Show me who was here last,* she ordered her magic.

It obeyed by showing her Neala's scarred face. Her fingers tightened on her occultarus. Pain shot through her nails as they elongated, darkening as they thickened and sharpened into wicked claws. She barely noticed as her whole form trembled. To think she'd felt sorry for Neala when she'd come into her space so boldly and stolen what she held dear.

She would pay. She would pay with everything she had.

"My love, do you have children?" she asked, turning to Marcus and drawing off her veil. The material snagged on her claws, drawing her notice for the first time. It bothered her to see the shreds of silk under the nails more than the sharpness of them and what that meant for her.

"I don't. Not yet, at any rate. Do you desire them?" he said, as obedient as to give them to her the moment she asked.

"Not a girl? With Neala?" She frowned, remembering her

clearly in the visions she'd somehow borrowed from his first life with Neala. The little blonde, playing on the beach.

Marcus repeated the words to himself before shaking his head. "She adopted two kids before I met her."

"Where are they?" she asked, grasping the front of his tunic. She would erase Neala for her trespass, starting with her children.

For the first time since he'd taken her potion, he seemed uncomfortable. He pried her fingers off of him. The claws were dipped in his blood, having gone straight through the material to make ten fingertip-sized holes. "I'm not sure," he said.

"How could you not be sure? Didn't she take them here?" she demanded.

"She didn't." He offered a shrug. "She left them with their grandmother, Gwendolyn. I'm sure she intended to bring them here eventually."

That was all she needed to know, nodding as she went back to her work station, drawing out her hand mirror and sucking in a breath. How could he even stand to look at her when she was in such a state? The veins were deeper now, framing her lips and turning her into a horror akin to the creatures that created this corruption.

The infection was speeding up, she realized. Once it got a foothold in her, it raced to turn her more and more Fell. She set aside her mirror and put the nearly empty vial of purification potion before her. Adrius hadn't gotten all of it out, leaving a smear that she retrieved with a dropper. She squeezed up what she could, suckling on the dropper to get as much of it as possible. A cringe seized her mind as it was paralyzed with visions.

Except this time, it felt like she was having a premonition, but she was stuck in a sensation of dark silence. Where was the future? Surely this wasn't *her* future, feeling like she was trapped somewhere pitch dark and cold, pressure pushing in on all sides. It didn't feel like she could breathe, but she realized she was holding in her breath as the sensation faded.

Marcus was looking at her with concern. "What is that?" he asked, gesturing to the vial she clutched to her chest in a death grip. With her usual, blunt fingernails. She was sure to check.

"It's a very powerful potion," she murmured, taking a good look at him. He smiled the too-wide smile she was used to seeing in her own reflection. Fell madness couldn't take him, too, she thought, scraping up what she could from the vial and offering the dropper to him. "Here, take some." With how fast it'd overtaken her in a few short hours, they couldn't allow the same kind of thing to get its hooks in him. She gladly fed him the last of it, knowing the rest would otherwise evaporate.

Like Adrius, he seemed to take it without ill effects. The visions seemed to be unique to her, her ability to see the future interfering as it often did at the most inopportune moments. "Feel good?" she asked.

"Like you made me a new man." He smiled a normal smile, free of any hints of Fell.

She put the potion away with a relieved sigh. "I *did* make you a new man. I made you my king," she said, not sure why his smile faltered for a moment. She'd given him the gift of a better life for him and his own. Last night, she'd made it official, giving him one of the priceless Fell Keys—the Winter Key to match the tempests of his passion.

She took him back to her quarters, liking that he seemed more aware, more like the powerful man he'd been before drinking her love potion. "So you're saying this is from another world," he said of the Winter Key he wore as an engagement band.

"That's right. Only the best for my love," she said indulgently. "It controls weather and the elements. Wind howls at your command, and snow dances. The sun and moon shine when you smile and hide their faces in the clouds when you anger. You will be as strong as a demigod when you learn to control everything it can do."

He held it up to a torch's light as they passed it by, inspecting the glowing motif of a snowflake hidden underneath the Key's opal stone. "Thank you. This is quite the gift." He gestured to her hands. "Which do you have?"

She proudly explained the Language and Mind Keys to him, showing her mastery of the former by speaking several different tongues to him fluently on a whim. "Those are both very powerful," he remarked.

"I need them to retain control at times. Vampire society only values the strongest, so I must continuously prove that I am indomitable." And sometimes she needed to force others to believe her way was what was right and good in the world. "You understand what that's like though. I can't imagine bringing together such a lawless group of men and turning them into as fine a fighting force as the Hartson Company."

"It's not as hard as you might think." He chuckled darkly. "Men like to be on the winning side. Who has a better guarantee of victory than a group of vampires against regular men?"

"It's almost cheating," she purred, finding something very gratifying about being on the side of overwhelming victory for once. The very world would fall to her rule in the same way, a massive vampiric army marching at her banner.

She felt that that day was very soon. With Marcus at her side, anything was possible. "Cheating is dishonor. We lost many of our men to mortal hands in fair combat. No hypnotism, no vampire tricks, just steel on steel."

"Some casualties in war are necessary. But imagine the victories you would have with a Sorceress by your side. Entire armies would bow and surrender when they hear that you're coming." She could practically see it in her mind's eye.

"Where is the sport in that? If a people are to be conquered, why not go down fighting first?" They passed by a guardsman, and his tone became subdued for that moment. "Of course, we want to lose as few men as possible."

"My dear Marcus, so honorable. The vampire world just doesn't work that way. One day soon, those who oppose us will have armies of vampires instead of mortals. You'll be glad to be the most powerful then."

He grunted, putting his arm around her as they drew near to the throne room and thus her quarters. "I'm glad for you, my love," he said, gruff.

Something about him was different, but she didn't question it as he kept her up until the late hours with his prowess. When she finally went to sleep, it was under a blanket of satisfied exhaustion.

Lucia woke to insistent rapping at her door. Few dared to bother her at this time of night...except she realized it was much later than usual as she listened to a distant clock tower chime the hour. Light streamed through the window, gracing her face with its silvery glow. She went to the door first, answering it to see Taryn towering over her. "Your Majesty, the council is waiting for you."

"Forget the council. Look!" she turned and pointed upward where through a window, they could see a crescent moon peering down at them, chasing away some of Nyixa's perpetual gloom.

"A good omen for your success, Your Majesty," he said, shifting closer to her subtly. She permitted him to touch the edge of her veil, the barest pleasure she could offer someone so obsessed with her every move and whim when she didn't want to encourage it.

"Where is Marcus?" she asked, after giving him a few moments and drawing a step away.

"He left your room earlier. I did not follow," he said.

"How odd. I would think he couldn't move," she remarked. The man could function on remarkably little sleep, but it was good he wasn't neglecting his men. "No matter. Leave me, Taryn. I will freshen up for the meeting."

She was refreshed and halfway to the map room, where she conducted her meetings, when she realized something was off. The Mind Key was no longer on her finger.

40

NEALA

Sometimes the darkness over Nyixa parts, and we see clearly the scythe of a crescent moon in the sky. Vampire magic is strongest on these nights. I suspect the veil between our land and the Fell Lands is thinnest on these nights.

-From Lucia's Journal

The moon was out. Neala sat on her balcony, watching it appear as if burning through Nyixa's shadows to shine upon them once more. It felt as potent as the rising of a harvest moon, the time when vampire powers were at their strongest outside of the island. The hair rose on the back of her neck as the moonlight struck the palace stones, lighting them to silver-white brilliance.

During times like this, she wondered at the necessity of their occupation of the old Fell island. They wouldn't have lost Nyah had they sunk the island, drowning the magic that connected their worlds. And she wouldn't be watching nature struggle with magic to shine moonlight down upon them. She'd seen countless crescent moons, and the one that rose overhead was shaped wrong, like it belonged to a much larger moon.

She almost missed the knock at the door as she watched the sky. Grumbling to herself, she answered, finding Marcus on the other end of the threshold. He grasped her shoulders, pushing himself into her space. "Neala," he murmured, peering closely at her face. "You look like hell."

So did he, with dark streaks under his eyes and a drawn expression. His eyes seemed fit to pop out of his face, startling her back a step. "It's okay." He lifted his hands slowly as if she were more crazed than he. There was a nondescript box in one hand. He held it like a shield. "I remember everything. I'm so sorry. I don't know what she did to me."

"Commander?" she said, puzzled. The title made him grow rigid with a hard gasp. *"What's wrong? This is unlike you."*

"Not commander. I'm not your commander." He tried to come forward and stroke her cheek. She flinched back from him, hands flexing at her side. They both knew who the better fighter was here if he aimed to force himself on her. "Neala…please. I'm your *husband*."

"I think you need to leave." She jerked her head, dropping her weight back into a defensive stance. Though she didn't know what'd gotten into him, she'd make him sorry he tried this when he thought she'd be groggy and disoriented.

It seemed he realized how foolish he was being, making himself more nonthreatening as he drew his shoulders in. He looked down at a glimmering object in his palm—she recognized one of the Fell Keys with a blink. A shadow creased his face as he clenched it in his hand. "I just want you to see her for what evil she is." He turned away and put it in his pocket. "I'll be back with help. I'm going to get you help."

"I don't need…help?" She watched him with puzzlement.

"She messed with you, too. I can see it," he said. "It's…it'll be okay. I'm coming back, you hear? I'm going to get someone who knows how to fix this." He gave her one last, lingering look before walking out the door.

She couldn't follow him out even if she wanted to, instead hunching over and clutching her head. It felt like claws sinking into her skull, nearly as bad as when Lucia had communicated to her across the world. "As you wish," she murmured into the carpet, swiping new crimson drops from her nostrils. Whatever command he'd given was lost in her mind, but the spirit of it lived on.

———————

When a page came to retrieve her for the council meeting, she was dressed in her finest armor, cleaned and primped. She'd considered her reflection earlier, taken in each scar and the crease which seemed imprinted between her brows.

Trying on a glamor was a whim of her mind, replacing her worn warrior's face with that of a doll-like lady. She batted thick lashes and forced a strangled giggle from her lips. And then she took it back off. It wasn't her. She didn't need Lucia's great beauty if it'd simply attract dogs like Marcus Hartson. And to think her family liked him so much.

She went to the meeting as her usual scowling self, ready to share just what a pig the man had been. Her entrance was heralded by a flurry of piteous looks from every single Blood Prince in attendance plus Adrius at the head of the table. Only Lucia and Taryn weren't there yet, and she wondered bitterly if they would join the pity party. "*What?*" she snapped, fitting herself between Korin and Jaromir.

"I'm sorry for your loss. I imagine recovering from what Marcus did is very difficult." Jaromir placing his hand over hers. It sounded like he was comforting Adrius over the loss of his mate, but he was clearly speaking to her and smiling kindly.

Puzzled anew, she wondered if she'd missed something. Else, somehow, they all knew of Marcus's early morning visit to her quarters. Embarrassment burned her cheeks at the thought. What a scandal, a knight such as herself caught with a man in her quarters. The rumor must've spread like flame over tinder with how they all looked at her. She studied her fingers, feeling a shamed blush rising to her cheeks as if she were a chastened girl once more instead of a warrior and a Blood Prince.

41

ADRIUS

From the beginning, we established a small council of the survivors. Blood Prince and advisor alike were to be similar in rank, with a voice to balance the power of the monarchy. Adrius and his band of sycophants were gone too long to know I've disbanded the council. This queen listens only to herself.

-From Lucia's Journal

Adrius was tired of sitting and waiting for his chance to strike. It wasn't going well for him. In fact, his plan seemed to be crumbling as the minutes passed by.

He sat with Korin at a conference table in the map room. Lucia held her meetings here, where there were maps of the outside world to reference for trade and the movement of troops. Korin was his only ally in this room other than Jaromir, Qin watching them with a keen eye a few seats away. He spoke quietly with Elandros, who'd picked a seat furthest from Adrius.

Sirius was gone. When they'd heard news that Marcus had left the island and taken his company with him, he'd followed without a word to anyone else. The memory of his brother's black eyes filled with hatred and vitriol haunted him. *You don't deserve to be king.*

He didn't, did he? He'd hesitated in his duty on multiple occasions, succumbed to Fell madness, and allowed Lucia to rule after banishing his wife and mother-in-law to great suffering, if not death. The vampire people deserved better. If he could pull off another attempt at the throne, he *would* be better.

"There is a test we have to determine whether a vampire has the madness within them," Jaromir spoke privately to him and Korin. He made eye contact with them both, less practiced in this than Neala. *"While I do not know why this meeting was initially called, I've brought the materials to conduct this test."*

"On Lucia?" Adrius asked.

"On all of us. After Sirius's outburst yesterday, we must take precautions." Jaromir's lips thinned. *"I suspect Lucia has it. Why veil her face otherwise?"*

"If she has the madness, she should be declared unfit to rule." Adrius realized this made him a hypocrite, but both his friends nodded in agreement anyway.

"She should be put to the sword," Korin said.

He didn't disagree, his fingers itching toward the knife he'd hidden on his person. This time, he wouldn't hesitate. He continued telling himself that as Neala came in next and sat across from them. They studiously tried to avoid mentioning Marcus to her since it was apparent from her distant stare that that matter was not up for discussion.

There was little time to discuss such matters anyway as a page announced Lucia's entrance. They all stood as she strode in, Taryn at her heels like a protective shadow. She took the head of the table while he lingered behind her, hand on his sword hilt as he gave Adrius a meaningful look.

Adrius sneered in return. Taryn alone, he could handle if it came to it.

"So, we are gathered here because Prince Wraith called a council meeting." Lucia laced her fingers as she turned to Neala. "What say you?"

"No pleasantries today?" Adrius remarked.

"Pleasantries would imply that I wanted a meeting in the

middle of this most unusual day. The moon shines upon us… Nyixa sparkles with magic. Why would I want to be here?" she scoffed. If he didn't miss his guess, she punctuated that with a sniffle under her veil.

Mourning what she couldn't have, he imagined. Marcus leaving meant he had broken free of her spell. Perhaps there was hope in his and his army's return, after all, but Adrius couldn't operate on hopes.

"So, why have you all demanded your blood right to a council meeting? This had better be good." Her tone was vicious as she turned her veiled head toward Neala.

There was a pause as Neala blinked, considering the grain of the table. *"It is time we saw underneath your veil."*

The other woman laughed, rearing back like a wounded horse about to kick. "What did you say?"

"This is why I wanted to call a council meeting," she said with growing surety as she looked the queen in her veil. Adrius could've cheered, as he wanted to see the same thing.

"Then that's the most ridiculous reason anyone's called a council meeting. Really, Neala? If you are jealous of my looks, that is a matter to keep to yourself."

"Well, why not?" Jaromir said as Lucia glanced around, cornered. He waved a dismissive hand to Elandros to keep him from interrupting. "If we were called together to see Lucia's beauty, I, for one, would like to be rewarded for my time."

"It's not unreasonable," Korin agreed hastily. The group of Fell hunters turned to stare at her.

Lucia's hand shook as she moved it up toward her head, but Adrius saw her trajectory was off. She was going for the occultarus circling over her ear. One spell, and Lucia would be able to continue hiding what she so desperately didn't want them to know.

He reacted faster, reaching across and grabbing the soft sheet of fabric from Lucia's head before she could touch her spell focus. A gasp formed at her pouty lips, echoed by a few of the hardened Fell hunters in the room. "How dare—!"

"Your face!" Korin exclaimed, banging the table with both fists.

Lucia smiled at them innocently enough, but her teeth were unnaturally pointed, and black veins seeped around her eyes like crow's feet.

"The most beautiful you've ever seen, yes?" Her voice trembled as she beheld their reactions.

"Fell madness," Neala breathed. There it was, exposed for them all to see. Lucia was hiding such a big secret in plain sight.

She'd meant to hoard the blood purification potions for herself, Adrius realized. With so little left and an affliction that severe, the queen needed every drop she could get. He had the last vial secured on his person—the last trace he had of Nyah. He wouldn't be surrendering it to Lucia no matter her state. "It's true," she said on a sigh. "Great power comes with great sacrifice. I struggle with this *just like Adrius.*"

He spoke up first. "We cannot have a mad queen."

"I am not mad, you cur," Lucia muttered, raising a cool eyebrow.

"We also cannot have a mad king," Elandros pointed out. "To rule one out would be to rule out the other."

He could practically hear Korin grinding his teeth. It was a fair assumption to tie them together. Both were slowly going mad under the pressure of the late Fell Emperor's last vestiges of power.

"I have seen the future," Lucia said. "We cannot continue down this path. It is poor form to be at such odds with ourselves."

Her darkening silver eyes beseeched all of them in turn. "The only thing that waits for us is war and death. Adrius is unstoppable, being unable to die, and I am the only vampire who can command the thirteen elements of Fell magic. Who would win? Are you willing to bet the future of the vampire nation on it? We are still a young settlement, a candle we lit to combat the darkest of nights. Fighting amongst ourselves is the easiest way to ruin."

"What would you recommend instead?" Qin asked.

Lucia took a deep breath. She hesitated and wetted her lips, glancing Adrius's way. "I am loathe to even suggest it. What if we had...a wedding? If Adrius and I unite, you will have the male figurehead you so desperately desire. We retain my policies and statecraft. No one fights, no one dies."

"That sounds reasonable," Qin said.

"*Absolutely not!*" Adrius thundered. His fury rose like a living thing, coiling around his chest to squeeze the breath from him. He would rather die permanently than disrespect Nyah's memory in such a way.

Jaromir laid a hand on his tense bicep. "Before we discuss solutions, I would propose a test for us all to take. We have seen three of the most powerful vampires have a fit of Fell madness now or are in the grips of it." He gestured to Lucia.

While they waited, Jaromir took out a stoppered glass bottle and a number of shallow glass dishes. "Oh, I remember this test," Korin said. They all should. Gwendolyn and Lucia had discovered a compound that reacted to high concentrations of Fell blood. When Fell madness could be caught early, it helped prevent undue deaths.

"Are we seeing if the rest of you are Fell mad like Sirius? Please, be my guest," Lucia purred, sitting back with her fingers steepled.

Jaromir cut his thumb on a scalpel, allowing a few drops of his blood to pool in one of the bowls. While he added the compound to those drops, he said, "If the results come back as I expect, we have a more serious problem than succession. One we must all work together on."

Though he didn't speak of the problem, a knife could cleave the air's tension, especially as his blood began to bubble and turn black, transforming into black foam.

"Jaromir? You too?" Adrius breathed, stunned by what he was seeing. The healer was the last person he'd suspect would descend into bloodlust like he had or madness like Lucia's grab for power.

He flashed a grim smile as he beckoned to Korin. "I have not felt like myself lately."

"Nor have I," Korin said before his blood even began to boil and fester. It putrefied even faster than Jaromir's sample.

One by one, they all had the same result. Adrius stared at the line of tainted blood samples, trying to find the words. None of them were safe, from the most gentle of them to him. He'd drunk a full vial of potion, and yet his blood smoked in this lineup.

A reaction sprouted within him, spreading bitter leaves through his emotions as he trembled to his core. "We need Gwendolyn," he blurted. "We need *Nyah*. We need her back. Do you see what you've done?" He turned burning eyes on Lucia, ignoring the sound of an unsheathing sword as he grabbed the front of her dress.

"Don't do something you regret," she said, grinning up at him. Darkness danced in her eyes even as he watched.

"Regret. You don't regret anything, do you?" He felt his vision swim with fury. "Without Nyah's blood, we cannot cure this. Her potions were the *only* thing we could use."

"And now Nyah is gone," she said. "*I* am queen."

He had his dagger in hand a moment later, its edge pressed to her throat. "Do you want the island to sink?" She looked him in the eye boldly. Behind them, Korin tackled Taryn before he could slice Adrius's head from his shoulders. "You have no magic. No magic, no Nyixa. Care to be responsible for thousands of deaths?"

The breath rattled in his lungs as he dug the blade in deeper. "End Gwendolyn's banishment. Do it!" he shouted in her face. Gwendolyn was magic in her own way—even if Lucia wasn't bluffing, Gwendolyn could control the portal and thus keep the island from sinking.

A line of dark silver blood ran from her throat as she continued to smile. "I will make a deal with you." He pressed the dagger in harder. *Don't hesitate,* he told himself, ready to cut.

"I know a cure." She made a choking sound, barely able to breathe the words. "I swear I'll get it to you. I swear on my blood."

"Call off your man." He wavered. His knuckles were white from strain around the dagger hilt, trembling with tension.

When he pulled the blade from her throat, shame seized him immediately. Who trusted a viper by their word? Only one who wanted to be bitten. "You have a week to show results."

42

LUCIA

The future is dark. My eyes strain to hear anything past the lapping of water, flowing and flowing and flowing like the funeral dirge of an underwater tomb.

-From Lucia's Journal

Lucia was truly desperate when she found herself before the Grand Occultarus, observing her reflection in its dark, glassy surface. Her veil seemed to shimmer, illusions of dark shadows coiling around her form and especially her face the longer she looked. The massive orb was an exquisitely powerful tool, but much of its ease of use had disappeared with Marcus's departure and his theft of every Fell Key in her possession save the Language Key bound to her soul and impossible to remove from her person.

She yearned to call out to him using the orb's power like she had immediately before that infuriating council meeting. With its power, she could magnify her voice across great distances, and she'd found Marcus's mind with pinpoint precision. "*Marcus, my love, why have you left me?"* she'd asked with all the pining of a woman after her first lover, yearning for more than the brief encounter they'd shared.

And like that lover, there for the fun and gone for the commitment, Marcus showed a different side of himself. His reply was clipped and ugly. He was gone, and she had not the resources to chase him with her attention otherwise occupied.

Adrius had her in a remarkably rough spot. She was over the barrel, needing to rush to find a cure for something she knew was incurable.

At first, she'd asked herself, did Adrius have the same curse as her? She'd taken his blood, studying it extensively. It responded to stimuli just as hers did. It turned corroded and rotten when left to dry and caused the same chain reactions in her potion making. She was fairly sure that, yes, it was the same affliction. Ultimately, it led to the same transformation—both of them would turn Fell eventually without intervention. However, her curse seemed keen to speed up the process in herself.

She posited that power itself was the curse but scoffed at the very idea. All of them would be insane with bloodlust in that case, being head and shoulders more powerful in body and mind than the common vampire.

She'd ultimately dried out her well of possible cures long before this ultimatum came up. Thus, the Grand Occultarus and its shadows. They seemed to jeer as she hesitated, her hand half outstretched to take hold of its power. So little would she be able to tap with only one Fell Key.

Hopefully, it would be enough. She reached out mentally across ocean and vast swaths of land, searching for the one person she was loathe to ask for help. But she'd sworn on her blood—she would ask Gwendolyn for help. What was the worst her old friend could do?

She projected her thoughts with difficulty, throwing them into the void and hoping they would hit someone named Gwendolyn Firetree somewhere in the proximity to the Roman occultarus. *"Are you there?"*

"Lucia?" a faint voice answered. She went weak-kneed with

relief that there was even an answer. Her increased consumption of the golden potion had melted her good sense as she also felt a pang of longing to see the other woman.

"*Yes. I'm glad I found you,*" she said in a rush. "*I need your help.*"

"*And you think I'll help you?*" Her voice oozed distaste, even from a distance. The hope in Lucia's heart withered away in an instant. It was nothing less than what she expected, but for it to unfold in reality stung in its own way.

She gathered her thoughts, reminding herself that she had the power here. She was queen, and when pushed last time, Gwendolyn had not pushed back. "*Well, of course. When it's Adrius on the line, you tend to step up. I need your help curing his affliction.*"

They steered the conversation into more tolerant waters. Lucia did most of the talking as she explained how Nyah's old potions weren't a permanent antidote. When Gwendolyn did speak, it sounded like the years had not been kind to her—she sounded elderly, her voice touched by the weakness that could only be brought on with age. She wondered if the former nephilim was truly fading away, even as a vampire, or if she'd simply refused to sustain herself properly with human blood.

Either explanation made her weaker, which was exactly the position Lucia needed her in. When she was finished, she added carefully to the end like it was her idea: "*So, I'm inviting you back to Nyixa. Your banishment is over. Adrius and I need you to help find the cure, and...well, you should know that I've seen signs of Fell madness in the other Blood Princes as well.*"

A little embellishment never hurt. Even if she didn't want to return for the sake of helping Lucia, she'd come back to save the others. "*This is dire indeed,*" Gwendolyn replied. "*I will need some time to decide.*"

"*Take your time, of course.*" She held her breath in the long pause that resulted. It dragged, going from moments to minutes.

As she waited, the shadows inside the Grand Occultarus surrounded her shimmering form, mocking with their silent laughter. The thread of mental concentration that connected them across nations began to fray. She didn't know if Gwendolyn replied or not because she lost the connection first. "No!" she yelled, slapping the glass surface. When she tried making the mental connection again, it was like the other woman had disappeared.

"Har har," she muttered, tracking the shadows as they swirled about. They weren't usually so active, but the moon was still up, lending extra power to the vampires who lived there. She decided to take a chance, peering into this massive tool of Fell magic. Even with one Key, it would answer to her whims.

Putting both palms on its surface, she made sure her command was spoken with the authority of a Sorceress. "Show me my future."

The shadows cackled, but the occultarus obeyed. The reflection of the city erupted into flame, haloing her in its blaze. Her own reflection withered down, unveiled and grinning a hideous Fell's smile as she relished in the destruction of the city around her. Nothing human was left in this reflection, no remorse as she held her hand aloft and thunderbolts rained from the sky.

Lucia turned with a gasp, but her island home was untouched behind her. The shadows frolicked as she shook herself off, giving it another try. "Don't play with me. I *will* sink this island if you don't show me what I want," she threatened. Immediately, she felt the mockery cease and the shadows truly focus on her.

She saw from her own perspective the moment she was wed to Adrius. Shock thrilled through her for a moment and then giddy delight. Though she'd offered forth a wedding to forestall a war for the throne, what she was truly after was his mating bond. If they became mates...she could steal the power of the Shield Key from him through that connection and then be rid of him forever. She would ascend to Sorceress and true immortal. She would be a *goddess*.

Through the Occultarus, she saw the tight disgust and defeat he wore as he gave her a limp kiss and her court burst into applause. The sound was deafening—more guests than she'd had reason to expect. She came out of that brief moment grinning up at her reflection. "That's more like it," she muttered, turning to Korin, who watched her with a suspicious eye. One of Adrius's allies was always with her, watching.

"I called her as you all insisted. It is up to Gwendolyn to show and help," she said primly.

Within the hour, Sirius returned to Nyixa, bearing news from Gwendolyn, with whom he'd presumably been squatting. The former nephilim would speak to Neala and Neala alone about coming to help them.

43

NEALA

My visions return only to taunt me. They show me Marcus throwing the Mind Key into the ocean and selling the rest like jewelry. He and his army are long gone, set to fight and conquer under Marcus's name instead of my own. Why would my love betray me in such a way? I would have given him the world, but he would rather steal it.

-From Lucia's Journal

Neala didn't find them; they found her right outside the abandoned ruin which concealed the Roman occultarus. Sorsha was first, throwing herself into Neala's arms with a flurry of giggles. "Mother! I missed you!" she exclaimed with the exuberance of a girl many years her junior. There were no complaints as Neala spun her like she used to when she was younger.

"*I missed you more.*" Neala smiled, feeling complete for the first time since Marcus had left Nyixa. It was curious how heavy that departure had made her even though a commander could be replaced. She rubbed at her forehead, a headache twinging there from even thinking about him.

So, she didn't. She grasped forearms with Keegan in a proper warrior's greeting. "Hello, Mother," he murmured.

"Hello, son. Have you kept them safe?" She inclined her head to Gwendolyn, who leaned on her staff but smiled to see her back.

"Yes, always." He leaned forward to add in a whisper, "All they do is sit around and make potions anyway."

"Do not! We make magic, too!" Sorsha exclaimed. Her perky, pointed ears missed nothing. Keegan made exaggerated snoring sounds in reply.

Neala grinned, hugging them to either side of her. *"We've just reunited, and already you're bickering."*

"It's constant." Unlike the rest of them, Gwendolyn was serious-faced. At first, Neala wondered if they'd earned her ire somehow, but the reaction seemed too strong to be cross with her children. No, something else was weighing on her heavily.

Her first thought was Lucia to get her this upset. *"We need to talk."*

"So we do," she sighed, beckoning as she turned, leaving the ruins. "Come. We're staying with a kind vampire couple. Much better than sleeping on the ground, I assure you."

She nodded in agreement, walking with her children slowly so she wouldn't overtake Gwendolyn's pace. *"I would rather not do that again soon."*

At this time of night, most of the city was asleep. She found herself glad to be free of Nyixa's constant bustle and crush of people, but it would've been nice to see more of the city as it was meant to be seen. It took a few minutes before she broke the silence. *"I imagine Lucia's request gave you a lot to consider."*

"Mmm, indeed. Did you and Marcus break up?" she asked, turning to give her a keen look. "Because he and his men marched out of Rome like bats escaping hell. Without you."

She expelled a frustrated breath. Why did everyone think she and Marcus were together? *"I suppose you could say that. He left without a word to anyone. Did he at least explain himself to you?"*

"He did, but it didn't make sense. He said he saw his future as the vampire with the largest coven in the world. Specifically those words. *Saw his future,*" she said, stopping at a stonework house and letting herself in with a key hanging around her neck by a rawhide cord. "And he asked me to help you."

"Help? With what?" Neala followed her children inside, shucking her boots out of respect to the unfamiliar building. She couldn't feel the auras of any vampires in the house and assumed they were out on the town at the moment. It gave her the opportunity to look around. This couple was well-to-do and apparently quite generous to allow Gwendolyn to also set up a mini laboratory in their kitchen. That was where her adopted mother went first, starting up a pot of tea.

"Only Sorsha and Lucia can see the future," she remarked, glancing to the girl. She was rubbing the fronds of a potted plant, coaxing it from drooping wilt into full bloom. "Lucia did something to him."

"It's no matter. He's gone to die to his own delusions." She shrugged, trying to hide the pang that left in her chest. That was her commander's life she brushed off, but it certainly felt like more.

"Lucia did something to *you,* too," she continued, her keen gaze focusing on Neala next.

She shook her head sharply. *"I would know if she'd done something to me. Look, we have bigger problems than Marcus or Lucia."*

"Do we?" Gwendolyn's hands rattled a saucer as she set out a few cups for them. "Because he stole her Fell Keys, too. They're gone! One's in the ocean, and the others were sold off like common jewelry."

The thoughts in her head went blank from the impossibility of that. He wouldn't be so stupid, would he? Even one of those rings in the wrong hands would be catastrophic. But…*"Why would he do that?"*

"He didn't want her to have them. I think he realized what happened and stole them from her for good reason," she said, sighing long and hard. "I wish he'd saved the Mind Key, but that's the one swimming with the fishes." Gwendolyn gave her a long, piercing look before shaking her head with a bitter frown.

"Maybe we don't need it, Grandmother. We have my magic," Sorsha piped up, sitting at the kitchen table with her brother, waiting for the tension to blow off between them with her head ducked.

Neala turned to her, brow raised, as if to ask *you too?* What were they talking about that she'd missed? "It's worth a try," Gwendolyn remarked, looking thoughtful. "Let's consult the spell books tonight."

"Okay!" she said cheerfully.

"Anyway," Neala said slowly. *"We have bigger problems than Lucia or Marcus, regardless of what he's done with the Fell Keys."*

Her adopted mother turned an attentive look her way, indicating that she should continue. She seemed inclined to believe nothing could be worse than the lost Fell Keys, but that skepticism faded to grim silence as Neala described Jaromir's corruption experiment. "So, you're saying that we all have some of that corruption in us." Gwendolyn bit her lower lip as she poured tea for them all and sat at the head of the table.

"In theory, yes. You were turned before Adrius drank the Fell Emperor's blood though. There's a possibility that you are not included in this." She sat at her side. The smell of tea, usually so soothing, turned her stomach today, so she left her cup untouched.

"It would be foolish to assume I'm not included, too. To assume we all aren't." Each word was heavy as a stone. "I know I don't speak of this much anymore, Neala, but it's time we did. We are damned. Each and every vampire down to a one. We accepted a supernatural curse from another race into ourselves, and now we act surprised that there are terrible repercussions for our decision."

Her tired voice picked up momentum, talking more to herself as if Sorsha wasn't sitting there with her eyes as round as saucers. "And that...that *woman* who sits on my daughter's throne decided to spread vampirism far and wide. How long until we transform into the very monsters we set out to fight? *How long?"*

"I don't know. But it does us little good to yell about it." She placed a gentle hand over Gwendolyn's shaking fist. *"We still*

have Sorsha's magic and your understanding of Fell potions. You can still do something to help us all."

She glanced to Neala's hand, turning hers over to hold it instead. "Your blood was corrupted, too?" she murmured.

"Unfortunately."

She bowed her head, shoulders sinking in quiet defeat. "You have a good heart. I noticed it from the first moment we met, back when I could see such things with my own magic. I can't see that destroyed by Fell madness."

"You cannot admit defeat before even trying to help with the problem," she said, thinking her adopted mother sounded like she was accepting some other necessity.

Gwendolyn gave her hand a last squeeze, nodding. "You're right. I am mourning you when you're right here with me. Please, drink your tea. Let us talk magic instead." She sent Sorsha off to fetch a couple of tomes of magic. Judging by Keegan's expression of censure as he went with her, he would try to calm his sister down over what she'd overheard.

"What of it?" Neala felt a twinge of unease.

"There's a spell I'm thinking will help you. We discovered a memory charm that gives recall to all the moments you've forgotten about in your life," she said. "It is…overwhelming. But I think you need it."

They were circling back to Marcus and her memory, and she was tired of him being brought up and whined about. Neala contemplated how much she'd possibly forgotten in her long life. *"That does not sound like the best idea."*

"We've refined it, don't you worry. Sorsha can specify what exactly she wants you to remember or just perfect your memory so you don't ever forget another thing." She put her palms up, beseeching. "There's no harm in trying, Neala. You've forgotten quite a large part of your life."

"It does not feel like I've lost a thing," she remarked, eyes narrowed.

Keegan returned at that moment, dropping a set of spell books in front of Gwendolyn with a thunderous clap. "It's true, Mother. You have forgotten your lifemate."

"But how is that possible?" Her voice softened upon his agreement, her mind racing with possibilities. They led in only one direction.

"Lucia," Gwendolyn said for her.

Evil, her mind whispered. Maybe she'd been onto something, after all.

She watched Sorsha return holding an occultarus as if it were pure glass as she returned to Gwendolyn's side. Together, they pored over a spellbook. Upon seeing her confused expression, Keegan whispered to her, "I got it for her from Nyixa. There's a few that aren't well guarded."

"That was incredibly dangerous." She frowned as he shrugged casually.

"She needed it for her spells," he said, gesturing to Sorsha whispering to it. It glowed from the inside with silvery light, levitating to her shoulder and orbiting her as Lucia's often did.

Still, it was the most dangerous thing she could imagine him doing. His glamor wasn't that strong, and the occultari were still linked to each other by magic. Someone could accidentally teleport here from the Grand Occultarus thinking it was the Roman connection.

Except she'd teleported between those two waypoints and hadn't felt a second so close by. She hummed to herself, wondering if the fae's proximity had camouflaged it just as they seemed to camouflage her from Lucia's scrying. *"Next time you do something like that, at least come say hello to your mother,"* she said at last.

"Okay. Sorry." A little smile lifted the corner of his mouth.

Meanwhile, Sorsha was stumbling over her people's difficult language as she recited a spell. It didn't necessarily inspire confidence, though her mentor nodded in approval after she'd managed the whole sequence twice without the occultarus going dark from an invalid spell. "Are you ready, Mother?" she asked, turning to her with nerves staining her enthusiasm.

"Do your best, sweetheart," she said, bracing herself as the girl seized her spellcasting focus from its orbit over her head and held it out to her. Neala didn't wince as it glowed brighter and

brighter, its hum drowning out the sound of Sorsha's spellcasting.

In that glow, she saw a great many things that she'd forgotten. Wetness dripped from her nose, eyes, and mouth, staining her trembling arms like liquid rubies. When darkness came, it was a blessing.

44

GWENDOLYN

For all my studies of Fell, I've yet to understand what triggers Fell madness in vampires. We've seen some enjoy the taste of blood too much. Others succumb to strong emotions and simply explode with a Fell's unearthly power. Once one crosses that threshold, it's nearly impossible to bring them back to reason.

-From Lucia's Journal

The moment the spell ended, an unholy roar escaped from Neala's throat. Sorsha startled backward with a gasp.

"How dare she! How dare she take him from me!" Neala screamed, her head thrashing and eyes rolling as the memory spell sank in, returning everything she lost. Her face bled, but it didn't conceal the darkness rising to the surface of her skin. Black veins blossomed around her eyes first, digging deeper as her open mouth filled with rows of sharp teeth.

"Sorsha—go," Gwendolyn said, shoving the girl behind her.

"But I could help—" she protested.

Neala turned to look at them, her eyes black as night. A growl escaped her parted lips as saliva dripped down one of her newly pointed teeth. "Get nephilim chains," Gwendolyn muttered. Such magical items were resistant to being retrieved via portal, so they needed to get a set the old fashioned way. The girl took off running.

"Mother?" Keegan said tentatively, attracting that black stare. "You have to calm down." He looked fit to run himself, blanching under her attention.

Neala roared, picking up one of the spell books Gwendolyn had used clever portals to retrieve from Nyixa. She threw it at Keegan, leaving a dent in their host's wall as the book impacted where he'd stood with a *crack*.

He flashed a desperate look at Gwendolyn as he retreated further. "Fell. I can't...If she bites me..." If she bore any hint of the Fell curse, she could cause him to transform into one of the monsters.

"Go, son," Gwendolyn nodded, stepping into Neala's path. The full blast of the female Blood Prince's fury felt like a scorching brand as he retreated as well. "She's not here. The one you want to kill is far from here."

For a moment, the Fell-addled woman cocked her head as if she would return to her senses. *"You'll do then."* She drew her sword. *"I've wondered—would your blood taste like sunshine? Is that the nephilim left in you?"*

"I'm your mother. You don't want to hurt me," Gwendolyn said, putting her back to a wall. She only needed to hold off Neala, knowing the fae children were rushing to help with one of the only items that could stop the Blood Prince in her tracks.

Still, she looked at Neala and saw nothing left of the redheaded girl she'd raised. Especially as she scoffed and spat, sword raised to slash. *"You're not my mother. You only adopted me because you wanted access to my children."*

Gwendolyn knocked her first blow aside with her cane. "You don't truly believe that, do you?"

"I see you clearly now." Neala gave a hoarse shout as she went for another blow just to be tackled out of the way by a blur of steel.

Keegan held her sword hand up by the bicep, clapping a gleaming shackle around her wrist. If she'd blinked, Gwendolyn would've missed the fluid twist he made to throw her to the ground, placing his knees on her shoulders to pin her. Beneath him, Neala thrashed and snarled like a wild animal, trying to buck him off. "Grandmother!" he called shakily.

Abandoning her cane, Gwendolyn jumped across the room to help, grabbing Neala's other wrist and forcing it into the matching shackle. The nephilim chains muted her preternatural power, but that wasn't why she suddenly slumped, unconscious. That was courtesy of Sorsha, her fingers flying in several motions of fae magic to throw her adopted mother into oblivion.

Gwendolyn stood, using a small portal to make her cane appear in her hand. She took in every detail of Neala's corrupted face, the sharp fangs that were exposed from her slack mouth. The sword she'd meant to kill with had slid several yards away, pristine and glimmering as morning sunlight started to peer into the shutters.

"God," she said, heaving a great sigh before a sob escaped her. "God save us."

45

GWENDOLYN

"The vampire race has a sickness rooted deep within it. And Lucia has spread it, unchecked, seeding ruin within the heart of every new vampire."

-Gwendolyn

For three days, Gwendolyn experimented and mixed potions, eventually perfecting a silver-tinged potion made with Sorsha's blood instead of Nyah's. It was a copy of the blood purification potion.

It didn't work. Not really. Every time Neala woke, she screamed with rage and made their patron couple quite nervous indeed. Gwendolyn hid most of the experimenting and paid them well to look away, but she felt the days numbering down on their hospitality. She fed Neala three vials of the silver copycat potion before asking Sorsha to remove the memory charm over her, hoping Neala would wake up whole and sane.

While her adopted daughter slept, Gwendolyn created a compound to test blood for Fell corruption. She tested Keegan and Sorsha. No corruption.

She tested herself.

No corruption.

Frowning, she'd done it again. The puddle of crimson mixed with the watery compound, but no bubbles or rotten froth resulted.

She considered what it meant as she paid a few random vampires on the street for a few drops of blood to test. Corrupt. Corrupt. *Corrupt*.

Returning to her borrowed house and testing herself a third time, she waited for the compound to mix in as she sucked on the small cut in her thumb. "Maybe you're special, Grandmother," Sorsha offered, watching too as the mixture remained inert.

She looked up at the girl, heart heavy in her chest. "It just means what you scried about me is true. I'll never have Fell madness." A unique blessing, it seemed. Maybe this was exactly where her nephilim powers went—unable to protect her further than burning away the little bit of Fell within her when she became a vampire. It explained why she could starve herself without going predatory, why her body had withered instead of pumping her full of corruption-fueled desperation for more blood.

"It makes too much sense," she confided to the girl. "We made vampirism from the blood of the Fell, so we took in their corruption, too. *Every* vampire will develop the madness, be it now or later."

Sorsha cocked her head, her eyes sparkling purple as she considered. Purple, Gwendolyn knew, was a sign of the girl's magic at work. All of her magic had that hue. "I already know what you're planning," she said.

"Will it work?" She expected Sorsha to try convincing her otherwise, to say it was too drastic. To say there was another way.

Part of her hoped for a reaction like that. But the girl merely grew solemn beyond her years as her lips pressed together. Sorrow dripped from a single word. "Yes." She took a shaky breath. "I'll help you."

46

NEALA

"Evil possessed you. It runs in your veins, ready to attack again when you're most vulnerable."
-Gwendolyn

When the darkness ended, Neala woke up angry. Angrier than she'd been in her life, seized with the instinct to tear and destroy. She lifted her arm to do just that when she realized it was shackled to her bedside by a set of nephilim chains.

She dropped her weight back onto the pillow behind her head, heart galloping hard in an attempt to burst from her chest. The last thing she remembered was Sorsha attempting that memory spell, and apparently it had backfired dramatically. Not only did she not remember what they'd set off to restore, but what'd led to her shackled to this bed was also a blank.

Blowing out a curse, she looked around. The room was tightly shuttered against the glare of daylight with only a few stray bars travelling along the floor in an inevitable creep toward her cot. She rattled her chains in a futile effort to remove them. Unable to press the knot attached to either set that served as the release, they'd remain on her, and their magic prohibited her from accessing her preternatural strength or powers of the mind beyond mental speech.

She rattled again, this time more obnoxiously in a call to anyone who could come assist her. Help came in the form of Keegan, looking tired and disheveled as he came in and stopped a safe distance away, inspecting her uncertainly. "Is that you again?" he murmured.

"The same me I've always been," she replied, tilting her head. He'd never shied away from her like this before. But he seemed truly afraid of her, chained and powerless on her cot. *"What happened?"*

Keegan wouldn't look at her, fixing his starry gaze on the floor. Biting back an impatient remark, she seethed silently instead as she grappled with the unnatural anger still brewing between her clenched teeth. He left the room abruptly, returning with a hand mirror that he used to reflect her face back to her.

At first, it seemed like an impossibility. That face held her features, but it couldn't be her. She'd last seen her expression as fully human, save for the fangs, but now her eyes were black, trailing dark veins around them like crow's feet. It felt like a fist squeezing her heart straight from her chest as she sat up, reminded of the restraints and seeing their need.

"Fell madness," she whispered. The dark veins, the too-wide smile, all remnants of the creatures they'd hunted. *"How long?"*

"You've been out for three days," he said quietly, setting the mirror aside after she had a good look at herself. "You remembered everything, and then you went on a rampage."

"I don't remember," she admitted. *"I'm just...very angry."*

"I know." His smile was gentle, but now she saw why he wouldn't approach her. Like a rabid animal, she was now infected with the one thing that would prove completely deadly to him. Keegan must remember what it was to be Fell, to be cursed with eternal hunger combined with constant death around him. Despite his uniqueness on this side of the portal, he'd enjoyed a life of luxury by comparison.

"Grandmother worked with Sorsha to make a potion for you.

She's wanted to deliver it herself," he continued. "She thinks it might be our only hope."

He left again, this time to retrieve her. It was a longer wait that had Neala fiddling uncomfortably with her wrists. The shackles had cut them all the way around, and those cuts didn't heal over with the haste she was used to. It'd been a long time since she was reminded of mortal frailty.

That was how Gwendolyn found her, trying to lick stray rivulets of dried blood from her hand. The older woman wrinkled her nose. "We were very fortunate Keegan could restrain you," she said, popping the cork off of a vial of silver liquid. It bubbled upon exposure to the air, fit to evaporate away if Gwendolyn weren't already by her cot, pressing the cool glass to her lips. She swallowed the thick mixture with a soft moan. It tasted like thick and rich blood, the kind from a healthy individual who could sustain her for a week or more.

"I'm sorry. Whatever happened was against my will."

Gwendolyn smoothed the hair from her face with a tender hand, her smile fleeting. "I know. That's why I made this for you." She gestured to the empty vial, watching her face closely as its effects started to course through her veins like purifying fire.

It stung her head to toe from the inside, but the feeling faded to numb relaxation before it became unbearable. *"But did it work?"* Neala asked, her chest heaving as she recovered and flexed her fingers. She sagged into the bed as her adopted mother held up the mirror again, this time showing her face as she was used to seeing it. As imperfect as ever but without the trace elements of Fell. *"I could kiss you. You've cured me."*

"How are you feeling though?" she asked, not quite making eye contact.

Upon some introspection, the seething anger in her was fading as if it'd never been. *"I'm not angry. What was that? What happened to me?"* She looked up at Gwendolyn with the same wide-eyed fear she hadn't experienced since learning the blade and self-defense. The Fell madness had stripped away that layer of assurance like a flaying knife through hide.

"Upon remembering…what we wanted you to remember, it seemed to trigger the Fell in you," she said. She reached over

Neala to release her from her chains, shaking her head slowly. "We decided to leave it be. If it doesn't bother you that you've forgotten something important—"

"That I was married to Marcus?" she interrupted. Gwendolyn froze, her gaze flying up to her face. *"It's all right. I believe it's true now, after all of this, which means Lucia stole him from me somehow, leading us to this moment."*

"That's right," she said, fidgeting with her fingers.

"She is evil. That's what Marcus wanted me to know." She was curiously numb as she said it, reaching for the sword hilt that was not currently attached to her hip. This time, rage was the sane reaction, but the other woman stepped away from her warily. *"I will kill her. We only need our council, not her."*

"I have a better idea, Neala. The potion you drank may be the cure for everyone, not just you," she said, putting a calming arm on her bicep. "We need the right setup to get it to as many vampires as possible."

"You want to give it to Lucia," she remarked, seeing the intent in her expression. *"And you're plotting something."*

Gwendolyn bobbed her head. "I have a condition for Adrius and Lucia both." Before Neala could even ask, she added, "You will find out when I am ready to reveal it."

"Do you have enough of the reagents to share it?"

This caused some hesitation and a stolen glance at her. "That was a potion made with Sorsha's blood." She flinched away before Neala could react, and it was a good thing she did, as her eye twitched from a sudden shot of anger.

"You used my baby daughter's blood in that?" she thundered. *"You fed me my daughter's blood!"*

"It worked, didn't it?" she said coolly. "It is the cure we all need, made from the blood of the race we stole Fell madness from in the first place."

"There's no way Lucia can know about Sorsha!"

She held up her palms defensively. "It'll be fine. Trust me. Don't you trust me?"

An undercurrent passed between them as they locked gazes. In truth, she did trust her, but her girl's life was not hers to use. *"How will you keep my girl a secret?"*

To her surprise, Gwendolyn bowed her head first. "I will make it a secret compound only we know about. Sorsha will never set one foot on Nyixa. It is not safe for her. She and Keegan are going to take shelter while we return there. I need to meet with everyone," she said.

"Let us not waste another moment," she said, breathing a sigh as she sat up and felt the extent of clusters of bruises and soreness over her body.

Sorsha refused to leave her side as she helped pack Gwendolyn's belongings for the trip.

47

GWENDOLYN

"It's not the same without her. But I will have reprisal in her memory."

   -Gwendolyn

Gwendolyn assembled a council meeting the moment she could. She walked through Nyixa like a ghost, sparing a fleeting glance for the Grand Occultarus.

"Will it blind me if I try to use it?" she'd asked Sorsha during her scrying.

"Yes," the girl replied.

"But will I find Nyah if I do?" It would be worth it if she could still hold her daughter.

Sorsha hesitated for a moment too long. "I'm sorry. I don't see it happening."

So, she didn't try, knowing she needed to be at her best for what was to come. She didn't use a portal to go into the palace, instead strolling through the city while Neala kept pace, carrying a few crates full of precious silver potion. They were nowhere near as powerful as the golden potions made from Nyah's blood, but she would sell them as something better and stronger anyway. Even a temporary cure was better than none at all.

"I apologize to hold you up. I simply am relishing seeing all of this again," she said, avoiding making eye contact where she could. Though she was different, older, than she once was, she didn't want to bring too much notice to herself.

"It is all right. I haven't taken the time to do this yet. Strange how you can come somewhere feeling so different, yet the place itself hasn't changed."

Gwendolyn nodded in agreement. It felt like an eternity since she'd stepped foot on Nyixa. Truly, she'd thought she never would again. Yet, it had changed little in her absence. "Just more people. Too many people for my tastes," she said, mostly to herself. Too many *vampires*, all seeded with a kernel of Fell madness. Just like the woman next to her, only cured on a temporary basis.

She brooded all the way into the palace, where a helpful gaggle of pages helped them to the map room. They waited together, Gwendolyn claiming the head of the table just to antagonize.

"Will you tell me then plan now?" Neala asked.

"Marriage. If they marry, they can get the cure."

"Adrius and Lucia? You would do better combining oil and water," she remarked.

Switching to mental speech as well, she clucked her tongue. *"Strategy. Think of it this way—Lucia confirms Adrius double for the throne. It is the expected move for them both to make to avoid civil war."*

"But...?" Neala prompted.

"But Adrius would rule much easier as a widower," Gwendolyn said, dusting off her hands as if washing them of Lucia.

Nodding slowly, the female Blood Prince said simply, *"Adrius will not like it."*

He didn't need to like it, Gwendolyn thought. He only needed to fall in line, and she was sure she could convince him of that.

48

LUCIA

"I will miss the person you used to be."
  -Gwendolyn

Knowing Lucia's luck, Gwendolyn was here to spit in her face. She wasn't pleased to see that her place at the head of the table was taken by the older woman when she walked in.

"Your Majesty, isn't Lady Gwendolyn trespassing? You had her banished," Elandros whispered behind her. *Always a step behind*, she thought, sparing him an amused glance.

"I invited her to bring forth a cure. Her knowledge of alchemy is unparalleled from all her experience with the late queen." Though she thought she probably had her on experience at this point. She couldn't see why the old woman would have a reason to perform alchemy without her daughter's magic to compel potions to new life.

Gwendolyn is my friend, she reminded herself. *Gwendolyn is my enemy.*

She wanted Nyixa to be successful no matter who ruled it. *But she was the rightful ruler, and she would bathe in the blood of all the council if they tried to take her throne again.*

It was very simple. Things were required to go her way, or the city would burn at her whims. She was, after all, the queen.

"What's in the boxes?" Lucia asked, going straight to Neala, who had placed two bulky crates on the table.

The mute Blood Prince pried off one of the lids with her bare hands. Inside, potions shimmered—dozens of potions, packed carefully. Neala turned, her face unreadable. *"It seems our people are saved, Your Majesty. How fortunate for you."*

What was that supposed to mean? Lucia's eyes narrowed suspiciously under her veil as she took out one of the potions to inspect it more closely.

"That is a gift to you only if you agree to its terms," Gwendolyn said. It disappeared from her fingers, reappearing in the slot she'd tried to take it from. The hair raised on the back of Lucia's neck as she sat.

"Gwendolyn. So glad you could come," she said, on edge as she sat down.

"As am I." Gwendolyn didn't look at her, gaze on the door as other Blood Princes entered, called away from their business for this meeting. The near-elderly woman stood only for Adrius, going to him to hug him tightly and murmur something in his ear.

Only once everyone was in the room did Gwendolyn look at Lucia. In her eyes, she saw the vision she'd tried to avoid. Cold darkness emanated from her, and the lapping of endless water filled Lucia's ears. She rubbed the ripples of gooseflesh that shivered up her arms. The vividness of the vision reminded her of the fire and death she'd once seen in Adrius's eyes.

"Greetings, everyone. I come with a cure to Fell madness." Gwendolyn met the eyes of everyone else in turn. "It comes with a price that Adrius and Lucia must pay for the good of the vampire race."

"Do tell." Lucia shifted uncomfortably at the other woman's grave tone.

"If you want this potion and the chance to avert a war…you two must wed."

Lucia expected the same outburst from Adrius as before, but he was thoughtful as he looked across the table at her and then back to Gwendolyn. "Fine," he said, more bland than stale bread.

Her eyes narrowed, suspecting some trickery afoot. "Fine? That is hardly romantic. How could I marry someone who thinks having my hand is simply *fine?*"

Adrius sighed through his nose. "I will wed you, woman, but I won't like it. That's politics, isn't it? Losing your freedom so you don't lose your head instead." His gaze flickered to the small scar on her throat where she'd almost done just that.

"Well said." Sirius spoke up with a tense glance toward his brother.

Their intentions couldn't be more transparent in the moment. Adrius wanted to wed her and then kill her to claim the throne permanently for himself and seek his revenge. She chuckled under her breath.

"Let us prepare for this joyous occasion and host it as soon as possible. In a fortnight," she said, smiling genuinely for her throne, which she would hold no matter what plots they concocted.

Adrius kept his stony expression, glancing toward his mother-in-law. Something passed between them privately, and his brows raised. Definitely plotting.

Just as Adrius had little use for her after their marriage, a similar story could be told in reverse. Either of them had a claim to the throne as a widow or widower. It would be cleaner that way, without a clash of personality or ideology.

"*Qin,*" she projected, glancing briefly to the quiet Blood Prince. She'd observed him carefully over the years, trying to suss out whose side he took. Generally wanting to be seen as neutral, time and again, he stood by her decisions and edicts.

Time to see if he would do the same for her now. "*Yes, Your Majesty?*" He continued flipping a coin between his fingers, observing the groups in the room as their meeting broke apart.

"*I would reward you greatly to put your observational skills to use in the coming days.*"

She waited, hoping she'd guessed right about him. Qin was not the type she could have followed. And Taryn and Elandros were both too obviously her hounds to call. *"You suspect foul play here?"* he replied, dry with meaning.

"Don't you?" Gwendolyn was looking at her again before Adrius was offering her a hand up to her feet.

"Something is off here," he agreed. *"You're scheming, and so are they. This isn't the way of Fell hunters."*

"It isn't."

"We aren't Fell hunters anymore, Your Majesty. I accept payment in gold for my services." And he named a sum that would denude foreign coffers. Not Nyixa's though, and certainly not in the face of a threat to her throne so close to her side.

"I accept," she said, waiting until Adrius left with his family to do the same. She went looking for her timid advisor, sharing news of the wedding and a warning for all the palace staff to be alert for anything suspicious.

Time passed, and the stalemate of inaction continued. Lucia ended up meeting with Qin in the early hours before her wedding. The throne room was transformed around them, boughs of silver chain and white rose garlands over the walls and railings of the coliseum-like court. With Adrius's utter lack of interest, she'd called for the space to be covered in her colors—white, silver, and black. Soon her two thousand-some guests would witness this affair, and it had to be perfect.

"Anything?" she asked, stopping in that shadowy nook between her throne and the concealed quarters behind it. The king's suite right next to hers was being prepared by a legion of maids and servants making ready for Adrius to move in. She kept her back to the wall so Qin's bulk hid her from view. He pressed intimately close in turn, ducking his face from view.

"They do plot against you, Your Majesty. They've left several echoes of conversation in the hallways and inside their rooms." He spoke of one of his unique abilities, clairaudience. He could hear any conversation uttered in a room, though they faded as time passed until they became echoing noise.

She grew tense, though this was of little surprise. But she

hadn't paid Qin a king's ransom for vague agreement, and he didn't disappoint. *"Lady Gwendolyn has asked Adrius permission to put her new purifying potion in the punch. She wishes to give his return credit for everyone's increased spirits,"* he continued.

Lucia pinched the bridge of her nose. It was too late to swap out the punch, made in part with human blood to entice the mostly-vampire audience with a refreshing treat. *"Go on,"* she sighed.

"Neala wants him to kill you on your first night together and make no secret of it. She is...very angry with you. She believes you have tampered with her memory."

"That must be the Fell madness talking," she scoffed. *"Does Adrius agree with her plan?"* Or lack thereof. In typical Neala style, it lacked finesse.

"No. But Sirius does. The two of them are calling for you to be butchered."

Though it came as little surprise to her, she sucked in an angry breath anyway. They would suffer dearly for even thinking such things. Adrius, she needed alive long enough to steal the Shield Key from, but those two...she would have fun reducing their pride to shattered bones and withered weeping. She would make sure to display their corpses so no one could whisper of hope for their traitorous return.

"But, let me guess, Gwendolyn is advising they exercise subtlety instead and bring me to ruin through some clever plan?" It was how the old woman worked. Though she preached honor, she wasn't above sneaking and cheating.

"That's right. And they're listening to her. So, the pressure is on Adrius to get close to you and bring her information they can use."

Lucia flexed her hands, wanting to rip and tear at something. The only thing within reach was Qin, but he was a slab of solid muscle she wouldn't dare try to attack. *"You will continue listening for their plots,"* she said, seeing that the true danger would begin after the wedding.

"Of course, Your Majesty. As long as you keep paying me," he said smoothly.

She rolled her eyes behind her veil as she dismissed him. His greed made him easier for her to control, with her lack of the

Mind Key. Acting as the spymaster she needed was all the better when she could keep his involvement with her secret.

She spent the rest of her early morning pacing, already tired by the time her maids arrived with the miles of silver and white fabric that was her wedding dress. "Have the guests started arriving?" she asked, allowing herself to be primped and unveiled for a rough treatment of brushing and braiding. Her bridal veil would cover her face for the public, though she was currently free of corruption due to the generous portion of potions Gwendolyn had given her.

"Yes, Your Majesty. It's the talk of the town. I think everyone will be there," one of the younger women tittered.

"Excellent," she murmured. By the time she was ready, she could hear the crush of people and voices amassing outside her quarters. An orchestra started up, conveniently placed within the pit the Fell had once used for entertainment by combat.

All was as it should be.

When it came time for her to reveal herself, that orchestra played the anthem of Nyixa, a stirring melody of strife followed by the harmony only string instruments could supply. She circled the entire throne room, letting everyone get a good look at their queen in her glory.

Her gown shimmered by torchlight, the silver silk hugging her slim-cut form and draping behind her in a lavish train lifted from the ground by three young girls. The front of her bodice was sewn with seed pearls in the pattern of her city's crest. She was nothing if not proud of what she'd created of Nyixa.

Her veil caught eyes and imaginations alike, glimmering with diamond shards but hiding her face and thus the beauty that was whispered about. She'd finished this off with a bouquet of white roses that she clasped to her chest as if she were a pure maiden at her advanced age.

At the end of her tour, Adrius waited for her at the foot of his throne. He looked just as uncomfortable in his kingly velvet as the last time he was married, but this time showed the death of his youthful glow. He barely looked at her as she took her place across from him.

Poor thing. He must feel betrayed, she thought. Gwendolyn

herself had made this wedding happen, throwing him right back into the political theater where he'd barely survived before. Now Gwendolyn stood in as Maid of Honor, her gaze dark as a tomb as she took the place of pride.

"You are sure?" Jaromir whispered, asking Adrius, not her.

Now was his chance. He could spurn her here, to devastating effect, but save himself the apparent travesty of having to marry her. But Adrius was Adrius, and he picked the path he'd already set his feet to. "I'm sure," he whispered back.

Jaromir's voice echoed from the vaulted ceiling as he began the proceedings. This was no solemn affair with him shouting, so most in attendance could hear and acknowledge the vows. When it came time for them to kiss, they came together like rigid dolls. Adrius lifted her veil and took a good look at her face. "I will do my duty to you, but nothing more," he said as he leaned in.

"Then don't put a knife in my back," she whispered back. Their lips touched. The audience sighed. And then Adrius pulled away as if burned, shoving her veil back into place.

"Ladies and gentlemen, the new king of Nyixa!" Jaromir exclaimed. Many in the audience jumped to their feet and roared, stamping their feet in approval.

"Shall we?" Lucia said under the din. Adrius offered his arm, and she took the invitation, leading the way out of the throne room. Gwendolyn and the Blood Princes followed them, each dressed in a fine suit...even Neala, who'd insisted so she could wear her sword just like her fellows.

Many of Lucia's guards began the work of herding the audience from the throne room to her banquet hall to enjoy a feast now that the ceremony was finished. The wedding party would join them shortly, but first there was another important ceremony to be completed outside of the public eye.

They went to the map room, where servants had dusted, cleaned, and laid out a tablecloth over the old table. Wine glasses glittered around a bottle of wine resting at the head of the table. "I wanted to surprise you," Adrius said while the Blood Princes milled about, preparing to swear fealty to the new royal couple. He picked up the wine. "This cost me a pretty penny, but I've saved it for such an occasion. Fine French wine for us to enjoy on this most special occasion."

He turned to them with the most genuine smile Lucia had seen from him in quite some time. "Let us have a toast first." His brother helped pass around glasses full of ruby red wine.

Lucia set aside her veil with a sigh, tired of how cumbersome it was compared to the simple silk screen she usually wore. She swirled her glass and inhaled its bouquet of dry flavor. A fine gift indeed, and with it in everyone's hand, she didn't expect foul play. "A toast, to Nyixa," Adrius said.

"To Nyixa." Something they could all agree about. Lucia waited a second to see everyone drinking and did the same.

"A toast, to new beginnings," she said. They drank to that.

It was only afterward that she realized Gwendolyn kept her mouth firmly closed over the lip of her glass. She hadn't swallowed a drop of wine.

Lucia's belly roiled. She set aside her glass, clutching her middle even as her limbs grew heavy with fatigue. It felt like the early morning caught up to her all at once. She simply wanted to lay down and sleep.

Elandros was the first to drop to the ground, his glass shattering under his palm. One by one, they all fell, crumpled like discarded clothing. Lucia's vision swam, but she saw the outline of legs as one person moved toward her without trouble.

Gwendolyn grasped her chin, jerking her head up none-too-gently. "Hello, Lucia," she practically purred. "Feeling a little dizzy?" She lifted her clenched hand and unfolded her fingers, blowing a fistful of powder into her open mouth and eyes.

It felt like Lucia's tongue was held down by a lead weight. She couldn't curse the woman or her blasted powder as it stung her eyes and spread bitterness over her tongue. "There, that should do it. While others around you sleep, you will be awake and aware for every moment of this."

Lucia stared, unable to do anything else. "I've been waiting for this moment for nearly two decades," the older woman continued. Pure loathing creased her face as she loomed over Lucia. She didn't look weak now, shedding that frail old woman act like a lady takes off her coat.

"You. *You* are the reason why my daughter is dead. My worst mistake was giving you the benefit of the doubt when you clearly were plotting something. I never thought you would stoop so low as to reopen portals to the Fell Lands yourself, but that's exactly what you did. Your actions killed a great number of innocent people and came closer to undoing everything I've sacrificed for." Gwendolyn trembled with barely leashed rage at this point. Helpless, Lucia knew this was how she died. She should have finished Gwendolyn off when she had the chance.

But she couldn't reply, and that's exactly what the other woman wanted. "You have done the world a great disservice as queen of vampires. Upon accepting the immortality of the Fell, we damned our mortal souls. You extended that temptation and spread it like a disease without thought for the consequences." She wanted to roll her eyes as the preaching fire entered Gwendolyn. Her beliefs hadn't faded an ounce upon becoming one of those she deemed damned. But she'd also always believed that she had a purpose in this world, something she still needed to fulfill before she left her mortal coil.

Lucia's face screwed up in censure, the best she could do to communicate her displeasure. She'd never seen vampirism through the same viewpoint as the other woman. It gave mortals immortality, strength, and beauty at the cost of bloodthirst. How did that define itself as damned? It felt like her thoughts beat at the window of her mind, wanting to get any words in edgewise.

"Now, there are consequences for that and everything else you've done. You've spread Fell madness, something which has no true cure. We had only Nyah—we could've been all right if Nyah was still with us," Gwendolyn continued, her speech faltering with the mention of her daughter. "...And I want you to know what comes next is because of you. Every life ruined is because of your actions."

Resentment stirred in her heart as her eyelids grew heavier. A tremor passed through the palace, shaking a map off the wall as it continued for a long few moments. "Feel that? That's the island reading its cues from you," she said, tapping Lucia's cheek. "We should've sunk Nyixa long ago. Good thing it's not too late."

It felt like a hand reaching into her chest and squeezing at her heart as she realized what might be about to happen. The lapping of water, a cold tomb. This deep in the palace, it would be nothing more than a watery grave if Nyixa sunk back into the sea. "Oh yes, I see you understand. The lion's share of powerful vampires are here in this palace, currently falling asleep from my mercy. They will pass on into the afterlife peacefully, but they will take their vampirism with them. It is your fault, Lucia. You, who've seen how deadly and evil Fell madness is. Every vampire is destined for that madness."

She released Lucia's jaw at last, letting her head thump to the floor as another tremor rocked the island. From how her head turned, she saw the resting faces of Sirius and Jaromir, but another was still aware. Neala fought off the pull of sleep, her face creased with strife. If only Lucia could peer into her thoughts and see what betrayal felt like when you trusted someone so blindly. Now, at least someone else knew that madness lurked in the heart of Gwendolyn Firetree as well as the rest of them.

"You will be aware of every moment passing. You will hear the screams as those trapped and aware drown, and they will curse your name for bringing them here," Gwendolyn continued. She stooped to stop something from moving—Lucia's occultarus. It was tugged from its orbit as she inspected it.

"That's the beauty of magic, isn't it? Even as you fall asleep, you will be awake, unlike everyone else who's drank my potion. That is my gift to you, Lucia. Even if you somehow survive, you will be aware every moment that this is what you've wrought on yourself. You've taken my family and…"

Her voice broke for a moment. There was a rustle of skirts as she knelt out of Lucia's line of sight. "And I must leave the rest behind with you. Every Blood Prince carries the risk to go mad on a moment's notice. Just ask Sirius or Neala." A sigh escaped her, filled with regret. Lucia supposed this was her way of apologizing to the family and friends she meant to kill as well. What did it matter? The only one awake to hear this part of the speech was Lucia herself. "Madness is the true legacy of vampire blood, and I will stop it from spreading even if it means leaving behind everyone I've ever loved."

She began to say her goodbyes, kissing the sleeping faces of everyone, save for Lucia. When she came to Neala, she closed her eyes gently and cradled her head as if she were still a babe. "I'll miss the person that you used to be," she murmured. Her stony face cracked at last, leaking tears like a waterfall.

Lucia struggled to keep her eyes open, and the tremors under the palace were becoming a continuous rumble. She heard the sound of Gwendolyn weeping and eventually teleporting away using her own magic. Inside, a tiny part of her raged. *How dare she leave them to die like this?*

But the other aware part of her shivered under her skin. She didn't want to die. Not lying helplessly as water crashed too close, promising to flood even the great palace once the island sank low enough. If only she could wake up—then the island would not get the cue to rest. But wrestling herself awake was as impossible as reversing her curse—the corruption was in her blood, as was the potion drawing her into a deep coma.

All she could do was call to the occultarus, which nestled itself between her hands obediently. Its dark magic may heed her for one last spell, and so she opted to save herself first, asking it to seal off this room and create air for them to breathe. A third command, to *wake up*, it would not listen to.

She wondered how Gwendolyn did it. Where she'd gotten blood strong enough to cast such a powerful spell over her and poison the wine so potently to cause a coma within a few sips. It felt like she would wonder it into eternity as the island sank and sank.

Unlike Gwendolyn's taunt, she didn't hear any screams as the majority of their race drowned with Nyixa. Only cold, numb silence and the endless lapping of water against the door to the map room, forever trying to work its way in but unable to breach the seal of her magic.

Lucia slept.

49

LUCIA

She made a new set of gravestones, nine in total, and hid them where no mortal tread. She honored all of their names, even Lucia's. Gwendolyn would return yearly and weep for what she'd lost.

Ａnd Lucia dreamed. Oh, did she dream. She was concurrently aware and asleep for it all.

Gwendolyn had devised the perfect revenge. She could beg for oblivion all she wanted, but the occultarus would not respond to a single command. It felt like her every word was shouted into the void of continuous dreams where the magical tool would never hear her.

Trying to talk to it that way would not unseal the door. It would not let her wake up. Her desperate last spell was her true doom. She could feel her curse embed itself deeper and deeper, no longer hampered by her potions and experiments. It shriveled her skin and stained her blood black. Curving claws and a set of razor-sharp fangs replaced her human features.

She couldn't see herself, couldn't open her eyes. But she knew, as time passed, she and a Fell were nearly one and the same. It stopped bothering her after a few decades of sleep-awareness.

No decay hit her nose. Not from the other bodies around her, or their clothes, or the furniture in the room. It was like they were perfectly preserved down here in the cold. A magical tomb not even water could breach.

Wake up. Wake up. Wake up!

She lived a hundred lives in one as she truly lost herself to her visions. She was Marcus, as he fulfilled the destiny he so richly deserved, for a time. Despite Gwendolyn's threats, she couldn't do anything as his army conquered a vast swath of the remaining European vampire covens, making him the reigning power in the region. Her pride for her true love swelled even as she watched him take lover after lover, creating a harem to fill the void left in his heart.

In the early hours of the morning, she watched Marcus look to the east and murmur a prayer for the woman he thought he'd lost. Not for Lucia—her love never mentioned Lucia again. The only prayer he would ever utter was for Neala, hoping she was in a better, kinder place.

Marcus didn't let love touch his heart again. Instead, she watched him discipline his sons for letting love stand in the way of duty. She wished she could reach out on those days and whisper to him that she was still alive. Simply trapped.

But life played out before her eyes, an endless stream she had no way of influencing. She watched Marcus die one day at his son's hand, and she'd screamed in her head for hours and hours until her nose dribbled with black blood from self-inflicted trauma.

Wake up. Wake up. Wake up!

When she recovered, she watched that son more closely. He'd killed his father with help from someone of Sirius's bloodline—a shapeshifter who served as leader of a coven of only four individuals. This little coven stayed alive by hiding what they were and staying in the shadows. They pretended to be mortal and rarely showed their powers.

She watched them take a ship over the ocean to a land they dubbed the "New World." The New World was where technology accelerated to a point that boggled her mind. Swords were exchanged for gunpowder weapons. And men grew softer and weaker as the world changed and war with it.

Vampire kind was at its weakest as mortals became more efficient and lived in denser populations. Gwendolyn flitted around the edges of her visions, acting as a curator of their kind. If anyone threatened to expose vampires for what they were, they would conveniently be gone. She sniped away the strongest and vilest of the vampires who remained, and so the rest remained on the fringes of society.

It wasn't right, and it wasn't fair. All of her hard work was gone, her people reduced to infighting and hiding. They no longer knew they were made for so much more, born from a legacy of heroes and sacrifices that'd saved the world from a greater evil.

Wake up. Wake up. Wake up!

Her mind would return to that little coven, and she watched it grow. Marcus's boy, Julian, played protector to the shapeshifter leader, Alexander. The initial rage she felt toward Julian for killing her love never fully cooled, so most days, it was unbearable to watch him. Instead, she watched Alexander.

Some part of her realized that Alexander would be important someday.

They would meet someday.

And on that thought, a tidal wave came into her visions. She saw herself free once more, her mind shaking itself awake after a full thousand years. She could but tremble with anticipation as events came into focus with her as the focal point.

With the proper guidance, Alexander would create the next Sorceress, a vampire with silver blood and magic such as Lucia. And with another push, she would share her blood with a second woman, creating a gold-blooded Alchemyst. These two women were the key to Lucia's salvation.

She didn't have to see herself in her visions to know she was ruined. If she were killed, her corruption would be shared with whomever took her life, and such a powerful curse would be an affliction no one wanted.

Gwendolyn hadn't wanted to personally kill her, and that was her true mistake. Lucia plotted to make her suffer worse than Lucia had as she felt herself wake more and more.

Fog clearing, eyelids lifting.

The sound of lapping water faded as Lucia's torment came to an end. She was still in her wedding gown as muscles unused but preserved flexed and spasmed with the agony that was *life*. Around her, the other vampire royalty were also stirring.

Nyixa was risen with her awakening. A city of ghosts and skeletons a thousand years submerged. Deep within its bowels were now nine of the strongest vampires to ever walk the earth. Even in slumber, their power was augmented by the passage of time.

Only Lucia knew what world awaited them beyond their island's shores. And she was ready for her revenge.

A thousand years later, these character return in the first book of the Blood Legacy Series...
Dream Walker: Blood Legacy Series Book 1

ABOUT ELISE HENNESSY

Elise Hennessy has developed a life-long passion for reading that inspires her imagination. She holds a master's degree in journalism and enjoys the process of telling stories. Now, she teaches future generations to love books too.

She focuses on writing tales of paranormal romance and young adult fantasy. Elise lives in Texas with her family and is owned by two cats.

Find out more about her books at: www.elisehennessy.com

Join her newsletter to stay up-to-date on her upcoming releases.

DREAM WALKER

BLOOD LEGACY SERIES BOOK 1

It was just supposed to be a simple delivery. It turned into a terrifying destiny...

Violet Reynolds is married to her job. Made the face of the campaign to name the facility's new lion, the junior zookeeper is exhausted and wishing for something more. But when the big cat finally arrives hours late, she's forced to flee for her life when the animal's handlers slaughter her coworkers.

Alexander Rehnquist never thought it would end like this. Drugged and trapped in the body of a lion, the five-hundred-year-old vampire's enemies plan to frame him for a massacre and delight in his humiliation as he's euthanized. So when a brave human woman frees him from captivity, he's grateful and determined to protect her.

Stunned when the creature not only talks but tells her he's a vampire, Violet finds herself the target of a supernatural conspiracy. And when he's able to enter her dreams through a previously unknown power, Alexander realizes this woman is much more than his rescuer. Especially as a millennia-old threat returns to claim her.

Can the fated pair survive an ancient fiend and find immortal love?

Dream Walker is the first book in the suspenseful Blood Legacy paranormal romance series. If you like action-packed scenes, strong-willed characters, and slow-burn connections, then you'll adore Elise Hennessy's thrilling tale.

Buy or Borrow with Kindle Unlimited

Made in the USA
Middletown, DE
26 April 2021